Praise for *All Over the Place*

"Filled with rich, deep emotion, engaging characters and dialogue, and plenty of intrigue that kept me turning the pages...Ms. Clarke is certainly an author to keep an eye out for!"
– Storm Goddess Book Reviews

"This book reminded me of a great chick-flick kind of movie, only in book form. And everyone knows the book is always better!"
– SMI Book Club

"One of the best, most romantic, awe-inspiring and awwwww-inspiring happily ever afters I've read in a long time. Brava, Serena Clarke! I plan to read more by you."
– Random Book Muses

Praise for *The Same But Different*

"You can't help but want to keep reading. It's not just romance literature, but also a story about sisterhood, loss and finding yourself. Extremely glad I found this book and *All Over The Place!*"
– Amazon reader

"Plenty of steamy tension...a recommended fun, feel-good story with some unexpected twists and surprises."
– WiLoveBooks

"A beautiful story about one woman's adventure of a lifetime."
– Written Love

All Over the Place

SERENA CLARKE

FREE
BIRD
BOOKS

First published 2013
This edition copyright © 2014 Serena Clarke
www.serenaclarke.com

All Over the Place
Free Bird Books
ISBN 978-0-473-28326-1

Cover design by Books Covered

This is a work of fiction. Names, characters, brands, media, and incidents are either the product of the author's imagination or are used fictitiously. The author acknowledges the trademarked status and trademark owners of various products referenced in this book.

For Adam, who always knew.

Sometimes, running away means you're headed in the exact right direction.

– Alice Hoffman, *Practical Magic*

Chapter One

W hen Livi Callaway ran away from the place that was, or wasn't, home, she planned to keep her distance. From there, and from others. Safety in anonymity.

The anonymity part was easy, but distance was a problem.

In her short time back in London, travelling on the tube had provided way too much direct experience of human anatomy. Her areas of unwelcome expertise now included overripe armpits and sweaty backs, as well as the endless varieties of Adam's apple (usually noticed while dodging malodorous morning breath).

Once in a while, though, there was a fellow passenger she wouldn't have minded getting closer to. Someone like the darkly handsome man she was catching glimpses of now, on the last Victoria Line train. Someone who provided a welcome distraction, until he got off at King's Cross, or Finsbury Park, or Seven Sisters, to continue his above-ground life.

Certainly not someone like the unsavoury character who'd pressed himself hard up against her on the evening commute one night, his expressionless face revealing nothing of what was going on lower down. The worst thing wasn't that he was doing it (think what those poor Tokyo women put up with), but that she didn't just turn around with a sharply aimed knee lift, instead of sidling away. I've reverted to Britishness already, she thought. Why didn't I go to New York instead? No self-respecting Manhattanite would put up with that.

Now, on this summer Saturday night, her carriage was jammed—but at least the passengers were cheerful. Although she was lightheaded with tiredness from a long, long day and night at work, she smiled as the people around her chatted and joked and jostled. Standing by the doors, at each stop she was forced to get off with the departing passengers and back on with the new batch.

After the third time, an American voice said, "You're like an onion tonight."

She turned and replied, without thinking, "*That's* not the kind of vegetable I'd choose to be."

The instant the words left her lips she knew it was all wrong. A mere second too late, it was blindingly obvious that he'd said not onion, but yo-yo. How could she *possibly* have imagined that anyone would randomly liken her to an onion? Now, as she looked up at tanned skin, dark eyes, glossy hair, and teeth that could only be from across the Atlantic, her heart beat out of sync. She took in distressed jeans, vintage polo shirt, and a battered leather satchel hanging from his shoulder.

Suddenly she was unsteady on her feet, not just because the train was lurching unevenly. Looking at his face, perplexed and amused, she willed the floor to open up and drop her on the tracks. She'd rather be electrocuted on the line than be a late-night crazy person on the Underground under his perfectly proportioned scrutiny. But there was nowhere to escape until the next stop, so she stood, cheeks flaming, praying he'd take pity on her and pretend he hadn't heard anything.

Instead, he said thoughtfully, "No, if you were a vegetable it would be something much more delicious. Sweet corn…cherry tomato, maybe."

Was he flirting? She chanced another glance. A rugged sweep of stubble and a scar on his jaw roughened his looks, making him even more compelling. Anyone who looked like that must flirt for a living. But suddenly she was uncomfortably aware of the harsh lights, and how tired she must look. She ran her hand through her hair, though she knew it wouldn't make any difference. "That's a nice thing to say," was all she could think of to reply.

"My mom always said, you know, if you can't say anything nice...she was English, she liked good manners. Plus, it's important to say nice things to nice girls, don't you think?" And he gave her a wink.

She couldn't help laughing, he was so shameless. "Don't think you can get away with being so cheeky, just because you do it in that accent."

"Okay," he replied, with a shrug and a grin. "But I don't think you spring from round here either."

Just then the train began to slow again, and there was a surge as people started to squeeze along to the doors. He put his arms out and made a protective space around her, shaking his head. "Oh, no. You can stay here this time. I'm not letting you go until I solve this mystery."

Up close he smelled warm and woody and clean, and she had to stop herself from leaning in and breathing deeply. At this distance he could probably hear her heart pounding. His full mouth turned up at the corners, a permanently tempting curve. Her hips threatened to arc towards him in a very inappropriate way. She wouldn't have been surprised at the crackle of blue sparks. If she actually made contact with any part of him, there seemed a real chance she'd just burst into flames.

Then the doors closed and the train started moving, and he grabbed the overhead strap to steady himself.

"Maybe that was my stop," she said, heady from their closeness. "Then what would I have done?"

"Come for a drink with me?"

She was enjoying this now, feeling a glow, forgetting her embarrassment, and her sore feet and backache from

3

standing in the salon all day. "At this time of night, unless you want to go clubbing, I don't know where you'd find somewhere to just have a drink. This isn't LA or New York."

"I'm not from LA or New York, I'm from Idaho." He looked at her closely. "And maybe I didn't mean *some*where."

"Ah," she said, and suddenly felt a little flat. That's right, she knew this story. Off she'd go to his place, with him and his charm and banter. They'd have a night that seemed unbelievable. And the next day it would be unbelievable, unbelievably awkward, as she pulled on yesterday's clothes and tried to find her way to an unfamiliar tube station, with unbrushed hair and uncleaned teeth. The walk of shame. She had no interest in taking it. There was a time, when she'd first arrived, maybe...but not any more.

Her change of mood must have shown. "Hmm," he said. "Maybe that's not something you should say to a nice girl from...?"

Looking at his expectant, handsome face, she gave herself an internal shake. Lighten up, she told herself. He's just a guy on a train, even if he does look like he stepped out of a catalogue. Just enjoy that someone, maybe, fancies you a little. And then she pushed her shoulders back, and put her smile back on.

"Actually, I was born here, but I've been living a long way away. Further away than you."

His face lit up. "Australia!"

"Uh, no. Sorry to disappoint you." Why was Australia always the first guess? Anyone would think there was no populated land beyond Sydney. Next stop Antarctica.

"Well then...ah, damn, this is my stop."

They lurched together as the train made a last jolt, and his satchel banged against her hip. All at once she was aware of the crush of other travellers again, as they began their relentless move towards the door. He was carried along in front of two large women, but called over their shoulders, "We could *try* to find somewhere."

She hesitated for a moment, not wanting him to be gone. Then, just as the two of them realised his bag buckle had caught on hers, the women swept him out and the doors closed. They looked at each other through the glass, his expression going from confusion to surprise to a sort of panic. And she was left holding his bag as the train pulled away.

Chapter Two

Livi pushed the American's leather satchel around behind her back, and plunged her arm into the depths of her own bag, feeling around for keys. When she was a teenager her mother had sent her on a self-defence course, where they taught the girls to always walk to the door with key ring in fist, keys poking out between their fingers, ready to attack any shadowy prowler. But by the time the train got to her stop she was usually too tired to be vigilant, worn out from a day of trying to be hair-salon fabulous behind the reception desk.

Getting sick of rummaging, and dying to get to the bathroom, she breathed a sigh of relief as her fingers finally came upon the keys at the very bottom of the bag. But as she unlocked the door and went to step inside, a voice called out from above.

"Come up the stairs slowly, we just need to…get organised. Won't be long!"

"Hurry up," she yelled back. "I'm bursting!"

Jiggling at the bottom of the stairwell, she smiled to herself and wondered what this one would be like. In theory, her flatmate Cass had the pick of London's men. Livi thought she was what a woman from a Renaissance painting would look like if, slimmed down several sizes, she stepped out of the National Gallery into modern London. Golden-red hair, creamy skin, long limbs, and brown eyes with a truly unfair length of lashes. Enough, really, for Livi—or any everyday woman—to cross her off their friend list.

But with Cass, she laughed like mad every day. Cass said what she thought, and what she thought others should say too. Men were her weakness, though. Since they started sharing a flat near the Blackhorse Road tube, Livi had marvelled at the unlikely guys who'd come through the door. Most of them seemed as amazed as Livi that Cass had chosen them, and she guessed they weren't amazed when they never got over the threshold again.

Finally the inner door to the flat banged open again, and Cass stood grinning and glowing at the top of the stairs in her gold satin dressing gown.

"Come on then, why are you hanging around down there?"

Up the stairs at last, Livi dropped everything in the entranceway and flew into the bathroom. She avoided the long mirror on the wall while she washed her hands. What if she saw something horrifying—a sudden pimple, smudgy mascara or, oh joy, something in her nose? After the embarrassing beginning, it was better to imagine that she'd looked her best for the American. (Ignorance being bliss, especially after midnight.)

But as she left the room, she gave in and looked, just for the briefest moment, and sighed. Yes, smudged mascara below her hazel-green eyes. An open face that invariably gave away her emotions, despite her best efforts. Unruly waves of glossy hair, once plain dark brown but now highlighted in chocolate and caramel (one benefit of sharing a flat with an expert colourist). And curves that were not runway fashionable, but had been her natural shape since her teenage years.

Those curves. She had to grit her teeth every time she saw another magazine headline shouting about how curves were back—while featuring long-limbed women airbrushed and elongated to within an inch of their pixelated lives. They may have had slightly more than an A cup, and a butt that actually provided some padding for sitting, but that hardly constituted radical curviness. She bet *they* didn't have any trouble getting clothes to fit. Womanly proportions were more difficult when they came in a package barely higher than an Olsen twin. Her curves would be fine, she'd decided, if she was several inches taller.

She came out of the bathroom to find Cass waiting.

"I never even noticed when we first met, but look, he's a mechanic and he bites his fingernails," she whispered. "His greasy fingernails! Honestly, I can't be doing with that."

Livi laughed. "Well, maybe you should notice a bit more before you bring the next one home. Now go in there and notice your hair, you're still all mussed up." She nudged her beautifully dishevelled friend into the bathroom, and went down the hall.

It always gave her a shock to see a full-sized man in their cosy living room. 'Cosy' being the word an estate agent might use, to make its smallness seem quaint rather than claustrophobia-inducing. As he sat on one of their squashy, mismatched sofas, this particular man's knees pressed against the coffee table.

"Hi," she said.

He leapt up, a copy of *Cosmopolitan* sliding to the floor. *Tease Him, Squeeze Him, Please Him: We Tell You How!* shouted the headline on the cover. She and Cass had read that article, and Cass had been keen to test the advice on the next guy to come along…which would be this guy. She tried not to laugh at his guiltily flustered expression.

"I'm Livi. Sorry about the reading material."

He held out his hand, and she tried not to look at his fingernails.

"Hi, that's okay, nice to meet you…I mean, I'm Steve."

As they shook hands, he went pinker still. Probably quite a sweetie, she thought, noticing his deep blue eyes. Better than the last one, who'd been flashy and overboiled, though still dazed by Cass.

Suddenly Steve's gaze was over her shoulder, and she turned to see Cass there, smooth and sleek and dressed again. Time to make herself scarce.

"I'm going to make tea, can I get you two anything?" she offered, just to get out of the room.

But Cass grabbed her hand and steered her out, saying in an extra-bright voice, "I'll just show you where I put the tea bags today."

In the narrow kitchen, she leaned against the cupboards and looked dramatic. "I must be getting old, if I'm actually considering a cup of tea afterwards," she said in a low voice. "Say it's not me. It must be the quality of the performance."

Livi laughed. "I'm sure it's not you, you're not over the hill yet, and I can't judge the other. Move across please, I need a spoon. Why do we never have any teaspoons, only big ones?"

"I don't know. And actually, it was nice."

She took a clean spoon from the dishwasher. "Just nice?"

Cass thought for a moment. "In a good way. I mean, he was hot...but there was something sweet about it. But I made him wash his hands first. You'd think that would've killed the mood, but no. Aren't men extraordinary, almost nothing seems to put them off."

She looked genuinely intrigued by this, so Livi held the spoon in front of her nose.

"Cass, look. Even upside down and concave, you're gorgeous, so no, I don't think it's extraordinary. Now, is he going or staying? Because I need to know if he takes sugar, and I need to show you something."

★

She put the battered tea tray down on the narrow coffee table, and flopped onto the sofa opposite Cass and Steve.

"When I suggested staying open later on Saturdays, I didn't mean *this* late. By the time we clean up, it's always a sprint for the last tube."

"It's a great idea for Nicolette," said Cass. "She gets to carry on with her fantastically stylish weekends, while we take turns at wearing ourselves into the ground making her even more money."

Nicolette loved owning Peach, her chic hair salon in deepest Soho—just as long as it didn't interfere with her aspirational social life. Every now and then, when things were quiet on her social calendar (between romances, in other words) she'd have a burst of business enthusiasm. Grand plans would be hatched, schemes would be proposed, and excitement would be in the air. Until she got distracted, and forgot about them again. Mostly, Livi and the other staff kept things ticking along themselves.

"It has been a big success," Livi admitted. "It's brought in a *lot* of money."

Her original idea was to stay open later to cater to the clubbing crowd. The girls (or guys) could come in after dinner, get dolled up to the nines—for an equally pretty price—and then head straight out and hit the clubs. But what she hadn't thought through was that no one hit the clubs until it was seriously late. On the plus side for Nicolette, as well as the extra income, it had gained the salon a wave of publicity (which Livi easily managed to keep her name out of, arguing that it should be all about Nicolette and the stylists).

The salon was the first place Livi had temped when she arrived in London. At the time, she hadn't cared where she worked. After a painfully public disaster and subsequent escape from New Zealand—that too-small country—she just needed an income. And while England (where she spent her earliest years) was the obvious first stop, in her mind she'd already stepped across to the next rock in the stream, on her way across the water to somewhere else again. Just keep moving, she figured. Any kind of action was good.

But somehow she found herself absorbed into the life of the salon, and months later she was still there. And good things had come of it—like meeting Cass. Without her, Livi knew, she might have sunk into a permanent slump.

Now she reached under the table into their secret stash, a shoebox full of chocolate.

"I think that place is in some kind of warp on the space–time continuum, though. Time goes more slowly there as the day goes on." She sat forward to pass Steve his tea, then ripped open a Galaxy bar.

"That's appropriate," he commented, as she held it out to him. "It'll be Planets next."

"Well..." Cass ducked to rummage under the table again and emerged triumphant with a dark brown packet. "Ta-da! Soft, crispy, or chewy?"

"Impressive," he said, accepting a handful. "Now just Mars bars and Magic Stars."

"Funny how so many chocolate things have space-related names," Livi commented. Cass offered her the Planets, but she shook her head. "I'd better not," she said, feeling around her nose. "Do I have any pimples that weren't there this morning?"

She leaned across, and Cass squinted at her. "We need another lamp. No, no pimples. Why, can you feel one coming?"

"No, I just...I was talking to someone on the tube tonight..." Then she remembered. "Sorry Steve, you don't need to hear about my pimples."

"You don't have any pimples," he said, looking perplexed.

"Wait!" Cass held up a hand. "You mean, you were talking to a *man*. Sorry Steve."

"That's all right," he said, shaking his head. "I'm just a fly on the wall."

"A *massive* fly...on the sofa!" She rocked back, laughing, then sat up again suddenly as hot tea sloshed onto her lap. "Oh, damn."

Steve looked down into his mug.

"Don't mind her," Livi said, feeling sorry for him as Cass dabbed at her jeans with a fistful of tissues. "She has a spare foot she keeps in her mouth."

But he sat up straight and put down the mug. "It's okay. I should be going anyway, it's really late."

Cass looked stricken all of a sudden, and pressed her hands on his nearest thigh. "No, Steve, honestly, I'm completely sorry. I just say things, it's a sort of disability, they'll name a syndrome after me one day."

Then he grinned at her, blue eyes flashing. "Like Tourette's," he said, and cupped a large hand over her mouth. Her eyes widened in surprise, then sank closed as he leaned in and replaced his hand with his lips.

Livi held the *Cosmo* in front of her face and waited. After a moment she said, from behind Jessie J, "Okay, now it's me who should be going."

"Sorry, you're all clear," Cass said, and this time it was her who looked pink, snuggled against Steve, her leg crossed over his. She fit perfectly alongside him, sheltered under his arm as though she belonged there. "Now, I haven't forgotten. What about this guy on the tube?"

"Okay." She went out and got the satchel from the entranceway, then came back and set it on the coffee table. "I need to know what to do about this."

Chapter Three

C ass and Steve rolled with laughter as Livi told the story of her humiliation, red-faced all over again.

"A bit of sympathy wouldn't hurt, you guys. Seriously, it was excruciating." She cringed just remembering. "And he was so gorgeous."

"Don't feel too bad," Cass consoled her. "If there was flirting he must have liked you, despite your oniony madness." Steve nodded in agreement.

She brightened a little. "I suppose so. Better for a *likeable* lunatic to have your bag."

The three of them turned their attention to the satchel on the table. Its presence in the room seemed larger than the physical space it actually took up. The deep brown leather was worn with age, but soft and pliable. Cass reached out and poked it thoughtfully, then went closer and breathed in.

"It's real leather, you know," she told them. "Look how supple it is, even though it's so old. Must have been expensive. Maybe Italian even. And look at the stitching."

Cass thought of herself as a bit of an expert, and was famous for her handbag collection. When they overflowed the wardrobe in her small room, she had just hung them on the wall, row by row, as a kind of art installation. Although she lusted after something from Hermès or Balenciaga, she made do with high street buys.

Steve and Livi couldn't help but smell the bag too.

"Oh, that's gorgeous," Livi said. "Like inside a saddler's." Then she laughed. "But it feels totally pervy, sniffing someone else's bag."

Cass shook her head. "You foreigners are weird. If you think it's wrong to smell it, how are you going to cope with opening it?"

"I'm not a foreigner, thanks very much," she said, wagging a finger at Cass. "I might still have a bit of an accent, but I was born here, same as you."

She was still surprised by how fast her accent had faded—soon it would be gone entirely. She supposed her brain was just reverting to its original programming. As a pre-schooler in Auckland, she'd spoken in the same tones as her English parents, her accent the same as if they'd never left England. It was only when she started school that it began to slip, and after a while she sounded as native as the next kid. (Apart from that brief, inexplicable phase, at about twelve, when she decided to try out a fancy English accent. She had no idea what her preteen self could have been thinking.)

In her mind, she'd thanked her parents a thousand times for thoughtfully being born in England, and for making sure she was too. It had made her exit much easier. Not to mention much more definitive—disappearing to Australia, the default setting for departing New Zealanders, just wouldn't have taken her far enough away. Now she adjusted the bag on the table, and wondered how far away Idaho was.

"It just seems so personal, opening a stranger's bag. I mean, there might be private things in there."

"He's not a stranger," Cass said. "You know where he's from, you know about his mother, you know each other's names…"

Livi shook her head. "Actually, we don't. All he

knows, probably, is what a ditz I am."

"Well, we already knew that," Cass teased. "And in that case, if you don't open it, how else will you find him? You have to find him. That's why you knew Nicolette ought to open Peach late, so you could be on the tube at the right moment to meet your dream man. Fate." She clapped her hands, loving the idea.

"Of course, he might be a gum-chewing, gun-toting evangelist with several wives," Steve pointed out.

Livi laughed at his deadpan stereotyping. "No, he said he was from Idaho, not Utah. I don't really know anything about Idaho. Do you?" She looked at Cass, who shrugged, but Steve put up his hand.

"I do. Potatoes. And fishing. I caught a fantastic trout when I was there."

He held his hands out wide to show them just how fantastic. Neither of them were impressed by the fish aspect of the story, but they looked at him with renewed interest. A man who'd travelled was a man with a story, a *past*.

"You've been to Idaho?" Cass asked.

"And a few other places. I did a motorbike trip across the States a few years ago, with some mates."

"That's extremely Ewan MacGregor of you," said Cass, and Steve looked pleased. She tipped her head and considered him again. Livi could practically see her thoughts rolling in a banner across her forehead: were motorbike adventures sexy enough to outweigh greasy fingernails? Maybe the nail-biting could be cured? Something to paint on, perhaps...

Steve leaned forward. "Well, Ewan MacGregor rode a BMW Adventure on his trips, fantastic bikes. But I'm happy with my Kawasaki KLR650 for long distance riding. It's cheaper than a BMW of course, but it's great off-road too, though it's a bit heavier than a specialised off-road bike..." His voice faded out. "Not so interesting?"

Livi rolled her eyes. "You sound like Cam."

"In New Zealand," Cass explained for Steve. "He's a motorbike nut too, which made him unacceptable as a boyfriend."

"Cass, no, it wasn't the bikes." A man on a motorbike could only be a good thing, in her opinion. (Well, apart from the unwashed gangster kind.) "We keep in touch, we always will, but he's just been a friend for years. It's not that kind of thing with us. Plus, he's been a student forever, I don't think he'll ever turn into a grown-up with a real life. And you know I was with Rob, anyway!"

Cass laughed and shook her head. "Honestly, Liv, it's just too easy. Take a deep breath now. Forget those New Zealand men. Let's get back to Mister Idaho, and his potatoes and fish."

"Potatoes and fish don't sound very promising," she said. She wasn't really clear on what her dream man was made of, anyway. So far she'd mostly struck slugs and snails and puppy-dogs' tails, so potatoes and fish would be an improvement. But the American didn't seem like a potatoes-and-fish type. More olive oil and apple pie and tooth-whitener...if those things could be so heart-stopping.

"Actually, it's beautiful there," Steve said. "Lots of wild country, mountains."

"Ooh, that probably means men in cowboy hats and tight jeans," Cass suggested.

"That's more appealing." Livi imagined the American in Wranglers and a black hat. Then she added boots, just as an experiment. The result was a walking cliché, walking in tooled leather boots, but oh boy, she *liked* it. "All right, let's do it then," she said. And, taking the bag on her lap, she undid the heavy buckle and opened it.

Inside was a big brown envelope, a parcel wrapped in brown paper, a London A–Z map book, and a packet of chewing gum. She took each one out and put them on the table.

Cass picked up the map book and flicked through the pages. "I haven't seen an actual A–Z for years. Everyone's got the app now."

"Old school," Livi commented. She kind of liked that.

"But look," Steve said. "Gum. And the A–Z is a sort of

tourist Bible." He was warming to his theme. "Do you think there's a gun in the parcel?" He picked it up and tested its weight in one hand, lifting it up and down. Then he squeezed it gently. "Bubble wrap."

"I think you're stretching it now," Livi said, taking the parcel off him and putting it on the table.

"No wallet or phone?" Cass asked. "Could they be in a different part of the bag?"

"No," she said, rechecking the inside. "And there aren't any zips or compartments."

"Of course there aren't," Steve said. "Men don't need fussy bags like you. He probably had his phone and wallet in his pocket."

"Men don't need fussy bags," Livi replied, raising her eyebrows at him, "because they can put their extra things in *our* bags, which we conveniently have with us at all times. You're right though, that explains it. But it won't help us figure out who he is."

She took up the brown envelope and tested a corner of the flap. It was loosely sealed, as though it had already been opened and closed more than once. She lifted the flap and pulled out the contents. There was a map of the Sussex countryside, with 'Cotchford Farm' circled in black marker pen, and the number '8/27'. Then a photocopy of one of the A–Z pages, with 'Golders Green, 3P, 9/1' in scratchy writing at the top. A Eurostar timetable, with a Post-It note stuck on the front reading 'Rue Beautreillis, 9/9'. And finally, a folding map of Wiltshire. She set them all in a row on the table.

"I suppose he's doing some travelling," she said, struggling to see any connections. "That's not surprising."

"What are the numbers for?" said Cass. "Street numbers?"

Livi frowned. "8/27 in the middle of the countryside doesn't make any sense…" Then she sat upright. "Dates! You know, in America they write their dates backwards, like they always say nine-eleven for the eleventh of September."

"Oh, well done you!" Cass grinned. "So 8/27 means

the twenty-seventh of August…"

"Which is next weekend," finished Steve.

There was silence while Livi and Cass looked at each other.

"Even I can see you're both thinking the same thing," he added.

"It has to be done," Cass said. "Fate."

★

To: cam.holden@nzuni.ac.nz
From: liviaway@gmail.com
Subject: Saturday night's developments

Here's what happened. Squashed on the tube after a long day and night at Peach. It was jam-packed and I got talking to an American. When he got off, his bag got tangled in mine and I ended up with it. There was no way to go back and give it to him, we were on the last tube. Cass is thrilled now we have this great mystery (you can imagine). She says I have to try to find him and return it.

How's academia? Any closer to finishing your tome? I don't know how you've concentrated for so long on it, especially something so impenetrable. Economics isn't exactly sexy. (No offence.)

By the way, please don't mention to Mum I've been talking to strange men on the tube, she'll have a fit. (Not that there's anything to have a fit about!)

Ugh, stopping now before I start to ramble on like a senior citizen, like I usually do. Must be getting old…

Goodnight down there.

xxx

To: liviaway@gmail.com
From: cam.holden@nzuni.ac.nz
Subject: Re: Saturday night's developments

Yes, I *can* imagine. Apparently women love a man of mystery—I remember your Mr Darcy phase.

Academia is fine, thanks. Now I'm lecturing too, the income makes it easier. I've almost finished the tome, but round here we call it the doorstop. Hopefully it'll be more useful than that though. My supervisor is pretty positive. And I had another paper published in the *European Economic Review*, so I'm starting to get some international feedback.

I know your eyes have glazed over by now. But it's about the interdependence of the whole world and the way it operates, right down to an individual level. That means you, miss.

I haven't seen your parents for a while. Someone told my mother that yours had gone on holiday, but no details. Grapevine still functioning here, no escape from the gossip network. That's where being a dull economics student comes in handy—no fodder whatsoever.

By the way, if you're getting old, I'm a complete fossil. Keep on rambling. It's part of your charm.

Have a nice day up there.

xxx

Chapter Four

G ossip was something Livi knew plenty about. For most of her teenage years it was as essential as air and water, as her crowd gossiped their way through school. When they finished, and went off to work or university or travel, they saw less of each other. But when they did get together, often at their favourite old waterfront pub, the Frigate, the gossip was even more vital, as they filled each other in on developments, disasters, and dramas.

Without any scandal in her own life, Livi could happily listen without worrying that she'd be the next one under the microscope, her actions analysed and her motivations speculated on. Oh, she knew getting together with Rob gave people a few hours of entertainment. From the start, even in the first days and weeks of their romance, she could see that they weren't exactly an ideal match. No one could say, 'Isn't it perfect, they're so right for each other.' One of her friends—not known for tact—summed up by saying it wasn't as if she and Rob weren't on the same page, they weren't even in the same book...if Rob had ever read one. Livi knew there was truth in it, but Rob definitely had his talents. He was funny, and lively, and carelessly good-looking. When he arrived with his grin and his straightforward confidence, any gathering suddenly felt like a party. He found something to talk about with everyone he met.

And if he talked too much about himself sometimes, oh, he made up for it at the end of the night when the talking stopped and it wasn't about Rob any more, it was all about her. Her in his big bed, holding her breath for his next touch, given over to fingers, lips, a lean, hard body against her curves, the sweep of her own hair against her skin, the brush of his rough jaw against her thigh. She measured her life from night to night, wading through the daytime hours, knowing that soon he'd be packing up his tools, leaving whatever building site he was working on, going home to have a shower before meeting her. She only had to think about it to feel all flushed. She'd never known anything like it. Of course she was ignoring their mismatch, but it was the most blissful denial imaginable. She still missed those nights, despite the disaster that followed.

And that disaster was what really gave people something to gossip about. Not just her friends, or everyone at the local pub, or the whole of Auckland, but the whole country.

By the time *Dance 'til You Drop* made it to New Zealand, from America via Australia, it was a smash hit. It was just another incarnation of the humiliate-yourself-for-fame television show formula, *Dancing with the Stars* mixed in with *Survivor* and, for the twist, *They Shoot Horses, Don't They?* Rob's mates secretly signed him up to audition, thinking it would be a hilarious joke. But his sunny confidence and simple enthusiasm, combined with his surfer-style good looks and work-hardened body, made him perfect for reality TV. The producers loved him.

"It'll be a laugh," he told a sceptical Livi as they sat on the beach the night he signed the contract. "And Liv, you've gotta love the prizes. I can't drive the old man's Toyota forever, you know. And, come on babe, a hundred thousand dollars!" In the late, low sun he glowed with the possibilities.

She wrapped her arms around her knees, and dug her toes into the sand beyond the edge of the old tartan rug.

"I don't know, there just might be more to it than you think. I mean, the whole point of reality TV is to make people look bad in some way for entertainment."

"You know I'm tougher than that." He screwed his beer bottle upright into the sand and pushed the pizza box from between them, to sit closer. "It's not a big deal, if you don't take it seriously."

"But on those shows they want drama and conflicts, they play up the negative side of things. And with the constant dancing everyone will be pushed to the limit." She'd watched more reality TV than she'd admit, and she didn't want them to make him look like a fool.

"Hey, they can't make me look any stupider than I already do," he said, reading her mind. He leaned against her and gave her a nudge. "Besides, I'll have my girl there cheering me on, right?"

She concentrated on covering each toe with warm, whispery sand. "I just think you should be really sure it's worth it." She didn't want to be dragged onto TV either, not for any prize.

"It's only dancing, hell, for the right money I can do that for a few days," he said, lifting her hair back so that he could see her face. "And think what we could do with that money. Maybe something a little sparkly, you know." He took up her left hand and traced a path along her ring finger, watching for her reaction.

"Oh." She felt the sun warm on her back, heard the waves fizzle on the edge of the sea, saw the twinkle in the grains of sand as they trickled off her feet. Each one a tiny diamond. "Oh..."

Rob took her cheeks between his hands and turned her face to his. "Babe, let's do it. I don't want to be without you."

The last rays of the sun were dazzling behind him, so that she had to shelter in his shadow. Close up, she looked right at him, and saw the desire in his eyes.

"You might not win the money," she pointed out, knowing she was ruining the moment but not quite able to give in to it.

"We'll do it anyway. It doesn't depend on money," he replied, and gathered her in, kissing her as though they were alone, not sitting on his father's worn car rug, amongst seagulls and dog-walkers, and children puddling in the shallows. As he tangled his fingers in her hair and pressed her close, she felt the irresistible shift inside and knew, again, that she had hopelessly and deliciously given in.

★

When Livi and Rob announced their engagement, their parents wanted to know if they'd set a date. His friends wanted to know when the party would be. And her friends wanted to know when the ring would be on her finger.

"I don't know," she admitted to Gemma and Bex, her two best friends from school days, as they sat under feathery palm trees outside their favourite seaside café. "Everything's on hold until this damn show is done with." She dropped a marshmallow into her usual hot chocolate and forced it under with her spoon.

Over their coffees, they both looked sympathetic.

"It's not too long, I suppose," said Gemma. "But could you start making a few plans in the meantime? We could help you."

"You don't need an excuse to buy bridal magazines, Gem," Bex said, stirring sugar into her cup. "You can just walk in and hand over the money."

Gemma went pink, and Livi reached over and gave her hand a squeeze. She had broken up with her last boyfriend a few months ago and was still single, but her wedding obsession was no secret.

"That's sweet Gem, thank you. Of course I'd love your help. It's only a short time, really, then we can start. It's just hard for him to concentrate on anything beyond the show, and I want him to be involved."

"How involved is he going to be, though?" asked Bex. "I mean, I can't see *him* going out to buy bridal magazines."

Livi and Gemma laughed at the idea. "Okay, point taken," Livi said. "I suppose it'd be enough to *feel* like he's involved, even if he's just nodding and smiling."

"Yeah, men are good at that." Bex rolled her eyes. "The clever ones, anyway."

"You're too young to be this cynical," Gemma said. "It's not like you've had bad luck with men."

"No, just with one man," she replied, with a grin.

Bex and Nick had been together practically since the beginning of high school, and despite—or maybe because of—a competitive and sometimes combative relationship, they were plainly meant to be. After a few drinks at Gemma's last birthday, Bex had confessed that the backwards and forwards battles kept things interesting for her, and making up was the best part of all. Both being chefs, they were guaranteed to have a tempestuous time.

"Speaking of men, what did Cam say when you told him?" Gemma asked.

Bex leaned in. "Yes, what *did* Cam say?"

"You mean about the show?" Livi occupied herself with her second marshmallow.

"No, the getting engaged!"

"Well, I haven't told him yet. Don't look at me like that! He's still away on that bike trip."

"He's going to be disappointed," Bex said. "He always thought he'd be the one."

No, he didn't. And he doesn't." She shook her head. "You know nothing's ever happened between us."

"I don't know why," said Bex. "If it wasn't for Nick, I would've been in. You seem oblivious, but he's flat-out handsome, you know."

"He is," agreed Gemma. "And so tall. And clever. Oh, and that motorbike..."

Of course she knew. You could hardly miss it. He was unarguably handsome, and tall, and clever. Amongst other things. But he was *Cam*. Their families lived opposite each other in their little street, and socialised together, so as kids the two of them were thrown together almost every weekend. And even though he was two years older, they'd always been happy in each other's company.

But when it came to budding romance, there was such a thing as knowing someone *too* well. She'd walked his dog, and stood on Lego in his hallway. She was there when he mastered the nine-year-old armpit fart, and years later when his mother told him off about the teenage wasteland that was his bedroom. And he'd seen her fall off her bike, and cry over the birthday kitten that came to grief in the street. When she cut herself to pieces, on her first attempt at shaving, he'd made no comment about the sticking plasters all over her legs.

On long summer evenings, they'd lain on his old trampoline, talking about everything and nothing, while their parents drank too much wine and burned sausages on the barbecue. She still tried not to think about the night just after she turned fourteen, when they stole an experimental bottle of chardonnay and she'd had to throw up behind the garden shed.

They saw each other across the road practically every day until he moved out of home, the first one of them to go. It wasn't that familiarity bred contempt—just too much familiarity. They were as good as family. In fact, with their almost matching hazel-green eyes and dark hair, they had occasionally been mistaken for brother and sister.

Now she raised an eyebrow at Gemma. "Well, it's not too late, Gem, if you feel that way."

"No, I think Bex is right," she replied. "I think he's quietly in love with you."

"Well, he's had plenty of chances to do something about it. We've known each other forever. If you're right, why hasn't he said something?"

"You never gave him an opening—look at all the

boyfriends you've had," Bex said.

"Not that many!" she protested. "No more than anyone else. Anyway, there was never any need for an opening. We're *friends*."

"He probably thought there was no rush," Gemma added. "You've always spent a lot of time together. When he came back from his time overseas, it was like he'd never been away. And then, this whole Rob thing did happen pretty quickly, you know. It was all go from the first day you met. I remember you bringing him to the Frigate that night. That was only, what, eight months ago?"

"I suppose so...but when things seem right..." she faltered.

They'd met at the beach, on the wild west coast. She and Gemma were sitting on towels laid out on the hot black sand, lazing in the sun, when Rob came up from the surf, running his hand through his saltwater hair, droplets falling from his lean body. He stopped to talk to them, and it was Livi he held a hand out to. He pulled her up, and she stood there in her retro one-piece, amongst all the long-legged, bikini-clad girls he could have chosen, and was captivated. And from that moment, it was all on.

Now Gemma sent a frown in Bex's direction. "Livi and Rob will be fine," she said. "I mean, it's true, we were all a bit surprised when you guys got together, but you obviously have a lot of fun and that's really important."

"Yes, we're all aware how much *fun* you two have." Bex wiggled her eyebrows at Livi, making her blush. "Why do you think we let you have the downstairs bedroom?"

"Oh my God." She buried her face in her hands, mortified.

"Bex, don't tease," Gemma said. "You're working nights at the restaurant anyway! She's only joking, we never hear anything."

Livi re-emerged, relieved. "Actually, we haven't been seeing each other as much as usual lately. He's had a lot of work on, and they've started meetings in town about the show." She watched an old ferry chug past on its way to the city. "It's all he can talk about. Which is fine, of course! I mean, I shouldn't begrudge him his fun, just because I'm not convinced about it."

"It's understandable, though," said Gemma. "Reality TV isn't everyone's thing."

"No," she said. "But I'll just have to get my head around it. There's a lot more to come yet."

Rob was keen to tell her all about it, which was good—but she was starting to feel like she'd scream if she heard 'Therese says' one more time. Therese, the director, was apparently the font of all television-related knowledge.

"Fifteen minutes of fame," Bex mused. "You might as well enjoy it, it's what everyone wants."

"It's not *my* fifteen minutes."

"But it could be. Don't they always do publicity and celebrity appearances for these things? You'll be going to the opening of an envelope and all that." She struck a pose.

"It might be fun," Gemma suggested. "Something to tell the grandchildren, anyway."

"Grandchildren! Gem, slow down there." Livi made a stop sign with her hand. "No, I'm just not convinced about reality TV, full stop. I mean, people have killed themselves after bad experiences."

"That's true," Bex said. "Some of those shows are brutal."

"Oh, stop!" Gemma exclaimed. "Now you're being melodramatic. Obviously Rob is not going to be killing himself. He'll have a fun time, hopefully win a nice car and some money, buy you a gorgeous ring, marry you, and have children and grandchildren and live happily ever after, the end." She picked up her coffee but put it down again with a clatter, looking flustered.

"Sorry hon, don't worry, of course you're right," Livi soothed. "I should be more positive. I will be."

She smiled at her friends, one sensible, one feisty. It was good to have back-up. The sun shone, the gulls wheeled, and they had chocolate cake. Everything would be fine.

Chapter Five

In the weeks before the show filmed, Rob was swept into a whirl of preparation, rehearsal, and promotion. Livi saw him less and less in person, but more and more in the media. It began as a story in the community paper about him being selected as a contestant, a sweet kind of 'local boy does good' piece. But by the time the publicity machine went national, Rob had been pegged as the sexy one, the ladies man—he had the looks, but would he have the moves to match? Livi was unimpressed, her positive resolve broken, but Rob was still enjoying the joke.

After one article in a women's magazine that asked readers to speculate on which of the twenty contestants might get together, Livi lay in his bed, officially engaged but without the diamond, and seethed.

"They know you're not single. Why do they write that stuff?"

Of the two women picked out for him, one was just pretty, but the other was stunning—blonde hair down to her handspan waist, a bust to compete with Barbie, and a face of cosmetic-company perfection.

"Don't worry, babe," he said, tracing circles around her belly button in the dark. "It's just their imaginary world. You know I love you."

She grabbed his hand and put it down on the sheet, too annoyed for fondling. "I know. I'm just not loving being invisible."

"I could take you with me to the next interview. Therese has organised it with the *City Standard*."

"No, that's not what I meant. I don't want to be in the papers. God, no." She felt panicky at the thought. "It's just, you are engaged, they shouldn't be finding you a romance."

"The trouble is, I wasn't engaged when I signed the contract, and Therese says that was what they really wanted."

There was silence as they both lay looking at the ceiling.

Livi cursed his friends for their great idea, cursed Therese, cursed the whole damn show. This wasn't the way things were supposed to go, in bed or out. She didn't want to be an unwelcome hanger-on, cramping the style of a dancing heart-throb. Hell, was she the only one who remembered that Rob couldn't actually dance? Although, after a few weeks of lessons with the show's instructors, maybe he could. The thought made her feel even worse, and she rolled away to get up.

But he rolled her back over towards him, winding his legs around hers and tucking her head under his chin. "Don't let it be more than what it is," he said. "Let's just play the game. It doesn't matter what some journalist writes."

She let out a long breath into the side of his neck. Once in a while, he surprised her by sounding quite wise. "Okay. But I don't have to like it."

"That's fine. Just remember to like me," he said, and ran his hand down, around her belly button once more, and then further down, until she was holding her breath again. This time she didn't take his hand away.

"I think every part of me likes you," she managed, before words escaped her.

★

Rob did say something to the show's publicists, and the next article talked about his fiancée and their romantic beach proposal. Livi was pleased to be acknowledged, and decided she wouldn't point out that it wasn't all *that* romantic.

By now he'd taken leave from work and, with a week to go until filming started, was all but swallowed up by the show. Some nights he let himself into the house after she was asleep and crawled into her bed, too tired to do anything but snore. In the morning she went off to work leaving him tangled in blankets, regretfully remembering the mornings they used to spend tangled together themselves. Once she heard him on the radio in the car on the way home, charming the female drive-time DJ, and had to smile. He *was* charming. And handsome. And sexy and funny. She decided to just be proud of him and let him enjoy the experience. If she was doing something so big, she knew he'd support her all the way. So when the publicists asked if she would join him for part of an interview, she said yes.

Bex and Gemma pulled out armfuls of their nicest clothes for a trying-on session. In the end they all agreed on a red dress of Bex's. It was cut so beautifully that somehow it made her waist look smaller and her bust look higher, and even managed to make her legs look longer.

"I know why that is," said Gemma, as they all considered Livi's reflection in the mirror. "I read that all skirts should finish at the point just below your knee, where your leg goes in a little. That's the most flattering spot for everyone."

"The other reason is that this is the most expensive dress I've ever bought," Bex said. "I got it last time I went to Sydney. It's a bit shorter on me, though."

"I do feel really great in it," Livi said over her shoulder, turning this way and that on black strappy heels. "And I love any outfit that makes me seem taller."

"It's perfect," Bex said. "Classic and just sexy enough."

"Classy," added Gemma.

"All good things," Livi laughed. "Thanks, you guys. You're going to make the best bridesmaids ever."

A moment's silence was followed by two cries of "Bridesmaids!" and Livi was sandwiched in a double hug that almost knocked her off her feet. For a few moments they rocked together, laughing, until Gemma exclaimed, "Wait! We're crumpling the dress."

After a flurry of smoothing and straightening, Bex said, "Livi, that's really special. Thanks for asking us."

Gemma nodded. "It is. I can't believe you're going to be the first one of us..." She wiped shining eyes with the back of her hand.

"Gem, it'll happen for you," Livi said softly.

"You're not the kind of person who'll be single for long," Bex added.

"No, that's not what I meant," Gemma said. "I just can't believe how grown-up we're getting. It only seems like the other day we were sitting around on the school field tanning our legs, and now look at us. We're adults."

"Apparently," Bex said. "But I'm still waiting for the grown-up feeling to kick in."

"Me too," said Livi. "Maybe the diamond will do it."

And they looked at their reflections, and wondered.

★

Sitting in the makeup chair the following day, stylists buzzing around with hair straighteners and lip liner and kabuki brushes, Livi thought she looked as much like an adult as she ever had. But although the red dress gave her confidence, it couldn't squash the butterflies in her stomach. She tried to distract herself by watching *E!* on the television in the corner, but the parade of red-carpet beauties didn't help much.

Then a battleship of a woman strode into the room, all in black, including her sharply spiked hair and crayon eyeliner. Over-glossy orange lipstick was the only concession to colour. Livi tried not to stare at her distractingly juicy lips as she spoke.

"Hel-low, you must be Liddy." Before Livi could reply, she continued, "I'm Therese. I'm getting everyone more or less in order for our filming today. You know what's happening, we're just doing a little piece on the background of each of our contestants, and you, of course, are background."

She smiled thinly, and Livi could only nod. So *this* was the famous Therese.

"Now, let's have a look at you then." She waved a hand at a stylist and he sprang into action, whipping the cape from around Livi, helping her to her feet and making a last hair adjustment. She tried a smile.

Therese narrowed her eyes, pursed her lips. "Mmmm." And, after what felt like a very long pause, "No, okay...that will have to do." Then she turned her back on Livi, leaving her decidedly wilted. "Five minutes, everyone," she announced to the room. And then she was gone.

Livi looked at the stylist in despair.

"No, you look great," he said. "She's always like that."

"I feel sick." Her butterflies had turned into bats.

But despite the horror of Therese, she felt a little better when she went into the studio and saw Rob sitting there, with his permanently beachy hair. He gave a low whistle at the red dress, and surreptitiously squeezed her bottom as he showed her to her seat. The shiny-suited interviewer was bouncy and enthusiastic, and sitting between him and Rob she almost managed to forget about the cameras as she answered questions.

When she went back to the makeup room to get her things, she gave her stylist a relieved smile. "Not so bad," she said.

An older woman who had taken her place in the chair looked up hopefully. "Really?"

"It'll be fine," she replied.

★

Later that week, Livi and Rob went to her parents' house to watch the finished programme. Full of nerves again, she stood in the hallway and peered around the door frame for their segment.

"Livi, you look beautiful!" her mother exclaimed when she appeared on screen.

"Evelyn, shh," her father said, grabbing the remote control.

"Well, she does, don't we all think so?" She looked around for support.

He stabbed at the volume button. "Of course she does, but shhh!"

"I was only *saying*, Ian." But she concentrated on the screen.

Livi was surprised how brief her appearance was, for something that took so much getting ready for. But even she, usually self-critical, had to concede that she looked quite nice and, okay, didn't sound too bad either. Rob was a star of course, arm across the back of her chair as though they were at a drive-in, chatting to the interviewer like they were mates. Which they probably were by then, she realised. With Rob, it was a smooth and speedy journey from stranger to acquaintance to friend.

"Come on, Livi," he called from her mum's floral settee as she and the red dress exited stage-left. "Your fans await."

Her mum ambushed her with a hug as she came back in, a bit pink. "Sweetheart! You were great. So professional, you looked fantastic. You did *so well*..." And more hugging.

She managed a muffled reply. "Thanks..."

Rob came to the rescue. "I need her in one piece, Evelyn. We don't want her all crushed next time she faces the nation." As her mum let go, he grabbed Livi's hand.

"Next time?" Although it hadn't been as traumatic as she'd expected, Livi wasn't planning on any more media appearances. "I've done my duty," she protested.

Rob sat her firmly atop the peonies and roses. "You *were* great," he told her. "There's nothing to worry about."

"He's right," said her dad. "I'm very proud of you. Let's have a drink."

"Yes, I'll put the kettle on." Evelyn headed for the kitchen.

"No." Her dad slapped the broad arms of his La-Z-Boy. "This calls for a proper drink." He hoisted himself up and went to get his latest bottle of whisky. "Rob?"

"Well, it'd be rude not to."

Livi left them to their manly ritual and joined her mum in the kitchen. "I'll have a cup of tea too, please," she said, over the noise of the old kettle. "Looks like I'll be driving tonight."

"Good idea," she replied. "You know what those two are like once they get started." She lifted the kettle, put in some more water, and resettled it on its perch. "Funny how stainless steel never looks really shiny again, once you start using it, no matter how much you clean it," she commented, while they waited.

"Like the toaster," Livi said. "How do you get off those melted-on bits of bread bag?"

"A scouring pad, and maybe some Ajax. Same for the shower glass. Anywhere really, as long as you're not too rough." Steam rose around her face as she filled the cups. "Keep it simple."

"Words to live by," Livi laughed, and her mother made a wry face.

"You have to take your wisdom where you can get it," she shrugged. "It's terrible, the trivia we're forced to fill our heads with. Men aren't thinking about that kind of thing."

"No, they're out there talking about sport, I bet. I suppose that's not much better, just man-trivia."

They smiled together, and Livi took the cup of tea her mum held out, handle first.

"So, when *are* you next facing the nation?"

"No, honestly Mum, that was a one-off. It was *supposed* to be a one-off." She blew on her tea and looked out the kitchen window, down to the neighbour's living room. The lights were off and the curtains were half-pulled against the warm spring evening, but she could see the colours from their television flicker and change, spilling out into the garden. Had they watched her tonight? She wondered how many people had. Her stomach twisted a little, and she held the hot tea close against her chest, the rising warmth dampening her chin.

"Rob seems to be enjoying it," her mum said. "It's a good adventure for you to have together."

"I suppose so," she replied, remembering what Gemma had said.

"It's not just wisdom, you should take your adventure where you can get it too. Life goes by very fast, once it picks up speed."

Had Gemma and Mum been talking? Livi wondered. And how many adventures had flown past, while her mum was busy raising a daughter, looking after a husband, building up their business, all necessary, sensible occupations. Did she see their blur, out of the corner of her eye, and pine for the unknown and the unexpected? Or was she focused, concentrating, filled up with the jobs at hand? The business was a success—her mum an accountant, her dad a solicitor. But running the office and doing admin, Livi had an inside view of her mother's life, and it wasn't exciting. She'd come all the way from England with her husband, an only child leaving her parents, taking her own only child, to do the most mundane and everyday things.

It dawned on Livi, looking at her mother standing in the same kitchen she'd stood in for years, that she didn't know much about her at all. Not the underneath things. A rush of guilt and love and an achy sort of poignancy surged in her chest, and she put down the tea and gave her a hug.

"Oh, sweetheart, thank you," she said, happily taken by surprise. Then, looking at Livi's face, "Are you all right?"

"Yes," she said, sniffing a little. "Mum, maybe you could help me find my next television dress?"

Chapter Six

The day the show began, Cam came back. Livi met him at the art gallery café, their place. It had started as a joke, years before, when she'd teased him about having no culture—so he challenged her to a trip around the art gallery, to see who could identify the most artists. He won, of course.

Afterwards, he showed her his parents' vast collection of art books. Amongst them was a heavy volume of art from the National Gallery in London. Inspired and intrigued, she borrowed it, and spent hours poring over the richly detailed landscapes, endless variations of Madonna and child, and angsty scenes of wrath and war.

Then, on a quiet page near the end of the book, she found a saint she'd never heard of—Saint Cecilia, patron saint of music and the blind. Her watchful beauty and her alarmingly gruesome end (in the best saintly tradition) caught Livi's imagination. She could only imagine the executioner's dismay when three strikes were not enough to sever Cecilia's youthful head. He gave up and ran away, and the determined Cecilia continued to preach for three days, until she finally succumbed. In the painting, she was wearing richly coloured robes, and flowers in her hair. (Livi doubted that she would have been so sumptuously dressed in real life, but it did make for a beautiful picture.) She was standing with her guardian angel, looking out at what her future held. It wasn't a showy painting, but it had a quiet strength that spoke to her more than any of the overly dramatic works did. Later, when Cam's parents took a trip to London, they brought her back a poster of it. She stuck it on her wall, and dreamed teenage dreams of going to the National Gallery herself, soaking up the art in a terribly sophisticated way, and hanging out in Trafalgar Square.

Also in his parents' library, Cam confessed at the time, was a book featuring significant paintings from Auckland's art gallery, which he'd used to do a crash course the night before their challenge. She had to give him credit—she was impressed.

She figured it was that same determination keeping him at university for so long. When he finished high school, he spent a couple of years travelling (years during which the street felt very empty to Livi, still stuck in class). But then he came back, and dived into his economics degree. He was the only person she knew who'd passed not only every paper and every exam, but handed in every assignment and aced every test.

Her own university record—two years out of a three-year arts degree—was less than perfect. Her parents had needed help with the business, so she took a year out. Well, they'd only meant it to be a year. In the meantime, working for the family company meant her employers were relaxed about formal qualifications. There were other benefits, too—obviously, she never had trouble getting time off for family commitments, and some of her friends were paying good money to learn the business management skills she was mastering on the job.

It also gave her a chance to save for the round-the-world trip she'd dreamed about for years. University would always be there, and Venice was sinking, after all. Along with any number of Pacific islands, apparently. She'd just have a bit of a look around, before she went back to finish that degree. After several years working with her parents, she had enough money to get started, and only needed to save a bit more for extras. Trafalgar Square of course, and a mule ride into the Grand Canyon. Hot air ballooning in Cappadocia, and maybe stop in and see George Clooney (oh, George) at Lake Como. When Rob came along, the plan had gone on hold. But she figured they could do it all together, soon enough. Except George, maybe.

She arrived at the gallery a few minutes late, and saw Cam sitting across the café in his usual jeans, white t-shirt and biker jacket. His dark hair was still in disarray from when he'd pulled off his helmet, and his fringe fell across his forehead as he squinted at the Sunday paper and stirred a coffee. As usual, he was not just on time, but early enough to already have a drink. She smiled at his familiar reliability and went to order her hot chocolate.

"Mixing it up with celebrities now," he said as she sat down, and turned the newspaper around to show her the full-page *Dance 'til You Drop* ad. Rob was right in the middle of the twenty contestants, underneath 'Premieres tonight at 8!', looking handsome, tanned, and shiny in a Spanish-style outfit. They'd somehow managed to slick his hair back for the photo. It was cheesy, but he got away with it—just. Next to him was the blonde, hair flying, spangles sparkling. Livi gritted her teeth.

"I'd rather not look," she said, turning the page to international news.

He grinned at her, his greeny-hazel eyes flashing with mischief. "I thought you liked celebrity gossip."

"I've gone off it lately."

"Funny that." He folded the sections of the paper together and cast them across to the next-door table. "I've been keeping up with my entertainment news though. Your man is a hit in the provinces."

"I'm going to ignore that," she replied, putting one of her marshmallows on his saucer. He drank coffee, but always said it was unfair that only hot chocolate drinkers got marshmallows on the side. Of all the unfair things in life, Livi figured this was one she could fix for him. "How *were* the provinces? Did you have a good trip?"

Every spring he took to the road with his friends, each on two wheels, with just a few essentials in a bag.

"Great. I'm glad I got the Kawasaki instead of that Honda. It handled really well, especially on the back roads. We went up over the old bullock track through Mount Shearer station. It was hard getting permission to take the bikes through there, but it was worth it." He grinned. "Blew out the winter cobwebs. Big sky and open space."

"That's good," she said. "You spend too much time at your desk."

"Academic life. I'll end up with a chair-shaped arse in a brown corduroy suit."

She snorted with laughter, then clapped a hand over her mouth, embarrassed, as people looked around. "God, sorry." She tried to steady her shaking shoulders.

"Don't frighten the horses." He passed her a napkin, and she pressed it against her face until the giggles subsided.

"Sorry," she said again. "It's just hard to imagine you on your motorbike with a chair-shaped arse."

"Best not," he suggested, and she nodded. He actually could compete with anyone as far as backsides went...but she didn't say so.

He took a sip of his coffee. "So how does this dancing competition work?"

"Well, it's kind of like an endurance competition, with official timed rest breaks and everything. They've set up studios in Downtown Square, so anyone can go in and watch during the day, and they're broadcasting every night with live dancing, and highlights from the day. Or lowlights, I guess." She frowned. "The judges have their say, but people vote, like *X Factor*, to decide who stays."

"And how's Rob's dancing?"

"Enthusiastic, but not all that great, last I saw. But they've been having lessons, so I don't know really. Anyway, I don't know how much notice people will take of the actual dancing, once they pick a favourite."

He raised an eyebrow. "A popularity contest."

"It might come down to that."

"In that case he probably has a good chance. He's got charisma."

She couldn't tell from his tone if having charisma was a compliment. Although Cam had met Rob several times, they were too different, she knew, to ever be good friends. But they each made an effort, maybe for her sake.

"Well, they have been talking him up." She grimaced. "They've made him into their ladies man."

"Yeah, I can see that," he said. "Do they know he has a girlfriend?"

She suddenly remembered what Cam didn't know. Girlfriend. Not any more. She cleared her throat, turned her mug, aligned napkin and spoon exactly along the edge of the table. Never mind Bex and Gemma, she told herself, just go ahead.

"Actually, he…" Her tongue felt wonky in her mouth. She swallowed, started again. "No, not a girlfriend. A fiancée." A minute adjustment to the spoon.

The silence felt just a little too long. She looked up in time to catch him rearranging his face into the right surprised-and-pleased shape.

"Congratulations," he said. "That's a big step."

"Thanks," she said. "Everyone thinks it's too fast, I think."

"Well, you have to do what makes you happy." He looked right at her. "Make sure it makes you happy."

She shifted in her seat. "Okay."

"A big step," he repeated, still considering her. She didn't know where to look. She resisted the urge to cover her face with the napkin again.

Then he slapped his palms on the table, making her jump. "Well!" he announced, standing up. "I'd better get home and unpack. And you must have things to do. Big night tonight."

She realised then that he'd arranged to see her even before going home. "Yes, I have to be in the front row, all dressed up." She stood up too.

"You'll look great," he said. "Good luck."

He came around the table, gave her a fraction of the usual hug, grabbed up his backpack and helmet, and was gone.

She looked down at her half-full mug and his uneaten marshmallow, and wondered if their art gallery days were over. His empty chair, still pushed out at an angle, seemed to reproach her. Had she ambushed him with the news? She had to tell him some time. She went around the table and pushed the chair in, then sat back in her own, thinking.

He was always there when she needed him—for help with maths homework, or lifting and carrying when she moved into her first flat, or just company on a difficult day. And that time he came to the rescue when she ran out of petrol, arriving on his motorbike like a modern-day knight on horseback.

She was always a little bit proud to have him as a friend. At school, some of the boys teased him for being a maths geek and a brainiac, but he was the first one to get a motorbike. Some of them laughed when he started karate, and called him Hong Kong Phooey. (He hadn't minded when Livi asked him who Hong Kong Phooey was—after all, he was the coolest kung fu dog ever. Not to mention the *only* kung fu dog ever.) But that martial arts training meant that the teasing never went any further. And it made him strong as he grew, and gave him a poise and centre that set him apart.

He may have lacked the endorsement of the cool boys, but his leather jacket, unruly fringe, and self-contained manner made him immensely attractive to the girls. There were plenty at school, and since, who made it clear they were interested, but although he'd had a few girlfriends, he never got very involved. She took back her marshmallow and chewed thoughtfully. For her, boyfriends had come and gone, none of them really significant until Rob. But how would she have felt, she wondered now, if Cam had got serious about one of those willing girls?

Beginnings and endings come in pairs, she thought. She liked beginnings better.

Chapter Seven

The premiere was as slick, loud and clichéd as anything out of Hollywood. Livi sat in the front row, between Rob's friends Darren and Angus, who'd started it all by signing him up. The crowd loved it. Putty in the host's hands, they cheered, ahhh-ed and gasped in all the right places. After a while, even she found herself getting swept up in the excitement.

When the contestants came out on stage she hardly recognised Rob, glowing and slightly unreal in television makeup and tuxedo, his hair plastered back. He looked amazing. The girls in the audience thought so too, whooping, squealing, and wolf-whistling. Let it wash over you, she told herself. Remember who he's going home with.

"He actually does look pretty good in that monkey suit," said Darren, recoiling as the camera panned past them again.

"Yep, not bad," conceded Angus, keeping his cool, with only a raised eyebrow for the audience at home.

Livi tried not to think about how many people were watching as she smiled evenly in her silver dress, until the camera passed and she could breathe again. The dress was a triumph for her mum, a slinky survivor from the seventies found in the back of her wardrobe. At first she'd been nervous about the slinkiness, wondering if she should buy some Spanx. But her mum was having none of it.

"Don't be silly," she said firmly. "You have *nothing* to worry about. I never had a figure like that, even when I was your age. It must have come from your dad's side of the family."

"I don't know," Livi said, looking in the long mirror in Evelyn's sewing room. "Maybe I'm a bit short for it. It's just, you know, the hips and everything…"

"No," her mum replied. "It's not. Look how flat your stomach is! Honestly, I would be delighted to look like you. Gok could have his way with me, I tell you. Now, just turn sideways while I pin it here…you'll see."

And once the dress was nipped and tucked to fit perfectly, teamed with spidery silver heels (and seamfree panties), she *could* see. It was fabulous. She knew Rob would like it, sleek and figure-hugging. She couldn't wait to see him away from the eager crowd.

The show rolled on. Demonstration dances from the contestants, Rob paired with the blonde of course, predictions and advice from the judges, and exhortations to watch every night for the next week and vote, vote, vote. By the time the glitter confetti fell from the ceiling, and everyone on stage had finished waving and hugging and slapping each other on the back, and the cameras had stopped rolling, and the audience had clapped itself out of the studio into the night, her head was spinning.

"I had no idea he could dance like that," she said to Darren and Angus, over the chatter of the milling crowd. Most of them seemed to be twiggy teenage girls, making her feel like an old aunty.

"Bloody hell, neither did I," said Darren. "We've created a monster."

"If he wins he'd better pass over a share of the cash," said Angus. "He wouldn't be here if it wasn't for us, you know."

"Thank you, Simon Cowell," said Livi. "But I think you're counting your chickens there."

"Where is he, anyway?" said Darren, looking around. "He can shout us a beer at least."

They went back to the main doors, but found them closed up. The stage door at the side was guarded by a large, black-suited, arms-crossed man who would neither speak nor be persuaded to let them in. After waiting around in the square a while longer, Livi started to feel cold in the silver dress. She checked her phone, but there was nothing.

"Maybe we should try his mobile," Darren suggested. "He said he'd meet us afterwards."

"No, let's go," she said to the guys. "I don't think he's coming. I'm starting to feel like a stalker." She wasn't going to call him.

"Yeah, bugger him," said Angus. "Better things to do." He took off his jacket and put it around her shoulders.

"He's probably stuck doing TV stuff," said Darren. "He'll turn up later on and leave makeup on your pillowcase."

She laughed. "Yeah, the price of fame."

But inside, a hard-edged misgiving was taking shape.

★

Rob didn't turn up at her place that night, so she went back to the studio at lunchtime the next day, feeling uncertain. She was struck by how absurd it seemed, the contestants changing their moves as the music switched randomly from one genre to another, the audience like wallflowers around the velvet-roped edge, the glitz of the dance floor giving way to the lunch-hour ordinariness of office workers and students. Amongst them were gaggles of teenage girls whose parents would probably be getting phone calls from school.

She stood at the back, avoiding the cameras, but Rob saw her from the dance floor and shimmied across.

"You looked gorgeous last night," he called as she came over, working a thumbs-up into his actions.

The girls nearby looked daggers at her, but she called back, "So did you."

He grinned. "I felt so wrong with that makeup on. Sorry I didn't see you, they booked us all taxis home after we had a celebration drink. Therese says they can't have any of us drinking and driving and getting in trouble."

She didn't say that they'd been expecting a drink with him too. Instead, she said, "Maybe tonight?"

He did a spin and leaned in. "Wear the dress," he whispered, and kissed her, one hand buried in the hair at the back of her neck, the other moving in time with the rest of his body.

She laughed, but closed her eyes, soaking in the closeness of at least a part of him. It felt like years since they'd been together. Then she tore away, scarlet-cheeked, as she realised the camera was right there.

"I'd better get back to work." She tried to maintain her composure. "We're really busy at the moment."

"Sorry, babe," he said, as the camera moved away. "That wasn't fair of them."

"That's okay," she said, fixing on a smile for him, the girls, and the lurking cameras. "I'll see you tonight. Have a good afternoon."

He gave her a wave goodbye, keeping up the dancing. As she went out, she heard the music change. She looked back to see him grinning again, being gathered up by the blonde for a slow dance. Obviously he was going to have a better afternoon than she was.

Then she saw Therese steaming through the entranceway. It was too late to hide. She braced herself.

"Ahh, yes, Rob's girl," Therese intoned. "We must do something more with *you*. He's *maaarvellous*, isn't he. Don't let anyone cut your hair this week, we'll sort it out. And keep Friday free for a special event." She threw the last words over her black-clad shoulder, already lining up her next target.

Livi emerged into the square hot-faced and annoyed. It was going to be a hell of a week.

Chapter Eight

The crowd was just as big and enthusiastic for the show's second night. More glitz, more razzle-dazzle. In the audience, Livi gritted her teeth as the lunchtime kiss flashed up on the screen during the day's roundup, and smiled determinedly as the camera came around to capture her reaction. She was relieved when the night ended and she was able to make her way out, laughing on cue at the jokes and teasing that came her way.

At home, she quickly took off the blue dress she'd worn to the show, and put the slinky silver number back on, wondering if Rob would come after all. He was tired when he finally arrived, but he brightened at the sight of the silver dress. This time, she'd left off the underwear altogether.

The dress didn't last, as she'd expected, but unfortunately neither did Rob. Before long he flopped back onto the pillow, leaving her feeling decidedly short-changed.

Then he sat up. "You know, I'd better go."

She felt a jolt of shock. This had never happened before. Usually, it was impossible to get him out of her bed, any time of day or night. Not that she wanted to, usually.

"Really?" She kept her tone casual.

"Well, Therese says we should all get as much sleep as we can, so..."

What kind of excuse was that, after all the nights he'd slept soundly beside her? She wondered what else Therese had been saying. At least he had the grace to look awkward about it while he pulled on his clothes.

As she watched him go, she told herself life would be back to normal in a week. Whatever the new normal would be, now that he was a women's magazine pin-up.

For the next few days, she saw him in the studio at lunchtime and went to the live evening show, but there were no more post-show visits. The dancers got visibly more tired as the days went by. Two dropped out, too weary and blister-footed to continue. Contestants were eliminated every night, but Rob was raking in the votes, running high on admiration. Cam was right, he had charisma, the judges were surprised and impressed by his dancing, and the audience loved him.

Each night, he gave her a wave as he left the stage, and she went home to her empty, unrumpled bed. And as she tossed and turned, trying to get to sleep, she found herself thinking about him. Their chemistry was blazing hot, until the show got in the way, but was that enough? Maybe they *were* in the same book—but was it only a bedtime story? If she was going to spend her life with someone, shouldn't it be a book that she couldn't put down, any time or place? She plumped up her pillow and lay flat under the duvet, forcing herself to relax. Everything had been turned upside down lately—she should probably just wait and see how she felt when it was all over.

One night, Therese swooped on her after the show. "We've decided to do something for you people," she said. "As you know, Friday is a rest day for the remaining contestants, so we're putting on dinner and a night in town for the families. Everyone will be there, even the contestants who've been eliminated. I hope you'll come and support Rob. I hear you're not keen on being in public."

"I'll come and support him," she replied stiffly,

ignoring the dig. "Of course I will."

"Good. We'll take care of hair and makeup, so you'll need to be at the studio in the afternoon. We'll put together a little feature to use on Saturday night's programme." With a critical look up and down, scrunching her sliced-tangelo lips, she added, "And Liddy, make sure to wear something stylish."

She restrained herself. For Rob's sake, for Rob's sake, she repeated in her head. Mercifully, Therese moved on before she had some kind of implosion. She'd never met anyone who could make her so furious, and yet so speechless. What would qualify as 'something stylish,' she wondered. Something black, probably. There would have to be a shopping trip, with some of her savings. Rob owes me, she thought, in so many ways.

★

After a late night at the mall, Livi showed up at the studios on Friday in good time, clad in a little black dress from a boutique she'd never dared set foot in before. The price tags within had confirmed her worst fears, but the dress was simple and gorgeous, with a plunging v-neck and a flared skirt that swung around her legs as she walked. She'd had to pin the sides of the 'v' to the edge of her bra, which involved some convoluted manoeuvring, but at least she didn't have to worry about an embarrassing mishap. If it was Hollywood, she thought, I would have just taped the dress right onto my magnificent implants. Therese would love that.

When she arrived, there was already quite a crowd of significant others—mums and dads, husbands, boyfriends, wives, girlfriends—all in their own version of something stylish. Therese was organising them into hair and makeup, armed with a large clipboard.

"Right, Liddy," she said, when she spotted her. "You can go through now, you might take a while."

She decided to stick up for herself this time. "Actually, it's Livi."

Therese was unmoved. "Yes, that's right, go on through please!"

What could she say? She went on through.

At dinner everyone had plenty to say about Therese, when the cameras weren't at their table. They were all looking forward to meeting up with the contestants later, at a club in town, although everyone agreed that it would have been kinder to let them sleep.

"I doubt any of them will be dancing," said one mother. "Jasmine is completely exhausted, I don't know how she's kept going."

"I've heard that some of them have *pharmaceutical* help," a husband said conspiratorially. "If you know what I mean."

Jasmine's mother gave him a sharp look. "Not *your* wife, I suppose."

He looked sheepish. "She was eliminated a few days ago."

"I heard that the ratings haven't been as good as they expected," said Jasmine's father. "Not terrible, but not fantastic either. It was on the radio this morning. They're worried it might not be renewed for another season."

"Would that be so terrible?" muttered a young man sitting next to Livi.

She gave him a smile. "I'm with you. I have mixed feelings about the whole thing."

The eliminated husband overheard. "Why would *you* have mixed feelings? Your man is probably going to win, you should be loving it."

"Well, I—"

"Or the blonde goddess," he continued. "Depends how many men are voting. I'd slip her my vote any night, any night she wanted. Jee-sus, she is scorching." And he poured himself another glass of wine.

Jasmine's father had to be restrained by her mother. "Keep the hell away from her," he ordered, "or I'll slip you a beating, you little..." He sat down abruptly as a cameraman headed their way. "Just watch yourself, unless you want me to have a chat with your wife," he growled.

Livi was glad when they ran out of wine. She had her own thoughts on Jasmine the blonde, but she wasn't going to share them with the table.

After dessert, and speeches thanking them for supporting their loved ones, they all walked up the road to Move-a-licious, the cheesily-named club that had been booked out for the occasion. As they walked, they gathered a following of reporters.

"Why are they making us walk like this?" someone complained. But when she saw the film crews waiting outside the club, Livi realised it had been planned for maximum drama. The manufactured hype felt cringe-worthy, but she smiled nicely from the safest spot she could find, tucked in the middle of the significant others. Cameras flashed as they passed along the red carpet (red carpet! oh, please) and into the darkened thud, thud, thud.

The first person she encountered was, of course, Jasmine.

"Hi!" she enthused, her hair glowing pale in the starriness of hundreds of tiny ceiling lights. "You're Rob's girlfriend! Wow, he is so great, isn't he! Hey, is it true, you know, how they say if a man's a good dancer, then he's good, you know, elsewhere?" She raised a suggestive eyebrow. "God, you lucky thing... Mum! Dad! Wow, it's so great to see you..." And she was gone, into the spotlight of a news crew.

Vodka, Livi thought. Vodka. She headed for the bar. Then, feeling strengthened with a drink in hand, she threaded her way through the crowd looking for Rob, skirting around the film crews doing interviews. Eventually she came upon Therese, in her element with a pack of black-garbed industry insiders.

"All alone!" she exclaimed over the music. "Have you seen Rob yet?" When Livi shook her head, she said, "Well, I'm sure he'd like to see you. I saw him going that way a few minutes ago." She pointed towards the back of the club.

This very small kindness was so unexpected that, after a hard week, Livi felt grateful out of all proportion. "Oh, thanks," she said. "Thank you."

Therese just smiled and watched her go.

The club was getting more and more jammed with people, and she had to elbow her way through to the back. In the corridor leading to the rest rooms there was a queue of women, jiggling and stepping, waiting to get into the ladies' bathroom. She waited for a few moments in case Rob came out of the men's bathroom, then went back out. A reporter from a late-night news programme was waiting, glammed up to blend in, cameraman hovering over her shoulder.

"Livi, right? Livi Callaway?"

She held up a hand against the sudden glare of the camera's light. "Yes."

"I'm Janet Walker, *Newsnight Tonight*. We'd love to do an interview with you and Rob. They're saying he might take out the top spot. What do you think about that?"

"I think he's doing really well, it would be great if he won. And an interview would be okay, I suppose." Her eyes strained into the dark crowd outside the pool of light. Was that Rob? "Excuse me," she said, struggling to see into the corner. "I'll just go and ask him."

She took a few steps, and Janet and her cameraman followed. "Oh, I'll be right back," she said, dying to be rid of them.

Janet nodded and held up a hand to the cameraman, and Livi continued towards the Rob-shaped figure. In the smudgy darkness, she couldn't quite see…

A girl reached out and pulled him close, the sequins on her dress catching and throwing back disco lights. She stood on stiletto-tiptoe to kiss him, one foot leaving the ground as her lips met his.

Oh, it's not Rob, Livi thought, and started to turn away.

Then she looked again. He buried one hand in the hair at the back of the girl's neck, and cupped the other around the shapely curve of her bottom, pulling her closer.

The camera lit Livi's face as she stood paralysed for the longest moment. She heard Janet hiss "Over there!", and the corner was suddenly illuminated. She had enough time to see the shock on Rob's face…and enough time to register that the girl was not Jasmine the blonde, but his other perfect match, as predicted by magazine readers.

Then her legs were moving, taking her through the mass of people, past Therese, out the door, back down the red carpet, into the city, beyond the reach of cameras, moving without any idea where she was going, just away from the spotlight and the jagged feeling in her chest. His words came back to her as she wove across the road, between Friday-night boy racers bumper-to-bumper on the main street. *We don't want her all crushed next time she faces the nation.*

All crushed. In the end, he did it himself.

Chapter Nine

A mongst greater London's eight million or so people, Livi counted herself lucky to work with some of the sweetest. Cass, of course. And Aidan and Will. They'd been together ten years, comfortably drinking the same green tea, wearing each other's clothes, and cooking dinner on alternate nights in their effortlessly cool Soho flat. For the last few years, they'd even worked together without any major upsets. They didn't hesitate to acidly point out the other's shortcomings, or poke fun at the other's mannerisms or bad jokes or latest experimental hairstyle, but there was such a *certainness* about them. They were a team, absolutely.

Today, at Cass's insistence, Livi was beginning the search for the mysterious American she'd met on the tube. All week, she'd found herself drifting off into daydreams, distracted by tantalising thoughts of him. Of course, it was nothing more than that—a daydream. If she did find him, she'd return his bag and the clues it held, and he'd return to America, probably into the arms of a feisty but glamorous Idaho cowgirl.

Maybe it was better that way. After all, when she arrived in London, she'd made a firm resolve—keep herself to herself, and avoid any more man dramas. Sure, there was temptation, but she was determined to stay out of trouble's reach. Lately though, after months of watching Aidan and Will happily teamed up, she'd begun to think that, maybe, she wouldn't throw all men out with the bath water. She told them as much that Friday morning at Peach, while they were waiting for the first client to arrive.

"No, no, no, you can't throw men out with the bath water!" exclaimed Aidan. "Once they're clean, it's a crime to waste them."

Livi could only laugh from behind the box of smoothing serum she was unpacking. "Honestly though, how do you stay friends, when you live together, and work together?"

"Oh, no, sweetheart, we're not *friends.*" Will shook his head. "We're lovers. A friend would never stand for what he puts me through. There has to be a greater reward."

Aidan looked apologetic. "It's true. I'm a nightmare. But I'm *so* worth it." He gave Livi a wink. He was so handsome, she believed him.

"So you do have disagreements, and fights?" she asked, putting down the inventory form she'd been ticking off.

"Oh, I love to start a fight, just so we get to do the making up," said Aidan. "It's the best fun getting him hot under the collar, I can tell you."

Will tutted, trying to maintain a stern look, but his smile won out.

"Of course," Aidan continued, "you have to get your fight started early enough in the evening, to allow plenty of time for all the making up. Never go to bed angry."

"To sleep angry, you mean," Livi corrected him.

He nodded. "You're right, those are two different things," he said. "It's the advice every mother should give before the wedding."

She sighed. "I wonder what my mother would have told me."

"Relationships are like hair care," Will said, holding up one of the bottles of serum. "You have to use the right products to keep everything healthy, smooth, and shiny."

Aidan clapped a hand to his forehead. "*Please* don't go into advertising," he pleaded. "That was terrible."

"No, it's true," Will said. "It may cost a bit more, but without it you're left with nothing but frizz."

"And split ends," Livi added, taking back the serum. "He's right."

Will took up his scissors from the plush cloth they'd been nestling on. "Well, I should know, you couldn't calculate the extra I've put into *you*." The scissors flashed under the salon lights as he pointed them at Aidan.

"And who was it that bought you those custom-made, monogrammed, top-of-the-line beauties?" Aidan asked.

"We're not talking about *material* things," Will said. "Don't you have more depth than that?" But then he smiled as he tenderly polished away an imaginary blemish on the blade. "You did."

Aidan was satisfied. "Well, then." He turned to Livi. "And don't worry, your mother will have her chance," he told her. "Someone will snap you up."

"I don't know if she wants to be snapped up," Will said. "She's not looking for true love with a crocodile. But sweetheart, you are a catch."

"Thanks, you two," she said. "I can't really say I'm looking for true love at all, at the moment. But I suppose I'm starting to think I could dip my toe in the water again. Even if it might be crocodile-infested."

"Just the fact that you're looking for something—well, someone, the American—is a good sign," Aidan said. "Hopefully *he* won't turn out to be a crocodile."

"He'd have to be an alligator, I suppose, being from over there," Livi pointed out. She went to the door and turned the heavy placard to show 'Open'. "Anyway, all I'm trying to do is give his bag back, remember."

Aidan and Will exchanged a look. "Okay," Aidan said. "If you want to rationalise it like that. But I heard he was an absolute honey."

It was true. He was. Since their Saturday night encounter,

the American had lingered in her mind. He was a teasing reminder that she was still the same Livi who'd once run hot, night after night, a tinderbox to the touch. Her wayward mind kept returning to the moments when they stood close together in the crowded carriage. In the aftermath of Rob, she'd almost forgotten that deliciously blurry, heated sensation—but the American had made her feel positively combustible.

Then the first client swept through the door, shaking raindrops off her umbrella, and they swung into action.

Livi hadn't had any salon experience before Nicolette hired her for Peach. But she was born to organise, and her experience in the family company had given her all the business skills she needed. She quickly learned the salon side of things. Officially she was the receptionist, but the longer she was there, the more duties Nicolette handed over. She answered the phone, ordered stock, managed the computerised appointment system and coordinated rosters. She looked after the junior staff, analysed salon turnover, kept up with all the new retail products, and maintained their Instagram and Facebook accounts. Nicolette came in less and less, and Livi did more and more.

Probably the trickiest job of all was molly-coddling their clients, who came on a spectrum from fussy to high-maintenance to hissy-fit. The fashion designer, the property developer's wife, the backing singer with ambition, the viscount's daughter, the TV presenter...they were hard work, but she'd started to think of them as from another species—they had their own characteristics and quirks, it was just how they were. They were so far removed from her own reality, it made her feel reassuringly normal. From this semi-detached view, it wasn't too hard to be patient with their obsessions and (mostly) unfounded anxieties.

Although she and the others were sometimes irritated by how little involvement Nicolette had in her own salon, there was a plus side. Livi made sure that the business was thriving, and then, within reason, she could organise things to suit them all.

She was leaving early that day, driving with Cass and their friend Mia to Hartfield, near Cotchford Farm—the first, and possibly last, stop on the trail of clues they'd discovered in the American's bag. She had no idea whether they'd find him, or even if they were on the right track with the dates. But once Cass and Mia got involved, the search was going ahead no matter what. They looked for the adventure in any situation, and if they couldn't find one, they'd make one up. With or without the American, she knew she'd enjoy the hunt.

★

Livi had never known Mia to be late. In fact, she was more likely to arrive early for any occasion, so she could sit and chat companionably while she waited for everyone else to get there, or be ready to leave too. So as the clock worked its way nearer to three, Livi kept glancing out to the cars hissing past on the wet street, expecting her to pull up with Cass (who was having a day off) at any moment.

But as she returned to the front desk after asking Katie, their most junior stylist, to sterilise some equipment, Aidan came and stood close alongside.

"Livi," he said out of the corner of his mouth, maintaining a casual expression. "Crisis alert. Client hysteria."

He flicked his eyes towards the salon's consultation area. Huddled on the dark leather settee was a young woman who must have been immaculately groomed when she left home, but was now obviously in the process of falling to pieces. Puddle water had crept up the legs of her jeans, and her red coat, unequal to the weather, was clinging heavily to her body.

"Nothing I say seems to be the right thing," he said. "Can you try? We could be in for a major drama if we don't get her defused."

Livi nudged him. "I thought you liked drama."

"Well, who doesn't?" he replied. "But I can't get any sense out of her, it's heartbreaking. Livi, please, be a sweetheart."

"I can't stay later than three," she warned him, reaching under the reception desk for a box of tissues. That morning she'd tucked the satchel under there too, keeping it safe until they set off to find its persistently distracting owner. For now, she pushed aside thoughts of whether the reunion might bring another round of flirting, or something more than that...

"Thank you, thank you," Aidan stage-whispered as she turned to go, relief obvious on his face. "I owe you one."

She made her way over to the crumpled figure and sat down. Holding out a handful of tissues, she said, "Hi, I'm Livi. Is there anything I can do to help?"

The young woman turned to her, with a tear-streaked face. Despite red eyes and smeared makeup, she was very pretty, and didn't look much older than a teenager.

"Do?" she repeated. "Help? I must look beyond help." She took the tissues and scrunched them to her face, shoulders heaving. "What could possibly help now?"

"Well, we'll do whatever we can," said Livi gently. "Who was doing your hair today?"

"I already *had* my hair done," she replied in a rising voice. "And now, *just look.*" She put her hands in her hair and flung the damp, dishevelled blonde curls upwards, letting them fall again any which way. A tissue drifted to the floor, landing next to her sodden suede boots, and she started to cry again.

Aware of curious looks from everyone else in the salon, Livi took her hand and levered her up. "Come on, let's go out the back and get you a cup of tea."

"Tea?" She shook her head but went along with Livi. "What good is tea, when my life is ruined?"

Here was drama to match Aidan any day. Livi steered her into the staffroom and asked Katie to take over at reception. Then she shut the door behind them, took the girl's coat as she peeled it off, and found a seat for her at the lunch table.

"I'm sorry, I didn't find out your name," she said, putting tea bags into mugs.

"Helena," came the snuffly reply, followed by a resounding nose blow. "Although my name will be mud now, thanks to him."

Livi came and sat with her at the table. "Him? What happened?"

"We organised this fundraiser together, for charity, you know. For cancer. It was his mother's idea really. She had cancer, you see." She blew her nose again.

"Oh, I'm sorry to hear that."

"That's okay, she's all clear now. Anyway, he— Edwin—he'd got into trouble at university, drinking too much, stupid pranks, and then he was caught plagiarising in an essay. And they said he was in danger of being expelled. So his mother made a deal with the head of department."

"To do some good works," Livi said.

"That's right," Helena replied. "But I ended up doing most of the work, while he got to look good. And now..." The tears flowed again.

"Now?" Livi prompted.

"Now, today, I went and had my hair and makeup done, then we met up for coffee, just, you know, to go over the final details. And he broke up with me, and he said I shouldn't go tonight. But most of the people will be there because I invited them, or convinced them, to go. I can't just not be there. But I can't go and face him. I'm such a wreck." She paused for breath and wiped tears and eyeliner from the top of each cheek. "He just wants to take all the credit. Damn it, why should he win?"

Livi reached out and took her hand. "He shouldn't," she said. "And he won't."

She managed a wavery smile. "I'm so sorry to make such a scene. I just had to get away, I just walked and walked and didn't look back, and then I realised what a mess I was, and then I looked up and saw your salon."

"Well, you came to the right place," Livi replied.

There was a hesitant knock, and Aidan peeked around the door. "Livi, just to let you know Cass and Mia are here."

She looked at her watch. Ten to three. Then she looked at Aidan. A plan was crystal clear in her mind.

"You know how you said you owed me one? I'm calling it in."

Chapter Ten

B y ten past three Livi was in the car with Cass and Mia,
heading for Hartfield. Helena was at a shampoo station
having a wash and deluxe head massage, and Will was
ready to give her a knock-out up do. Livi had convinced a
makeup artist from the spa along the road to come at short
notice, with the promise of a free colour in return (figuring
Cass wouldn't mind when she knew why). And she'd
rescheduled Aidan's last client so that he could race home
and pick out his most stylish outfit, befitting the dashing
companion of a successful young society fundraiser. All
Helena had to do was put on her party dress and hold her
head high. Livi hoped she could carry it off.

"I'm sure she will," said Mia, stopping the car to let a
soggy backpacker scurry over a pedestrian crossing. "Aidan
is so gorgeous, with him on her arm she'll be flying."

"I hope you told him not to play up though," Cass said
over her shoulder. "He's great at coming out with
inappropriate comments."

"It'll be fine," Livi replied. "He's under strict
instructions. And Helena's so sweet, he really wanted to
help when he heard the story."

"She's not the only one with a story about appalling

61

man behaviour," Cass commented, raising an eyebrow in Livi's direction.

She looked out at the endless-seeming streets of London going by in the drizzle. "I just thought, yes, why *should* he get to treat her like that and come out looking like the winner?"

"I'm glad Rob didn't get to be the winner. Karma. You had that satisfaction at least," said Cass.

"I don't know if satisfaction is the right word exactly," Livi replied. "But I probably would have lost all faith in human nature if he'd won."

"Did he get any votes at all after that?" Mia asked. Cass had told her the basics of Livi's brush with fame, but Livi hated talking about it.

"Some. I would have preferred none." Ideally, she would have preferred him to have choked on a stray sequin. Or been struck by a bus on the way home. Or by lightning. Or a meteorite. She was flexible. Just as long as he didn't win.

If he had, she wouldn't have been there to see it, anyway. By the time Rob was doing his last night of shooshing around the dance floor, she was on a plane to elsewhere. Because once footage of her humiliation screened on *Newsnight Tonight*—that same night—every other TV channel, website, radio station and newspaper in the country picked it up. Even she could see it was too juicy a story to leave alone, but it was no fun being the one in the spotlight.

The next day, the phone rang incessantly, and Gemma and Bex stepped in to fend off reporters, shocked friends, and women's magazine editors, while Livi wished she hadn't volunteered to put her name on the phone account, making her number so easy to find. She left her mobile turned off.

Mid-morning, reporters started turning up at the house, knocking and calling out inane questions. "Livi, how do you feel?" She hardly needed to answer that one—the photographic evidence said it all. "Livi, what do you want to say to Rob?" Well, nothing that wouldn't be peppered with beeps (or asterisks). "Livi, will you be at the show tonight?" They seemed undeterred by getting no response. She supposed they could whisk up a dramatic story out of that, just as well as they could from any actual answers.

The girls sat with her to watch *Dance 'til You Drop* that night. They didn't think it was a good idea, but she felt compelled to find out what they'd show, so they ignored the intermittent door-knocking and turned the volume up.

First, there was the usual recap of the previous day's events. A tightly edited montage of clips showed the contestants relaxing on their day off. Then there were scenes from the dinner (although none of the complaints), and the faux-Hollywood red carpet walk. Livi was pleased to see that she was only just visible in the crowd.

But then everyone was suddenly walking in slow motion on the screen, and the shot came in close. A little oval of light appeared around her, while the rest of the significant others were in shadow. The voiceover became more dramatic.

"Livi Callaway is engaged to Rob, one of the show's hottest contenders. She has no idea that her night is about to take a turn for the worse..."

Then, an ad break. Livi leaned back in her chair.

"Maybe we shouldn't watch," said Gemma.

"No," she said. "I want to see it."

But when the moment arrived, and she saw herself walking away from Janet Walker, towards her unpleasant surprise, she picked up the remote and switched the television off. "Actually, I don't want to."

Gemma nodded. "Good call. There's no point in torturing yourself."

Bex fetched a bottle of wine, the most expensive one in their small collection, and three glasses. "I think you've earned it," she said. "And we'll keep you company."

Eventually, the last reporters gave up and left, and the neighbours stopped twitching their curtains and started turning out their lights. They sat in the living room with their wine, and a bit of peace at last.

But then there was one more knock at the door.

"For God's sake," Livi said. "Don't they ever sleep?"

Bex got up and twitched their own curtain back a few millimetres. "It's not another reporter," she said. "It's Rob."

Livi started to get up, but Bex had other plans. "No," she said. "You stay there. He should work for it."

She went out of the living room, and they heard her open the front door. "What took you so long?" she asked.

They couldn't help smiling at each other. She obviously had no intention of going easy on him.

When he replied, Livi could hear the change in his voice. "You know why. I had to dance during the day, then I had the show."

"Right, the show."

There was a long silence. The girls imagined Bex giving Rob her steely-eyed look. That fierce face could stop a bear in its tracks. Finally, Rob said, "So...can I see her?"

She must have relented, because in a moment she appeared, Rob following behind. Livi stood up.

"We'll leave you to it," Gemma said. "Come on, Bex."

They went out, closing the door behind them.

Livi looked at him. His hair was full of product and his face still bore traces of the stage makeup. His t-shirt was a white v-neck, made from cotton so fine she could see the outline of his muscular, newly waxed chest. Where was her rough and ready builder? She missed the old Rob. The Rob whose work-roughened hands could also work gentle magic. Whose idea of dressing up was a scalding hot shower, aftershave balm, and his best jeans. And who would have laughed a hairless, v-neck-wearing builder off the premises.

"I'm sorry," he said. "That wasn't meant to happen."

She must have looked as sceptical as she felt. At least he didn't start with 'Therese says'.

He began again. "We were just friends. I mean, we *are* just friends."

She sighed at the cliché. "You know, I've had a lot of time to think lately." Once, she spent her days remembering what they'd done the night before, and imagining what they'd do again that night. But with most of Rob's nights devoted to the show, her empty bed had given her plenty of opportunity to think. And without the nights, the mismatch appeared in plain daylight. "We're not really right for each other, are we?"

"It felt right to me," he said. "All those nights. I know you felt it too…over and over again." He reached for her, but she stepped back. The old magic was gone, the denial no longer blissful.

"It's just not enough."

"It used to be," he said. "We were dynamite, you know that."

"I know." She looked at the hand he held out, and remembered the touch that she'd risen to meet, hungry for more. She looked at the lips that had travelled her body with intoxicating precision. Then she looked in his eyes, and remembered the truth. "But it wasn't enough to build something real. Something that would stand up in the real world. You should be looking for more than that too."

He shook his head. "Last night, that was just one mistake. I don't even know why it happened."

"Rob," she said. "If you really don't know why, maybe you need to do some thinking too."

He shook his head. "It's just been a crazy time. Therese says ups and downs are inevitable when you're in the media."

There it was. Therese says. She held herself steady, as she'd done so often when faced with the woman herself. "That might be true," she said. "But it doesn't make it okay."

"Babe, just think about it. Don't make any decisions. There's only one more night to go."

As she saw him out, she gave nothing away. But her decision *was* made. The next day, she grabbed a last-minute ticket online and packed a suitcase. Time to resume her original plan.

On the way to the airport, her mum assured her the business would get along fine. Her dad didn't say much, but his face was grim and his knuckles were white on the steering wheel. She sat in the back seat watching the familiar green landscape passing by, and said a silent goodbye, to more things than she could bear to think about.

★

Now she pulled herself back to the present, a different city rolling past the window. She squinted out through the London rain. She was moving on. She *had* moved on.

"I think it's lovely that you're helping Helena so much," Mia said, catching her eye in the rear view mirror.

"Yes, women should stick together more than they do," said Cass. "I don't know why we're so competitive and judgemental with each other. We should back each other up."

"I'm glad you feel that way," Livi replied, "because I had to promise the makeup artist a free colour to get her this afternoon. She had to rearrange her clients."

Cass laughed. "Take me for granted, why don't you! That's okay. Anyway, you're in charge of my appointments, just tuck her in somewhere secretly."

"We should probably do it when Nicolette's not there."

"Do it at my place, if you like," Mia offered. "I've got a full range. I could do dinner afterwards."

Cass had first met Mia at a product launch for colourists. Ending up in the same group to watch a demonstration, each recognised a kindred spirit in the other, and they were tucked up in a bar, wine glasses in hand, before the model's last foil was in place. Since then Mia had decided she was fed up with working in a salon, no matter how swanky. She only took a few select, desperately grateful clients at her house in Notting Hill.

And each of those desperately grateful clients had a clutch of desperately hopeful friends waiting for a chance to get through her front door. Mia knew, with only a look, which combinations of tones and highlights would flatter and frame even the most sallow, tired face. Those lucky ones stepped back out, almost unbelieving, looking and feeling brighter, lighter, and ready to take on the world. They invariably stopped for a moment between the pillars outside the door to feel their locks, glossy and new, before proceeding down the white steps like pageant contestants. Not surprisingly, Mia felt perfectly justified in charging a small fortune for her talents.

Not that she needed to earn anything if she didn't feel like it. Her father was a Swedish baron (or a count, or a knight, Livi had never figured out exactly which). After her mother died, when Mia was only three, they moved to London with her grandmother. While her father immersed himself in using the family money to build a property empire, Mia and her Farmor Ingela made a home in England.

"Dinner? Don't say you've given in and started cooking now that Farmor's gone," Cass teased.

They'd come to know Mia's grandmother so well that she insisted they also call her Farmor, explaining that it was the Swedish name for your father's mother. In her opinion, Farmor said, the more granddaughters the better.

"Oh, no," Mia said now. Her neat blonde bob swung and settled again as she shook her head, and she patted her (only slightly rounded) middle. "But we'll have real food. Farmor would be on the first flight back if she thought I was eating fast food. I found a place that does ready-made meals to reheat at home. I had a divine duck leg confit from there last week."

Cass screwed up her nose. "I don't think I could eat any part of a duck." She paused. "Though I suppose it's the same as eating chicken, when you think about it..."

Livi stretched her seatbelt to lean forward. "Is Farmor enjoying being home?"

"Well, she lived here for such a long time, she says she's not sure where home is now. So she's experimenting. Testing it out."

"What about you? Have you thought about moving back too?"

Mia shook her head. "No, not me, I won't go back. But I've been here all my life. All the life I can remember, anyway. England is home for me."

Is home where you begin, or where you grow up...or where you end up? Livi wondered. There were times when her heart hurt for the things she'd left behind. Little things, mostly. The sweet, soft air. Walking in bare feet. The heavenly ice cream. But bigger things too. Friends. Family. The ease of being in the place that's yours. Even if it was only yours for a while.

"I love that you stay Swedish enough for the Saab though," Cass said, patting the tan leather seat.

"Of course! It was that or a Volvo. But I'm saving the Volvo for when I have some kids to put in it. Touch wood." She pressed her fingers to the glowing woodgrain on the dashboard. Then she stopped at an intersection, and squinted through the rain at a cluster of road signs. "Could someone check the map? The Saab is great, but it won't get us out of London by itself."

Cass looked at her phone. "Right," she announced, with an air of authority. "The A23 to the M23 to the A264 to...oh, but there's the A22, that looks better. How would you get onto that? Just a minute..."

Mia turned to Livi with a grin. "Lucky we're not expecting your American until tomorrow."

★

Although it wasn't much more than an hour's drive, thanks to the rain they arrived in Hartfield in a gloomy half-dark. Mia found a spot in the pub car park, and they made a dash up the stairs and fell gratefully through the old wooden doors.

"This is great," Livi said, looking around at dark beams, comfy seats, and a sea of cheerful faces.

Cass elbowed her and pointed out the handsome bartender. "I agree."

Before long, they were ensconced at a table with beer and crisps.

"I don't know why we let him talk us into this," said Livi, tentatively sipping dark liquid through the foam on her Westerham Grasshopper. "Whew, I see why they call it a bitter. Thank goodness they're only halves." Cass had refused the barman's offer of pints, insisting that a half was much more ladylike.

"This experiment seems to have an animal theme," Mia said. "You with a Grasshopper, me with Black Sheep Bitter, and British Bulldog for Cass. Do you think he was having a laugh?"

"Well, if he was I can't bring myself to mind," Cass replied, watching him pull another smooth pint. "I'd put myself in his hands any day. Although one of these will be enough, I think. It's a bit manly for me."

"Good. You don't want a hangover for tomorrow." Mia sent her a firm look. "Now, I've done some finding out, as promised."

Because Mia was even more organised than Livi, and definitely more meticulous than Cass, she'd volunteered to do some research before their visit. She pulled a folder out of her bag and found space for it on the table.

"A dossier!" Cass said. "I'm terribly impressed."

"Mock if you like," Mia retorted. "This is good stuff." She brushed away crisp crumbs and opened the folder.

"So, clue number one—Cotchford Farm. Date, 8/27— tomorrow. Home of A.A. Milne, author of *When We Were Very Young, Now We Are Six*, the Winnie-the-Pooh books. And of his son, Christopher, as in Christopher Robin. If we have good weather tomorrow, we can go exploring in the Hundred Acre Wood. Apparently all the places in the books are based on real places around here."

"That's sweet!" Cass exclaimed. "But why would Livi's American be interested in Pooh Bear? That doesn't seem right."

Livi frowned. "It does seem a bit strange. He didn't seem that type...whatever that type would be."

"Ah, but wait." Mia made a show of turning to a new page in the folder. "There's more. A.A. Milne and Christopher Robin weren't the only famous people who lived at the farm. Brian Jones lived there too, in the sixties."

Livi looked blank. "Brian Jones?"

"You know, the Rolling Stones," Cass explained. "He was the guitarist. Who replaced him, Ronnie Wood? Maybe there was someone else first. My dad will know, he loves the Stones. But didn't Brian Jones drown?"

"Yes." Mia paused for effect. "He drowned in the swimming pool at Cotchford Farm. It was ruled death by misadventure, but some people believe he was murdered."

There was silence at the table while they absorbed this information.

"That's not so sweet," Cass said, looking at Livi.

"And best of all," Mia continued, "or maybe worst of all, the Brian Jones Fan Club was selling actual tiles from the swimming pool. All numbered, with a certificate of authenticity."

"No!" Livi was horrified, but couldn't help laughing.

"Yes, one hundred and thirty pounds, plus post and packing. A bargain."

"I really don't know what to make of that." Livi shook her head. "But I think I'd prefer him to be a Pooh Bear fan."

"Still," said Cass, "on the positive side, that may have solved my birthday present dilemma for Dad." And she gave the barman a wave and her sweetest smile.

"Maybe he just knows the people who live there now," Livi suggested.

"Maybe," said Mia. "But I had a look at the other locations too. I'm not sure about the 'Golders Green 3P' that he wrote on the A–Z page—it could be anything. I need to spend more time on that. But there is something significant about Rue Beautreillis." She looked at their expectant faces. "Jim Morrison had an apartment at number seventeen. He died in the bathtub there."

"No!" Livi said again. But this time there was no laughing. Another watery death. She could see the others struggling to think of something positive to say.

"I didn't want to say anything before, in case it put you off coming today," Mia said.

"It could just be a coincidence," offered Cass, always the optimist.

"I suppose so," Livi said. But if it *was* just a coincidence, it was an uncomfortably unpleasant one. She took a bracing sip of the Grasshopper. He'd looked pretty clean-cut...but under the surface, it could be a completely different story. If they did find this American, she'd better be ready for anything.

Chapter Eleven

The clear, bright day that dawned seemed to lessen the misgivings of the night before. After a cooked breakfast, with plenty of tea, they all felt ready for action. Armed with Mia's research and a collective sense of purpose, they headed down the high street and out of the village. In the morning light, Livi felt like she was being driven along the top of a chocolate box, the city weight of London falling away.

"Oh, this is gorgeous," she enthused. "Such beautiful buildings, and look, Pooh Corner!" She practically bounced in her seat, Tigger-like. "That looks so lovely, we *have* to stop there on the way back."

"Maybe your American will be in there, hanging out with Piglet and eating a pot of honey," teased Cass. "Honey for the honey."

"I hope so. Better than the alternative."

Cass nodded. "Shame it's not actually on the corner though."

Soon they were in green fields on both sides, up and back down a steep hill, and then they were turning right into Cotchford Lane. Livi suddenly felt her stomach cramp with nerves. She looked down at the leather satchel sitting on the seat next to her, and held her middle. There's no need for that, she told her belly. All we're doing is returning something lost.

Mia and Cass looked over their shoulders at her. Apparently that last part had come out louder than she intended.

"Returning something lost, did you say?" asked Mia.

"Yes, and finding something new for you too," said Cass, sitting up straighter as Mia stopped the car in the lane. They all peered down a leafy driveway. "Something good, I'm sure. And he could be just down there."

"Cass, less drama, not more, would be good," Livi pleaded. "My insides are all twisty-turny."

"Sorry," she replied. "But fate can have that effect on people," she added, looking in the direction of the farm.

"Less fate, more action," Mia said decisively, unbuckling her seatbelt. "This is what we came for. Bring the bag, Livi."

As they walked down the driveway, the house came into view, warm red brick with deeply pitched roofs, two chimneys anchoring it into the slope of the hill. Flowers bloomed in front, and climbers swathed the walls and tickled the white window trims.

"Now *that* is chocolate box," Livi said, forgetting her nerves for a moment.

"Definitely more Pooh Bear than sex and drugs and rock 'n' roll," said Cass. "Although, it has a bit of Miss Marple about it. It's very quiet."

She was right. There were no cars in the driveway, and the windows were all firmly shut against the morning air. Livi's stomach relaxed a little, but disappointment shuffled quietly up behind her.

Then a man came around the corner of the house, and they all jumped, along with her stomach.

"Can I help you?" he asked.

Cass and Mia both looked to Livi, two sets of raised eyebrows, but she shook her head. He was tall, and not completely unattractive, but he was carrying garden shears, and he wasn't the American.

"Um, we were looking for someone. An American, um, visitor..." She realised she didn't know where to start explaining, but he saved her from further fumbling.

"Nobody's here today. They've gone up to London." He narrowed his eyes. "It *was* to meet an American. He was supposed to come here. Do you know him?"

Disappointment now gave her a hefty shove in the back. So near and yet so far. She searched about for what to say. "No, actually, we were hoping you did."

Suspicion hardened his expression, and he swung the sharp-looking shears around in front of him. "And you are?"

All three of them looked nervously at the long blades. Then Cass stepped forward, smiling.

"We're sorry to have troubled you, we're just doing a tour of Pooh Bear country and we were hoping to find a friend."

His face only softened a little as he looked her up and down. "Well, this isn't a tour stop, this is someone's home. Between you crazy toy people and those Jones fanatics, there's no peace. Honestly, a bit of respect." He brandished the shears. "I've got edgings to trim and a pool to clean." And he stomped away.

They took their chance and scuttled back down the driveway, hearts on hold. Once they were all bundled into the car, they breathed sighs of relief.

"Whoa," said Livi.

The others could only nod.

"We were on the right track though," she said. "He could have been here. We were so close."

"Fate delayed is fate denied," said Cass sadly. Then, "I could go a drink about now."

"That's justice delayed," Livi pointed out. "And denied. But I could do with something to steady my nerves too."

"It's too early for that," said Mia. "Although, there is something else soothing we could do. It's a surprise." She started the car and turned it back to the main road. "I don't think it's far."

Livi and Cass wanted to know more, but she wouldn't be drawn. Soon they were turning into a car park, still in the countryside. They all got out and Mia herded them down a path.

"Trust me," she said. "And while we're walking, find some sticks."

"Sticks?" they both asked.

But she just kept walking, stopping every so often to gather up a fallen twig or branch, so they did the same. Eventually, after going through woods and meadows, they were in the trees again. The sun speckled gently through the summer leaves, and a rustic wooden bridge arched over a narrow river.

"This," said Mia with obvious satisfaction, "is Poohsticks Bridge. I read that you can walk here from the farm, but it was probably better to drive, given the circumstances."

Livi's face was stuck in a big grin. "Oh, that's what the sticks are for!"

"This is too sweet," Cass said. "I love it!"

"It's *exactly* how it should be," said Livi.

"Good," said Mia. "Let's play then."

They happily lost track of time dropping sticks off the bridge and running backwards and forwards like children, until some tourists arrived and, suddenly self-conscious, they realised they'd better let someone else have a turn.

On the way back to the car, they all had an extra spring about them. Livi twirled a Julie Andrews impression on the open path. "It's so nice to have some *space*. Being in the city all the time, your eyes forget what a horizon looks like."

"I know what you mean," said Mia. "A city needs lots of green places."

Livi nodded. "Yes. But it's not just space for its own sake."

"Not just for spinning?" Cass tried out a few turns and twisted her ankle on a rutted part of the track. "Ow!"

"No, I mean, having physical space gives you mental space, and emotional space. Head space. I think that's one reason why the world's gone so wrong. People just don't have space for mental health. They're squished in little flats, in cramped buildings, in crowded streets, in teeming cities. Their hearts can't breathe."

"Well, you *are* comparing with your little piece of paradise. I don't know if things are that much worse here than before," Cass said. "Who was that old Roman guy who complained about the state of society? Or was he Greek? Anyway. The youth of today, and all that."

"I think it was Socrates," offered Mia. "Greek. We had to study philosophy at school," she explained.

"Don't sound so apologetic," said Livi. "That's very impressive."

"Yes," Cass added, "with youth like you there's still hope for the world." And she gave her friend a squeeze.

"I don't know about youth," laughed Mia, "but at least we're old enough for that drink. And I'm already hungry for lunch. Let's get going. The first of September isn't far away, we should start thinking about Livi's next move. Unless you want to go to the Pooh shop?"

"No, let's not sully the magic of Poohsticks Bridge with commercialism," said Livi. "Nothing could better that."

"Yes, let's sully it with alcohol instead," Cass laughed. "Ooh, I wonder if that barman is working today..."

She gave her ankle one last rub and set off, happily anticipating her own next move.

★

That night, when Mia dropped them off at the flat, Livi and Cass found a small figure with a large suitcase sitting on their front step. As they came through the front gate and the figure stood up to meet them, Livi had to rub her eyes, cartoon-like, to believe what she was seeing. Surely not.

"Mum? What are you doing here?"

She gave a little shrug, a little smile. "I thought I'd come and visit."

"Where's Dad?" She looked all around, as though he might burst out from behind one of the raggedy shrubs in the front garden.

Her mother's voice was casual, but her face gave away something more. "He's at home, I suppose."

Livi remembered Cam's last email. *Someone told my mother that yours had gone on holiday...* Her brain strained to pull the pieces together, but refused to process what it came up with.

More tea, she thought, opening the door for her mum and picking up the suitcase. Though she knew hair, makeup, and borrowed arm candy wouldn't fix this one. After tea, she had no idea where to begin.

★

To: cam.holden@nzuni.ac.nz
From: liviaway@gmail.com
Subject: Another night's developments

These developments less fun than the last. Mum's here. We got home from looking for the American (who we didn't find) and she was waiting at the front door. Apparently she's been here for a week, staying with her cousin June, who I've never heard of. Thinking, she says. I can't understand why Dad hasn't phoned, or come over even. She's determined not to phone him, and I'm not allowed to either. She's full of apologies, but she won't tell me what happened. This is obviously NOT a holiday. I don't know what to do, or what she's going to do. Thank goodness I could go back to work today. (Never thought I'd find myself saying that.)

This is all the wrong way round, surely my parents should be the ones worrying about *me* still. We're not supposed to worry about them until much later.

Sorry for the depressing message. Hope you've had a worry-free weekend.

xxx

To: liviaway@gmail.com
From: cam.holden@nzuni.ac.nz
Subject: Re: Another night's developments

I'm really sorry—that's no good. I don't know what you should do either, except maybe give her time and space to do her thinking, whatever it is she's thinking about. I'm sure she'll talk to you about it when she's ready, and I'm sure you'll do the right thing. Tell me if there's anything I can do here.

This weekend I've been worrying about trying to meet a deadline for a paper. It's about how poor countries are being forced to compete with each other, and with rich industrialised nations. It's a downward spiral—reduce wages, use cheaper resources, lower standards—which only makes people poorer in the long run. Can be an argument against globalisation. I'm writing it with James. Remember him? The only one who didn't shave after Movember last year. Looking very dodgy by now.

Also worrying now about whether to order Chinese or Thai. Some problems are more easily solved.

Good luck with the rogue mother.

xxx

Chapter Twelve

L ivi couldn't remember a time in her life when her parents were apart for more than a few days. They weren't perfect, she knew—there had been disagreements, like any two people who'd stuck together for almost thirty years. But now, to have them not just apart, but literally on opposite sides of the world, felt totally wrong. They were her foundation, and she'd taken their solid grounding for granted. Now she felt like she was sagging in the middle. Obviously there were people in the world with unimaginably large problems—her own life was a dream in comparison—but somehow that didn't make her situation less upsetting. Just knowing that someone else has broken their leg, she thought, doesn't make your sprained ankle less painful.

That morning Cass was extra solicitous, rolling a spare stool across so she could sit instead of stand behind the reception desk, leaping to answer the phone first, and intercepting Katie heading her way with a complaint.

"Sort it out yourself," she instructed. "You've been here long enough. Let Livi have one quiet morning at least."

But the enforced peace didn't last long. At ten thirty-five, bang on time, Mattias came through the door and up to the desk.

"Good morning, Miss Callaway," he said, holding out one of the cups he was carrying. "Here's your hot chocolate."

On the inside, Livi heaved a sigh. On the outside, she smiled nicely, just as she did every morning. "Thank you."

"You are *very* welcome," he said in his charmingly accented English, just as he did every morning.

A lot of things were charming about Mattias, and Livi knew he ticked all the boxes. He dressed very well. He had lovely manners. His golden blond hair looked very healthy. He was extremely intelligent. He worked hard. He was really very nice. All in all, he should have been the ideal guy. And yet, for her, the sum was somehow less than its parts. After an initial collective breath-holding, everyone in the salon had stopped waiting for romance to bloom. Mattias hadn't stopped waiting though (as they all loved to remind her). There was an awkward patch, when she'd tried to gently make it clear that she simply didn't feel that way. But he just kept bringing the hot chocolates, charmingly, and it didn't seem polite to try and give them back. So she didn't.

He worked at a translation company not far from Peach. Mia, being a good cousin, had brought him to the pub with her one night after he moved to London from Stockholm, to help him meet some people and find his feet in a new city. But when the morning visits started, she apologised on his behalf.

"He's always been single-minded," she said. "I suppose you wouldn't get to be fluent in four languages otherwise. But it can be very trying."

Or very flattering. Livi discovered that, for a person whose heart had been thoroughly squashed, perhaps a little adoration wasn't *completely* unwelcome. She decided to put aside the awkwardness. If Mattias was determined to keep coming, without any hope of romance, where was the harm?

As he settled in to while away his morning tea break, leaning against the counter, the door swung open. A woman with a glossy sheen and impeccable posture entered the salon. She was so beautifully styled and made up, Livi couldn't pick her age—somewhere in her forties, or maybe fifties. Her smooth blonde hair swept elegantly to the side, and her red wrap dress hugged a killer figure. Behind her came a lesser mortal, a young man carrying a laptop bag in one hand, and a snakeskin briefcase in the other. Mattias stood upright as she approached the reception desk.

"Livi." It was a statement, not a question.

Livi found herself straightening up too. "Yes, that's me."

Mattias slipped away out the door with his coffee, feigning a scared expression.

"I thought so. She described you well," the woman said, in beautifully modulated American tones. "I need your help."

"Of course. What can I help you with?"

"I should be back in LA right now, but I decided to stay on for an industry function this evening," she said. "I can do my own makeup well enough to be presentable, but not my hair." She smiled, and immediately looked less intimidating. "My usual stylist is away, so my niece Helena recommended you."

"Oh, Helena!" Livi smiled back. "Are things going well for her?"

"Yes, very well, thanks to you. Although I think she's fallen in love with your Aidan."

Livi laughed. "Well, she wouldn't be the first. He's not here today, or you could have met him."

"Oh, that's a shame. I heard he was quite something."

"He really is," Livi agreed. "But it was Will who did Helena's hair, and he's working today. I think he could fit you in."

"Will it is then. I'm Rachael Radner. And this is Scott. We might need some extra space."

Before long she was settled in a corner of the salon,

juggling black coffee and an iPhone, Scott frantically finding papers and taking notes. She and Will bonded immediately over some mutual Aidan admiration, and soon they were laughing and joking together while he started her hair.

Cass came and stood with Livi at the desk, admiring. "She's quite something herself. Really classy."

Then they saw her take a call, and her face hardened as the conversation progressed. She held up a hand for Will to wait and they strained their ears, resisting the urge to sidle closer.

"We'll have to keep negotiating then...no, I don't want to offer any more money yet...was that what the author said himself?" She tapped a manicured nail on the arm of her chair. "Damn it, I'm going to get this one. I'll call you shortly."

She sat back, pressing the phone against her chin thoughtfully while Will hovered. Livi gave in to her curiosity and went over.

"Is everything all right?"

She sighed. "I'm trying to get the film rights for a book. An amazing book. You know, one of those forget to feed the children, stay up all night, read until you're cross-eyed books."

Livi and Will nodded. "Except for the feeding the children part," he said.

"Well, apparently the author isn't convinced that my company is the right one for his book. But if I could talk to him directly, I think I could convince him."

"Will you try?" Livi asked.

"I'll have to. The difficulty is, he's Estonian, and he doesn't speak good English. I read the book in translation. His publisher there is doing all the negotiating, and they seem determined to tangle up every production company in the Western world. I think time's running out, but if I could just tell the author how I feel about the story before someone else gets to him..."

Will looked at Livi. "Isn't that one of the languages

Mattias-the-genius speaks?"

"I think so." She hesitated. Mattias would love this. Well, while she was in the swing of doing good deeds... She turned to Rachael. "Mattias is, um, a friend, who works for a translation company near here. Would you like me to contact him?"

"Yes! You would be a superstar. Thank you very, very much."

"You're welcome. Hopefully it will actually help."

Will raised a warning eyebrow at her as she turned to go. "You do realise, now *you'll* owe *him* one."

★

Unsurprisingly, Mattias was more than happy to drop everything and come back to Peach when Livi called. Before long he and Rachael—hair beautifully done—and Scott were ensconced in the staffroom, ready to do battle via speaker phone.

As Livi left them to it, she could hear him talking. "Swedish, of course. Estonian and Finnish, which are not completely different. But it's cheating a little to count Finnish as a foreign language, because my father is from Helsinki. And you really can't count English, everyone has English..."

Smarty-pants. She smiled and shook her head as she taped a 'Do Not Disturb' sign on the door. Back to the day's regular jobs.

Then her heart sank as she looked across the salon and saw her mother talking to Cass. Please, she thought, please, no drama. She braced herself and went over.

"Hi, Mum."

"Hello, sweetheart. Sorry I didn't see you before you left this morning. You look lovely."

She took Livi's hand and held it out to one side, the better to appreciate her swing skirt and sheer blouse, both in regulation salon black.

"That's okay, you must be tired. You look lovely too."
And she did. In a dark blue suit with a neat nipped-in waist,
her hair shorter than it used to be, and even heels, Livi
thought she looked years younger. "What are you dressed
up for?"

"Thank you! I'm off to my orientation this afternoon,
for work. I'm going to be a walking tour guide. Sights of
Royal London."

Livi practically fell off her own heels. "You…what?"
Her head pounded. "Work?"

"Yes. You girls have both been very kind, but I know
I've been in your way. I'd hoped to stay on at June's, but
her daughter was coming back from abroad. Now that I'm
working, I'll be able to give you some money and find my
own place."

"But what about…" Words jostled and elbowed each
other on her tongue, but she couldn't get anything sensible
out. "Dad. Home."

"Mmm." She avoided Livi's eyes. "No, not right
now."

"Not right now? What does that mean?"

"It means June has found me a great job, and I'm
going to have some fun, and a change. I think you know
about that."

"No, this is not the same. It's not the same at all."

Tears threatened but she held them back. Cass stepped
in and gently steered them both to the sofa, luckily empty of
clients. They sat in silence for a while, one pulling herself
together, one waiting.

Finally her mum spoke. "Livi, I'm sorry, sweetheart,
but a lot of things changed after you left."

"Don't say you're blaming *me*." She pulled a tissue
from the box she'd offered Helena not many days before. In
the life she had before this.

"I'm not blaming. I'm just saying I started to…think.
And after my birthday, I knew I had to do something.
Another year had gone, and it was just…gone. One after
the other, faster and faster."

"What about Dad?"

She looked uncomfortable. "Well, I left him a letter. And I arranged for someone to cover for me at work. You know, Melanie, she helps us out quite often."

"So...you didn't tell him yourself?"

"No."

"So he found your letter, and then he went to work, what, the next day, and Melanie was there at your desk?"

"Yes. I have to admit, that wasn't the best thing to do." She screwed up her nose, had the grace to look rueful. "But I needed a clean break."

Livi looked at her, agog. Who was this woman? The mother she'd last seen, conscientious, steady, patient—an accountant, for God's sake!—seemed completely unrelated to the runaway sitting next to her. Someone who would plan her getaway so secretly and carefully.

Then something occurred to her.

"Mum, I have to ask. Is there someone else?" She didn't want to know, and she had to know.

"Yes, I suppose there is." Livi caught her breath, but her mum continued. "It's me. The other me. The me I forgot." Her voice broke, and she reached for a tissue too.

Livi felt her heart give a little. "Oh, Mum. But couldn't you remember yourself together with Dad? Doesn't he remember you too?"

"I don't know." A small sob escaped. Livi slid closer and gave her a hug, not knowing what else to say or do.

Just then the staffroom door opened and Rachael emerged, followed by Mattias and Scott. All three looked elated. Livi stood up as quickly as she could, composing herself.

"We got it!" Rachael raised triumphant fists in the air. "Livi, I don't know where you found this man, but he is brilliant." Mattias demurred modestly, but looked thoroughly pleased. "What were the odds? Thank you so much, both of you."

Livi's mum stood up and quietly tried to edge away, tucking the tissue in her pocket, but Rachael saw her. "Oh,

I'm sorry, you were with someone."

"This is my mum, Evelyn," Livi said. "Mum, this is Mattias, Rachael, and Scott."

"Oh, it's a pleasure to meet you," Rachael exclaimed. "You must be very proud of Livi, she's just great. I have kids too, you know, I only wish they were as helpful. I suppose most moms would say the same."

Mattias stepped forward. "Lovely to meet you, Evelyn," he said, shaking hands in his formal northern European manner. "I agree, Livi is wonderful. As you must be. You obviously did a very good job."

Livi repressed the urge to roll her eyes, but her mum, with her small hand still engulfed in his, was completely charmed. "Oh," she managed. "Oh, thank you."

"Well," said Rachael, looking around at them all. "This has been a very successful day so far. I have some time left before my function starts. Can I take you all out to lunch? My treat. Evelyn?"

"Oh, I wish I could, but I have to go to work." She looked terribly disappointed.

"And I'm afraid I have to go back to work too," Mattias said regretfully. "I have a very long and boring Finnish government report to translate for an EU meeting."

Livi looked at her watch. She'd barely done any work herself today. She started to decline too, but Cass, whose ears were flapping enough to lift her off the ground, called out, "No, you have to eat after all, go and enjoy yourself."

But as she was gathering her things to go, with the worst timing, Nicolette rang. She was on her way. Cass and Livi both knew there would be no lunch breaks now. Her visits were always a whirlwind of purposeful activity, everyone rushing madly around until she swirled back out the door.

"Next time then," Rachael insisted, giving Livi her business card. "Definitely next time."

"Next time," Livi promised, and they hugged goodbye. "Say hi to Helena from us."

Mattias paused before he followed Rachael and Scott

out the door. "I think now you might let *me* take you out," he said. "Tomorrow night? Shall I meet you here after work?"

"That will be fine," her mum told him, still entranced.

"Mum!" Livi said. But then she realised Will was right. Time to pay the piper. "That will be fine," she echoed.

He nodded with satisfaction. "Good. It was very nice to meet you, Evelyn." Another gentlemanly handshake, and he was gone.

"Oh, Livi," her mum sighed, straining her neck to watch his tall Scandinavian form disappear down the street. "He is *lovely*."

★

Nicolette swooped in, not so much a tornado as a diminutive blonde waterspout, spilling over with plans and determination.

"It's time to get serious," she announced. "Peach is a success, in itself, but we can do so much more. I want to get this place whipped into shape, and then we're expanding. I want more Peaches. A tree-full!"

Livi didn't know what had brought on this latest sudden urge for empire-building. Maybe it was the departure of another toy-boy. But she knew there'd be work ahead, at least until Nicolette got distracted by her personal life again—which probably wouldn't take long.

As she was handing over a list of jobs, Nicolette saw Rachael's card tucked under the corner of the telephone.

"Mingled Yarn Films? That's the production company Jake invested in."

Ah, Jake. Livi got ready for a repeat of Nicolette's Jake Michaelson story. One party night in the eighties (one night among many), she met him in a club when he was visiting from LA. He wasn't single then really but, you know, he only had to raise one wicked eyebrow... She was always coy on the details, thankfully, but apparently he nicknamed her his peach. And thus the salon, when she opened it years later, had its name.

Now, despite her everyday cougar tendencies, she took a persistent interest in all of Jake's activities, and had managed to maintain contact over the years. From what Livi had seen of their few emails (which Nicolette couldn't resist showing off) there was a hint of half-heartedness on his part, but she supposed he wasn't one to burn bridges with an attractive woman of any age. Now Nicolette held up the card.

"Where did this come from?"

When Livi told her the story, including how they'd helped Helena (but not how they'd juggled clients), she was pleased.

"You did very well, Livi. I hope she tells Jake about it. Maybe he'll want to catch up next time he's in London." Invigorated by the idea, she clapped her hands sharply. "Come on then, let's get this project underway. I'll be back soon to see how you're getting on. In the meantime, I think I'll send Jake an email."

Once she was gone, everyone breathed freely again. "I suppose she *does* realise how old he is now," Cass commented, to no one in particular.

Livi just shrugged, and looked at her list. Review client database, get quotes for bathroom renovation, research new inventory control software...the bullet points went on and on. She mentally added another: pay rise for long-suffering staff members. Mind you, the way things were going with her personal life, the extra work could be just the distraction she needed.

Chapter Thirteen

The next morning—the morning of the date—was the first in weeks that Mattias didn't show up with hot chocolate. This inspired a new round of teasing.

"He's hoping you'll wonder where he is," Aidan said. "And worry that maybe he'll stand you up tonight. Then you'll be super-glad to see him, for once."

"Ooh, psychological games," Cass said. "That's very sly."

"Maybe he isn't coming. Maybe a delegation from the EU has him in a dark room, shining a light in his eyes, determined to extract government secrets." Will made spooky finger-wiggles.

Livi just shook her head at them. "Seriously, aren't there things you should be doing?" She was more than busy herself.

Despite their speculation, Mattias arrived at five thirty, looking clean and shiny. "We missed you today," said Will.

"EU," he replied gravely.

"Ah," Will nodded, with suitably serious eyebrows, then had to turn away to stifle a laugh. If Mattias noticed that they were all suddenly deeply occupied elsewhere, he didn't let on. Livi decided to ignore them.

"I'm ready," she said, pulling on her green coat and turning him towards the door. "Shall we go?"

As they walked, Mattias said, "I hope you don't mind, I got tickets to a Swedish movie. When I saw it was showing I really wanted to take you. It came out years ago, but it's very good. *My Life as a Dog.*"

She frowned, not quite with him. "Your life as…?"

"No, *My Life, as a Dog. Mitt Liv som Hund.* I know, it sounds strange, but I think you'll like it."

"Okay. I'll trust you."

But she wasn't hopeful. All she knew about Swedish movies was Ingmar Bergman, and she hadn't seen any of them all the way through. Something about strawberries came to mind, and playing chess with Death. Black and white. Depressing.

But to her surprise, she did enjoy the movie. She had misgivings at first—maybe it would be too sad—but as it continued she was mesmerised. Mesmerised, that is, once Mattias stopped leaning over every few minutes, translating.

"Mattias!" she finally hissed. "I can read the subtitles!"

"I know," he whispered, "but they leave out so much detail. I don't want you to miss anything."

She gritted her teeth, formulated a polite reply. "Every time you give me the details I've just missed, I miss what the *next* subtitles say, so I fall even further behind. It's better to just let me read."

"Ah. Sorry."

He turned back to the screen. Even in the half dark she could see he looked a little sheepish. He held out a bag of Minstrels, a peace offering, and they settled back to watch.

After the movie, he took her to a French restaurant. "Not a Swedish restaurant?" she teased as the waiter showed them to their seats.

"Well, to be honest, not everyone is a fan of Swedish food," he replied earnestly.

She decided not to try and make any smorgasbord jokes, and instead picked up her menu.

"Oh, ratatouille—" she began.

"That's a vegetable stew, very nice," he said.

"Mmm." She had a feeling where they were heading. "And cassoulet—"

"Yes, now that's made with sausages and beans and—"

He stopped when he saw her face.

She knew she shouldn't, but she couldn't stop herself. "You know, I watch the Good Food channel. I've lost count of how many times I've seen Rick Stein cook cassoulet. Also, I did actually study French at school, probably just as much as you." In truth, she'd forgotten most of it—but she could manage restaurant French. "Plus, there are descriptions of each dish right here on the menu. So thank you, but I really don't need you to interpret for me."

He blinked, looking a bit stunned, and she realised that irritation had made her words sound harsher than she intended. They both studied their menus for what seemed like a long while, and she felt very sorry that she'd said anything. It would have been better if she'd turned down his invitation altogether, despite her mother's enthusiasm. But then he cleared his throat.

"Mia always tells me I'm a know-it-all," he said. "But I'm worse when I'm nervous. I'm sorry." With a slight blush showing below his soft blond hair, he looked like a chastened schoolboy.

Now she felt terrible. He really was a lovely guy, and it wasn't his fault if his niceness wasn't enough to spark anything in her.

"No, no," she said hurriedly. "*I'm* sorry. You were just trying to help, thank you. Let's just order and enjoy our dinner, it's so nice here."

He smiled at her, obviously relieved. "I'll order some wine while you choose."

For the rest of the night she was as patient and carefully well-mannered as she could be. After two glasses she refused any more wine, for fear her tongue would loosen and get away on her again. By the end of the evening, when she said goodnight at the Leicester Square tube—receiving a genteel kiss on the cheek—all the graciousness was a weight in her chest. She ran down the stairs, feeling it dislodge a little more with each jolting step. She decided not to wonder whether it was some deficiency in her character, that such a perfectly decent person could make her so cranky and impatient. He didn't deserve that. So, whatever the reason, this would definitely, definitely, be her one and only date with Mattias.

★

She arrived home to find a date going on in her living room. A date with a chaperone—Cass, in the corner, looking unimpressed. On the more comfortable of their two settees sat her mum, glass of wine in hand as she chatted happily away to a middle-aged man. He was tanned and solid, with a well-weathered face that spoke of a life in the sun. It was still handsome, despite an alarming arrangement of greying facial hair.

Livi made a silent appeal to Cass, who could only shrug. Then her mum noticed her.

"Livi! How was your night, sweetheart?"

Her cheeks were prettily flushed and her eyes shone. Livi hoped it was due to the wine, not the man beside her. With his arm resting along the back of the sofa, he looked perfectly at home.

"Oh, it was okay," she said. "How was your first day of Royal London?"

"Marvellous!" she exclaimed. "Len and I were just saying, it's a wonderful thing to have a city so stuffed full of history. That's something you just don't get in New Zealand."

"Or in Australia." Len arose and put down his glass. He smoothed his moustache down on each side to meet the thin line of beard that led up to his ears. Then he held out his hand. "Len Mortlock," he pronounced, in an unmistakable twang. "It's a real pleasure. Evelyn's told me all about you."

He had the smoothly provocative air of a man who might or might not be flirting, and knew he could get away with it. But tonight, Livi just wasn't in the mood. She considered the whisker-tainted hand, then switched her bag over to her own right hand. She'd already used up all her good grace for the night.

"Really? When did she have time to do that?"

Her mum gave her a sharp look, but Len appeared unmoved.

"Well, tonight of course. She was my guide today, my angel of London."

There was a sort of snort from the corner. Livi looked at Cass, who sought refuge in her wine glass.

"I'm sure she was," she replied. "You'll have to excuse me, I have an early start tomorrow."

There was nothing more she wanted to see here, especially in her Mattias-saturated state. Bed was the only place for her now, preferably with the blankets over her head. A state of denial is best maintained in the dark, she believed.

"Ah, what a shame. It was a pleasure to meet you, love."

Len reached again for her hand, but she side-stepped neatly and waved around the room instead.

"Goodnight, everyone. Don't let me ruin the *party*."

Her tone was obvious to the women in the room, but Len, seemingly oblivious again, lifted his glass with a jovial wink.

"Always a party when Mortlock's in the house, you're right there," he said, stroking down the tufts under his nose as he looked at her. "Another time, love. Another time."

Avoiding her mother's eye, she escaped to her bedroom and shut the door. Teeth and face would have to wait until the coast was clear. She could hear the continuous bass of his voice, running over the top of her mother's, through the wall. How long would he stay, she wondered, as she put on her pyjamas. With her mum sleeping in the living room—also for an unspecified duration—there was no way to avoid hearing them. Oh God, she suddenly thought, please don't let me hear anything...you know... Mercifully, her brain refused to form the rest of the words in her head, but it was too late. The idea was there. She burrowed under the covers and put a pillow over her head. From the muffled darkness she sent out a fervent plea, willing it around the curve of the earth, into morning light in the far distant south. Come on, Dad. Come *on*. Come and get her. Where *are* you?

★

Some hours later she woke with a jolt, panicky and overheated in her cocoon. She flung off the comforter and felt around in the darkness for her bottle of water. There was silence in the flat. She sat on the edge of the bed, flapping her pyjama top in an effort to cool off, and considered whether to risk going out there. In the end, a desperate need for the toilet decided it.

Outside her bedroom door, she paused in the narrow passage and strained her ears. No muffled, suspicious sounds, no voices, no man-snoring. She crept along to the living room and peeped in. Her mum was tucked up asleep on the sofa, alone, the length of her only just fitting between its rolled arms. She breathed out. Relief.

In the bathroom, she used the toilet and then cleaned her teeth, banishing any remaining hints of the infamous but delicious cassoulet, the red wine, the luxurious chocolate bavarois. Then she pulled out a cleansing cloth and wiped away what was left of her makeup. Barefaced, she assessed herself in the mirror. A challenging night, manners-wise. She decided to put it down to extreme provocation. Her mother might be an angel of London, but she saw no sign of a halo in her own reflection. Nor was she aiming for one. Just keeping on top of earthly things was enough for now.

★

To: cam.holden@nzuni.ac.nz
From: liviaway@gmail.com
Subject: What happened next

The rogue mother is now employed. A walking tour guide of Royal London. She won't say how long she's planning to work for, only that she'll be able to find her own place when she gets paid. No idea what this means for her and Dad, but I do know that he'd go nuts if he knew she was bringing men home from work with her. Well, okay, just one, a silver-tongued Australian.

On the plus side, we had a brush with Hollywood. A movie producer came in to get her hair done. She was desperate to get the film rights for an Estonian book she loved, and I organised for Mia's cousin to help her with some translation to close the deal. It was a glimpse into a whole other world.

Hope you and the hairy James got that paper wrestled into shape.

xxx

To: liviaway@gmail.com
From: cam.holden@nzuni.ac.nz
Subject: Re: What happened next

We nailed it. James has decided to shave in celebration if it's accepted, so keep your fingers crossed—I'm sick of looking at crumbs in that moustache.

Your mum is full of surprises. (Bit like someone else I know.) I hope she'll figure things out, for all your sakes. I suppose a lot of people start to reassess things once they hit a certain age. I'm planning a really expensive bike at around fifty. Ducati maybe. Or, if I'm an old fart by then, a really high-spec Goldwing. It takes two.

Your visit from Hollywood sounds good. Maybe you'll get a mention in the film. There are so many obscure jobs in the credits, surely 'book deal translation facilitator' could be included.

Have a good weekend.

(Beware dodgy Australians.)

xxx

Chapter Fourteen

Nothing is ever like it is in the movies, Livi had come to realise. Since arriving in London, she had never once seen Gwyneth Paltrow dashing to catch a tube, or not catch a tube. There was no old lady sitting on the steps of St Paul's, imploring her to feed the birds, though who knew what tuppence was worth these days. American werewolves were nowhere to be found (probably a good thing, she had to admit). Henry Higgins had never appeared to suggest they must do something about her accent. And, most disappointingly of all, although she once hovered around eighteen yards or so from *that* doorway on Portobello Road (no longer blue, sadly), Hugh Grant didn't bump into her, apologetic and endearing. Maybe she should try again, armed with a large pair of sunglasses, though she drew the line at a beret. Most days she felt more Bridget than Julia, but still, when she visited Mia in Notting Hill, an unreasonable hope persisted, a feeling of possibility. If not Hugh (or Colin) then maybe…something.

So when Mia suggested that she and Cass should come and stay at her place during the Notting Hill carnival, Livi was keen. Plus, it would distract her from her family difficulties and the issue of the (possibly warped) American while she waited for September the first and Golders Green.

"You do realise it's an absolute zoo," Cass said. "I mean, a million people, or some other ridiculously huge number."

"Really?" She tried to imagine almost the entire population of Auckland crushed into the streets of Notting Hill. "That *is* a lot."

"Last time I went, I ended up with the most terrible hangover. Are you sure you want to go? It's not a romantic occasion. Hugh won't be there, you know."

It was no good fighting the blush that coloured her cheeks. "I know that! But I'd like to go, and we're not opening on the bank holiday anyway."

"All right then. But you'll have to rebook my Tuesday clients. There'll be no getting out of there on Monday night."

"Really?"

"Well, there could be, but you won't want to, believe me. And I certainly won't feel like doing any work on Tuesday. Ah, you sweet, wide-eyed country mouse. What a lot you have to learn about this big old world," she teased, patting Livi's shoulder.

She got a shove in return. "Watch out, or I'll be rostering you to work every Saturday night until Christmas." But they both knew she was safe—after all, they needed *some* Saturday nights to go out together.

"Will you bring your mum?" Cass asked. "Do you think she'd like to come?"

Livi frowned. "Maybe. But she has a date on Sunday night."

"A date? Not with..." She made a whisker-twiddling gesture, and Livi shuddered.

"Yes. Well, she's not calling it a date. They're both interested in *theatre*, apparently, so they're going to see *The Mousetrap*. A cultural evening at the world's longest-running play."

"Right, because Len is simply overflowing with culture."

"I would really, really like to stop talking about it now."

She could feel herself getting tense. Len was clearly a ladies' man from way back, and normally she would have just had a laugh at the whole suave rascal routine. But things were far from normal.

Cass was sympathetic. "Say no more."

On Carnival Sunday, Livi sat with her mum for afternoon tea at the little Formica table in the kitchen.

"Are you sure you don't want to come too?" she asked. It was worth a try.

But Evelyn shook her head, and dunked a digestive biscuit in her tea. "No thanks, I'm too old for all that." She sighed as the bottom half of the biscuit disappeared into the mug. "Something more sedate will suit me better."

"That's not true, you shouldn't talk like that. You're not too old at all. But if you feel like sedate, I suppose there's nothing more sedate than a fifty-year-old play."

"Sixty, actually."

"That should make you feel young then, the play's older than you are."

Her mum smiled. "Only just."

"We won't quibble over numbers." Livi gave her a hug, and picked up her overnight bag. She didn't want to mention Len Mortlock, and she couldn't bring herself to say anything about having fun with him. "Come home safely."

"You too."

★

The mass of passengers compressed sardine-like into their tube should have prepared Livi for the scene at street level. But as they shuffled up the stairs and out of the station, into the music and buzz, she was amazed by the number of people. Around every corner, and the next, and the next, were people. People dancing, people singing, people eating, drinking, jostling, partying.

Cass saw her face. "This is nothing. Wait until tomorrow."

They made their way in the humming evening air to Mia's house just off Talbot Road, clutching their overnight bags in front of them. She had given them strict instructions to watch out for pickpockets. As they started up the steps, the shiny black front door flew open.

"Finally! I've hardly eaten anything today, and now I'm starving." She hustled them in and up the stairs. "You're in my old room. Let's just throw your things on the bed and go."

"Why haven't you been eating?" Livi asked over her shoulder, as she propelled them along the hallway.

"Carnival food. You have to try some of everything. You'll see."

Before long, they were back out in the streets. As they wound through the crowds, past DJs pumping out hip hop, reggae, and music Livi didn't have labels for, they were surrounded with laughter and sound and the smells of a faraway, tropical place. Stallholders called out as they passed by, urging them to try all kinds of Caribbean temptations.

Livi breathed in deeply. "This smells amazing. What should we eat first, do you think?"

Cass looked disappointed. "I was actually thinking about rum punch. But I suppose we *should* eat first. Not there though!" She came to an abrupt halt as they approached a stall festooned with flags.

They both turned to look at her. "Why not?" Mia asked.

"Honestly? Curried goat?" From her expression, they might have been asking her to eat curried slugs.

"But you can eat a cow, or a pig, or a lamb. What's the difference?"

Mia had a point, but Cass stuck to her guns. "Curried goat just sounds seriously unappetising."

"What about jerk chicken then?"

"Well, that's just rude. It's bad enough that we have to eat the chicken, do we have to disrespect it too?"

Mia rolled her eyes. "You should know that you are the million-and-first person to make that joke. And it doesn't get any funnier."

"Can I have my rum punch now?"

In the end they all had plastic cups of rum punch, and paper plates of spicy jerk chicken, and rice and peas, and fried plantain, and Cass was even persuaded to try the goat, and then Mia was satisfied that they'd 'done' carnival food.

They stopped outside the Duke of Wellington to watch a pair of DJs behind their turntables, playing up to the crowd. Although the Duke himself was unamused on the pub sign above them, collar stiff and arms crossed, they were quickly caught up in the music and atmosphere, bumping and jumping with the rest of the revellers. It felt like hardly any time before Mia announced over the *thump thump thump* that they should go.

"But we only just got here," Cass protested, balancing her drink as she swayed to the beat in front of the speaker stack. "Everything's going strong." She shook her booty in her best Beyoncé imitation, and the young men nearby whistled in appreciation.

"And it will still be going strong tomorrow," Mia said firmly, removing her from the enthusiastic advances of a hopeful partygoer. "Come on, we have to pace ourselves. You don't want to be hung over for the parade."

So, with a reluctant Cass lagging behind, they headed back.

Mia had converted her childhood bedroom into a luxurious guest room. Now she filled large bowls with ice cream, and they propped themselves up in the king-size bed with pillows and cushions and comforters. It made a perfectly cosy nest for the three of them.

Cass passed a bowl across to Livi, a mischievous expression on her face. "Did you tell Mia about your date?"

"Ooh, a date! Who did you go out with?" Mia leaned forward to savour the details.

Livi sent Cass a scowl. "It wasn't *really* a date. Well...I suppose it was." She wasn't keen to relive it. "I went out with Mattias."

"You didn't!" Mia was a picture of astonishment.

"I promised to go out with him because he helped a client with some translating."

"Oh, I got all excited on your behalf just then. I thought there was some fantastic new man on the scene." She leaned back again, shaking her head. "But Mattias— no, you're off the hook there. I'm going to tell him so."

Now she felt bad again. He'd made a lot of effort, after all. But Mia was definite.

"No, Livi, we know he's not the one for you, so don't let him talk you into anything. You have other projects underway, remember." Looking at their questioning faces, she added, "Like a rendezvous in Golders Green in a couple of days."

"Yes," Cass said. "You have to go and find the one who *is* for you." She settled happily back against the pillows, empty bowl wobbling on her knees. "The one who's meant to be. Fate."

Common sense wrangled with fantasy in Livi's head. "You're both forgetting that we have no idea *where* in Golders Green this fated man might be. And that he might be completely twisted."

But as she stirred her ice cream into chocolate-chip-studded whip, a whisper of anticipation crept in. Maybe she did believe in fate.

Or maybe it was just the rum punch.

Chapter Fifteen

The carnival was like nothing she'd ever seen. From their vantage point on Westbourne Grove, Livi watched, spellbound, as the endless ribbon of the parade wound past. Above them, locals hung from upper-storey windows, making the most of their elevated views.

All manner of creations, animal, vegetable, and mineral, swept by. Colour-coordinated flocks of birds and assortments of flowers progressed exuberantly along the road. Richly adorned kings and queens preceded an enormous white dragon, and a truck laden with a steel band provided a deafening soundtrack for its joyful, bikini-wearing, flag-waving followers. Behind them, a metallic bronze and red and green tyrannosaurus rex stomped and flailed along, teeth menacing, a metal rooster inexplicably perched on its back.

She did a double-take as a giant replica of Rio's Christ the Redeemer statue was pushed past, teetering slightly as if in the spirit of the music. Equally gigantic Caribbean folklore characters jogged along, atop the heads of black-clad figures hiding underneath. Barely clad dancers with expansive jewel-coloured wings were followed by small girls dressed in samba outfits, snowflake costumes, and the fairy princess dresses of their dreams. She wondered what their innocent wee minds made of it all. And everywhere, feathers, feathers, feathers.

It felt wrong to stare, but she was entranced by those exotic creatures wearing nothing but body paint, nipple sequins, gargantuan feather headdresses and teeny-weeny thongs. Well, some of them were thongs. Others were nothing more than a tiny triangle at the front—less than Eve got by with—and at the back, a little jewel emerging cheekily from the top of taut (and sometimes not so taut) buttocks.

She grabbed Cass's arm. "Look! How do you think those stay on? I can't see anything around the sides holding them up."

"They must be totally wedged in. You'd think that would be uncomfortable."

"And unhygienic," Mia commented, making them laugh.

Even the police lining the parade route were caught up in the festivities, whether they liked it or not. Livi held her breath as a large policeman became the filling in a gyrating, sweating, drag queen sandwich. He struggled to maintain a neutral expression as he was swayed about. Then, just as Livi thought he would snap, they twirled away, winking and blowing kisses, leaving him resettling his hat, his earpiece, and his dignity.

There seemed no end to the swirling, waving, drumming, flapping, bumping, and grinding. Anything that could be found in earth or sky or imagination seemed to be there, everything bigger, taller, wider, and more vivid than in the real world outside those streets. Watching the parade pass by in a happy daze, she did feel a little like that country mouse, though she wouldn't admit it to Cass.

Then she suddenly snapped to attention. On the other side of the road, in the gaps between a flock of enormous bejewelled birds, a figure caught her eye. Was that...? It couldn't be. She craned to see as he began moving away through the crowd, further down the road. Dark, glossy hair, faded polo shirt, tan... Now a troupe of gold-painted dancers, shimmying and jiggling, completely blocked her view.

"Excuse me. Excuse me." She tried to move along a little, but she was jammed in on three sides, and there was no getting past the barrier and the policeman in front of her. Straining desperately to see past the swarm of extravagant headdresses, she thought she caught a glimpse of a perfectly white smile. A feeling of urgency overtook her and she struggled to elbow her way out. "*Excuse* me!"

But Cass reached out and grabbed the back of her dress. "Where are you going?"

"I thought..." She wobbled about on tiptoe, trying in vain to see him again. "I thought I saw the American."

She bobbed up and down, hoping for a clear view, but the parade rolled relentlessly past, oblivious to her drama, the very small drama of one in a crowd of thousands.

★

Late that night, merrily fortified, ears still ringing from the onslaught of samba, garage, steel bands, and calypso, they fell back in Mia's front door.

"Does anyone want tea?" she asked, playing the good hostess despite the hour.

Cass groaned and clutched her forehead dramatically. "No, no. Definitely no more liquid. Why didn't someone stop me drinking? I'm completely ruined." She swayed a little, as if to prove her point.

"Maybe horizontal would be better than vertical," Livi suggested. "That was *huge*. I'm wrecked too."

"Bed bed bed bed bed." Cass kicked off her shoes and began to climb the stairs, Mia and Livi trailing behind. In her late-night, rum punch state, Livi thought the staircase seemed to have grown extra treads since they left that morning.

Finally in the bedroom, Cass pulled her pyjamas out

from under her pillow. "Honestly, I'm all boobed out. I don't even want to look at my own while I'm getting changed."

"At least yours bear looking at," Mia said, perched on the end of the bed. "If I let mine loose they slump around like drunken aunties. Carnival boobs seem to be relentlessly perky." She regarded her bust with despair. "Thank God for structural lingerie."

"It was full on in every direction," said Livi. "Drunken aunties and all the other relations. That was a *lot* of bumping and grinding."

"Yes, little mouse." Cass grinned, then ducked to avoid Livi's well-aimed pillow and fell onto the bed. "You'd think it would put you in the mood, but it was just too much of a good thing." She sent a theatrical sigh towards the ceiling.

"You might not say that if you had someone to be in the mood *with*," Mia pointed out.

"Which reminds me, it's a shame you couldn't grab your American when you saw him," Cass told Livi.

She sighed. "I don't know now, I don't think it really could have been him. I mean, how many hundred thousand people were out there today? It must have been wishful thinking."

She finished buttoning her pyjama top and climbed into the big bed with Cass, who shook her head emphatically. "No, no, not wishful thinking. Clear sign if you ask me."

Mia played mother hen, adjusting pillows and straightening the covers. "You two look very sweet."

"More sweet if we were less drunk," Cass replied.

"Speak for yourself," Livi said. "I'm always very sweet."

"More sheet and mess drunk," she chortled. "Sore feet press hunk."

Mia shook her head. "Tragic. Definitely lights out time. Goodnight. *Sov gott*. Sleep well."

She flicked off the light as she went, leaving them

giggling like twins awake far too late on a school night.

★

There was no giggling when they woke the next morning, heads bursting and tongues like desiccated dishcloths.

Mia popped her head around the door. "Good morning! Come and get some breakfast when you're ready to eat."

"Eat?" moaned Cass. "I'm never eating again. Or drinking again." She rolled away from the light coming through the curtains, and wriggled further under the comforter. "Never. Again."

Livi swung her legs out of bed and sat up gingerly. Okay, not as bad as she'd feared. And was that feeling hunger? Maybe, after Nurofen and a drink, she could eat. She ran her tongue around her teeth. Ugh, toothbrush first.

She emerged from the bathroom fresher, but still feeling shady. Mia, on the other hand, was bright and chirpy, laying out tea cups and pastries.

"I can't believe you're in such good shape." Livi lowered herself gratefully into a chair and leaned her elbows on the stripped pine table. "Do you not feel hung over?"

"Pfft. Not me. I've had so much practice drinking *snaps*, a bit of rum punch is nothing."

"Oh, do you mean schnapps?" When she nodded, Livi said, "Don't tell Cass that. She'll probably want to embark on some kind of desensitisation programme, like for allergies."

But when Cass finally appeared, she swore that carnival rum punch would be the last alcoholic beverage ever to pass her lips. Well, until her birthday anyway.

107

Chapter Sixteen

By the time they left Mia's house, Livi wasn't feeling too bad, but it was a rough ride home for Cass. Every jolt and bump of the train brought forth a new moan or whimper.

"Why so much punch?" she lamented. "Why the curry goat? Look what it's done to me."

"You can hardly blame the poor goat." Livi felt compelled to defend him or her.

"I told you it wasn't right," Cass grumbled, clutching her stomach.

"What's not right is blaming an innocent wee creature for the after-effects of your indulgences."

She groaned and closed her eyes as the train lurched yet again. "Kill me now."

They were both relieved to finally stagger in the door and up the stairs. Cass made a beeline for her bedroom, with an apologetic wave to Evelyn, who was sitting where they'd last seen her, at the table with a cup of tea.

"Cass doesn't look very well," she commented, as the door banged shut.

"It was a pretty big day in the end. So much fun though. I think you would have really liked it." She supposed she'd better ask. "How was the play?"

"Oh, the play was great." Her voice was bright and over-polite. "Great." She looked away out the little window, across the rooftops on the other side of the road. "Lovely."

Livi didn't know what to say next. Clearly something was not great, or lovely. Should she ask? She had no idea of the protocol for dating-related conversations with your mother—when your mother is the one dating. If it was a date. She prayed not.

When the doorbell rang, she sprang gratefully to her feet, despite her own rum punch headache. "I'll just see who that is."

Steve the mechanic stood on the front step, looking clean-scrubbed and hopeful and smelling good. When he saw Livi a flicker of disappointment showed on his face, but he quickly regrouped.

"Hi. I was wondering if Cass was home?"

"Hi, Steve. She is, but...she's just in bed. Come up though, come up."

He hesitated, one foot over the threshold. She couldn't help noticing that there was not a trace of engine oil under his slightly ragged fingernails. Clearly he hadn't just been passing by, but Cass in bed was a circumstance he obviously hadn't been prepared for.

"Come on up," she urged. "She's in bed by herself."

He blushed, as she thought he might, and stepped in and followed her up. She tapped gently on Cass's closed door.

"Cass?" Silence. She knocked again, sharply this time. "Cass! Steve's here."

There was a muffled sort of groan from within. "Steve? No. Queasy..." Then silence again.

They waited a few moments, but nothing more was forthcoming.

"I'm sorry," Livi said. "She wasn't feeling very well."

He couldn't manage his disappointed face this time. "That's okay. When I phoned, your mum said you'd be back, so I just thought…" He turned to go. "Thanks anyway."

Her heart ached for him. "We had such a late night," she said. "She's really worn out."

"That's okay," he said again, with a determined shake of the head. "I knew I was aiming high. I'd better get back to work."

She saw him down the stairs, closed the door on his purposefully upright figure, and went straight back upstairs into Cass's room, without knocking this time.

"Hey, Cass." She shook the batik-printed mound. "Wake up."

"Nooo."

The mound travelled to the other side of the bed, but Livi was merciless. She pulled back the covers and tugged the pillow out from under Cass's head. "Wake up!"

"What…why did you do that?" Cass was indignant. "My head is absolutely killing me, that doesn't help, you know."

She grabbed the pillow back and put it over her head, blocking out the light and Livi's reproachful face.

"You should have seen him. If you'd seen him, you wouldn't have sent him away. He must have taken time off work. He looked so sweet. And well-groomed."

"If you were in this head, you wouldn't be receiving visitors either."

"But it was such a big deal for him to come here. I mean, it was brave. He said he knew he was aiming high."

"Oh!" She emerged from under the pillow, surprised and pleased. "Did he? He *is* sweet. You know," she added, "I have been thinking about him an awful lot."

"Don't say you might actually, properly, like this one?" Livi teased.

Cass looked pink. "Maybe. I would like to find just one. You know, the right one. It's not *my* fault if it's been taking a long time." She was suddenly struck with remorse. "Oh God, do you think I hurt his feelings?"

Livi's teasing had unintentionally hit home. "Yes, you probably did. I think—"

But her reply was cut short by her mother's raised voice. Although they couldn't tell what she was saying, she sounded upset. Livi turned and made for the kitchen, and Cass heaved herself out of bed and followed, dropping the pillow on the floor.

They found Evelyn leaning out the window. From below, they could hear a familiar voice shout, "Just let me come in and explain! Come on love, open up…I'm telling you, it would really be best if you let me in." Then he started hammering on the door.

Livi and Cass looked at each other. "Is it locked?" Cass whispered.

Livi nodded, grateful for the automatically locking night latch. Then, seeing her mum's distressed face, she went and stood with her at the window.

In the front yard, an agitated Len Mortlock was pounding on the door and yelling up, "Evelyn! Come on now, Evelyn!" The suave demeanour was gone. Now his well-tended hair was in disarray, and his moustache was askew. She would have laughed at the sight he made, grim expression, beetroot face, and flying spittle, but he looked so incensed that she felt quite afraid. She was glad to be a storey above.

"Len, please go away," Evelyn pleaded. "I really don't want to hear any explanations."

"Evelyn! Just open the door and we'll talk about it." More hammering. "I'm starting to get really angry now…"

Evelyn turned away and started to cry. "Oh Livi, I'm so sorry. I didn't think he'd do this."

As reassuringly as she could, Livi said, "It'll be okay." She gestured to Cass, who came over and put an arm around Evelyn's shaking shoulders. Then she leaned through the window, and tried to use her most authoritative voice. "Len! You need to go now."

"This is between me and your mother." He sent her a look that made her go cold, but, with Evelyn crying behind her, she stood her ground.

"Len, if you don't go I'll have to call the police."

He snorted. "I'm coming in." And he started kicking at the door.

Before any of them could think what to do next, they saw a figure charge through the front gate and grab Len by the back of the collar. As he jerked backwards, his face was a study in scarlet surprise, and any menace he held for them evaporated as they watched Steve effortlessly spin him around and fling him into the hawthorn hedge. He howled with pain as the thorns connected with a dozen parts of his anatomy.

"Sorry about the hedge," Steve called up to them as he hauled him out, scattering glossy green leaves and berries, and manhandled him to the street.

"Another time, love," Len managed to get out, despite his head being wedged between his elbows. "Another—"

He was cut short as Steve hustled his sorry form, still flailing and fighting, along the pavement, around the corner and out of sight.

With his removal the street was quiet again, as though nothing at all had happened. They found themselves laughing, and crying a bit, with the sudden release of tension.

"My God, he's quite mad," Evelyn said, still shaking. "Thank goodness the downstairs neighbours weren't home." She lowered herself into a chair.

Something occurred to Livi. "Mum, what did he want to explain?"

"Oh...well, yes. I suppose I'll have to explain myself now."

The girls sat down with her, and she reluctantly began.

"Well...after the play we started walking to find somewhere to eat. We went down a little side street, and then we came to one of the old red phone boxes, and he said he needed to make a call." She stopped, rubbing her forehead.

"And what happened then?" Livi prompted.

Her cheeks reddened, but she made herself continue. "Well, then...he sort of pressed me into the phone box, and…I'm so embarrassed…he tried to pull up my skirt, and, you know…" She swirled her now-cold tea in its mug, avoiding their eyes. "Luckily someone came past just in time."

As her meaning sank in they were both incredulous, and furious.

"*You* shouldn't be embarrassed about that!" Cass exclaimed. "That's absolutely scandalous."

Livi felt a hot anger in the middle of her chest. "It is, it's disgusting. Especially when he tries to make out that he's such a gentleman."

"He did seem so charming and funny," said Evelyn. "I thought he was just a bit cheeky, a bit of a larrikin. But…obviously not."

"I really do want to call the police now," said Livi.

"Oh no, I'm in one piece. Unsullied. But, speaking of gentlemen, thank goodness Steve was here." She neatly changed the subject.

Livi looked at Cass. "Yes, what do you think of your Steve now?"

"Well, I know we're not supposed to be impressed with manly displays like that any more, but that *was* impressive." She got back up and peered out the window and down the street. "I can't see a motorbike. Maybe he had to park around the corner. Do you think he'll come back?"

"I hope so," said Evelyn. "He deserves a big thank you."

"I know how *I'd* like to thank him," Cass said, grinning, her headache apparently forgotten. "Surely he'll be back."

Livi looked doubtful. "I don't think so. He looked pretty flattened when he left the first time." She felt for him. She knew the feeling all too well herself.

"You could call him," Evelyn suggested.

"I don't have his number," Cass said, dismayed. "I never asked him for it."

"Then you'll just have to wait for him. That'll be a

change for you," said Livi, not able to resist.

Cass wasn't offended. "Now you and I will both be on the hunt for missing men. But," she said to Evelyn, "I hope yours stays missing."

"So do I," she replied wholeheartedly.

"Me too." Livi tried not to think about her going off to work the next day, out on London's streets with only a blue flag and a gaggle of disoriented tourists as protection. If her dad was here, none of this would have happened. She made up her mind to call him as soon as her mother went to bed. She couldn't imagine why he hadn't phoned before now. And, despite Evelyn's strict instructions, she had every right to talk to him. After all, it was her family too, even in this crumbled state. She just hoped it could be reconstituted.

★

To: cam.holden@nzuni.ac.nz
From: liviaway@gmail.com
Subject: Mothers and madmen

Drama. We'd only just come back from the Notting Hill Carnival (which was fantastic, by the way) and Len the Australian turned up, pounding on the door like a crazy man. Mum had gone to the theatre with him, and afterwards he tried to *take advantage of her* in a phone box. Sorry to sound all Jane Austen, but I can't manage the direct description when it applies to my mother. Anyway, luckily one of Cass's admirers, Steve, stepped in and got rid of him. We're expecting that will be the first and last of the walking tourists Mum brings home. Hopefully it'll be the last we see of Len too.

I phoned Dad last night but I got the voicemail at work and home, and on his mobile. What can he be doing?

You're lucky to have nice steady parents. Say hi to them from me.

xxx

114

P.S. Can just see you and James cruising the countryside on the Goldwing, his moustache tickling the back of your neck...

To: liviaway@gmail.com
From: cam.holden@nzuni.ac.nz
Subject: Re: Mothers and madmen

He's trimmed it. But even so, no more of those jokes, thank you.

Think we know now that there are no guarantees on steady parents. But your dad would be worried—for all of you—with lunatics at your door. Anyone would be worried. Remember your self-defence. And get Cass to keep her Steve handy. He sounds like a useful guy to have around. Be careful out there.

xxx

Chapter Seventeen

T he next night, Mia phoned. "This is your personal
Google service calling."

Mia loved a project, and prided herself on her online
search skills, so she'd risen to the challenge of helping find
the American. Now she put on her efficient voice.

"Right, clue number two. Golders Green, the first of
September. I've done a bit of research for you."

"Thank you!" Livi said. "What did you find out?"

"Well, I don't go up that way very often, so I didn't
know much about it. Let's see. There's the London Jewish
Family Centre. Did he look Jewish, do you think?"

"Um...I don't know." She thought back to dark eyes
and exotic golden brown skin, perfect teeth revealed in that
mischievous smile. Even standing in the kitchen under a
bare light bulb, dirty dishes cluttering the worktop, just the
picture of him in her mind's eye was enough to give her a
little rush. "More Italian, probably."

"Okay." There was a pause, and Livi could imagine
her inscribing a neat cross next to item one. "There's the
Hippodrome theatre."

"Hmm. What about the '3P' he wrote on the A–Z
page—could it be seat 3P, maybe, in the theatre?"

"Maybe, but it hasn't been a theatre for years. Now one of those hands-in-the-air churches owns it. I haven't been to church for a long time, but I can't imagine they've introduced numbered seating. What else...oh, there's a big bus station outside the tube station."

"Could a 3P bus go from there?" There were great swathes of London Livi had travelled under countless times by tube, but she had no idea what they looked like on the surface. She sometimes thought she should take the bus more, and actually *see* this city she was living in.

"I don't think any of the buses have letters and numbers together. Except for the night buses, but they start with N." A longer, weightier pause now. "The most famous thing in Golders Green is the crematorium. It was on that A–Z page."

"Oh." Her heart sank. From a drowned Brian Jones to the crematorium, en route to Jim Morrison...this was turning out to be a less than uplifting search.

Mia was sympathetic. "I know. Not very encouraging. But it's not necessarily the crematorium. I just thought, graveyards are organised into sections, so you can find people. It looks like there might be a section 3P."

"So he might be going to see someone buried there."

"Well, someone scattered. Or possibly in an urn. There are lots of famous people there, apparently."

"Great, another famous dead person."

"But he said his mother was English—maybe she's there. Or some other family members."

This was a much nicer idea. American boy crossing the Atlantic to pay tribute to his English forebears. It sat much better alongside Pooh Bear, who she obviously much preferred to Brian Jones. But, even assuming the crematorium was the right place, who knew if he'd be there at the same time she was? All she had was a long lunchtime—she couldn't spend all day sitting in section 3P, whatever that was. The whole exercise was probably, almost certainly, a wild goose chase.

But. *But*. The memory of him, the electric sensation of

117

standing just a whisper away from his body, breathing in his closeness. Without even touching her, he'd flicked a switch, and she was humming. No one had had that effect on her since Rob. Life is too short to be sensible *all* the time, she reasoned. And she was sensible in so many other ways. Before she knew it she'd be an old lady, saving her cling film, reusing her tea bags and wearing a warm coat in hot weather. In the meantime, before she took possession of her bus pass and orthopaedic shoes, surely she could take a chance or two.

So she set out from the salon the next day as planned, hung about with her own bag of synthetic origin—pleather, as Cass liked to call it—and the fragrant genuine leather satchel. The heavy glass door had only just swung closed behind her when Mattias appeared.

"I was just coming to invite you to lunch," he said. "Are you free?"

She didn't know what to say. How could she explain what she was doing?

"Um...I'm going...I'm going to Golders Green."

"I haven't been there yet. I'll come too and keep you company." He gave a firm nod, as if it was all decided. "Let me take that bag for you."

He took hold of the satchel's strap and began to lift it from her shoulder. There was a polite sort of struggle for a moment, Livi insisting she was fine. It didn't seem right to let him carry the satchel (though she couldn't say why). But then she gave in to his absolute determination to be chivalrous. What were the odds of them actually finding the American, anyway?

They made their way through the lunchtime bustle to the Tottenham Court Road tube and waited for an Edgeware train to come along. She noticed that the satchel, not having any hint of man-bag, actually gave him a slight (a very slight) edge of cool. Quite an achievement, she thought.

As they rocked northwards, he made conversation. "Do you have an appointment in Golders Green?"

"Um, no." She was tempted to tell him she was off for some intimate procedure, just to see his face. A Brazilian wax, or colonic cleansing. Or a smear test. She smothered a giggle. He looked sideways at her, but she resisted the urge. How could he be so well-mannered, and yet blunder along doing things ordinary people wouldn't dream of?

He continued on. "Where are we going today, then?"

Damn. She was backed into a corner. "Golders Green Crematorium."

His eyebrows flew up. "Oh!" Then something occurred to him, and he organised his features into an expression of mournful sympathy. "Oh. I'm so sorry." He put a large square hand over hers on her lap.

"No, no, it's okay," she said. "No one has died. Well, not just now, anyway." Finally she hit on an idea. "I'm going there to research some family history, for...um...for my friend Gemma." Brilliant, Livi, she thought.

Then she looked down at his hand, still resting on hers. Was it creeping sideways onto her thigh? For once he took the hint, and removed the hand. Mia obviously hadn't had a word with him yet. She'd have to say something before this outing was finished. But for now, they continued the journey without any further discussion.

They arrived at Golders Green, above ground for once, and trooped out with the other passengers. They followed the iron fence around the edge of the paved forecourt, full of red buses, and she looked around for Finchley Road. "It's only about five minutes walk," she told him. But it could be a very long five minutes, she added to herself.

Luckily, he was happy to walk along in silence. She wondered if he felt any residual awkwardness after the wandering hand. Probably not.

Soon they turned into Hoop Lane. It was getting hotter, and she was glad of the trees that reached out and cast speckled shade onto the pavement. On their left a cemetery stretched out behind brick walls, crammed with the substantial, upstanding gravestones of another era. Beyond those they could just see a section of the cemetery where the graves were horizontal, one simple rectangular sarcophagus after another.

"I think that's the Jewish cemetery," she said, breaking the silence as they regarded row after row of memorials. "It's not part of the crematorium."

"Yes," he nodded. "Jewish tradition is to be buried, not cremated. Respecting the body is very important. And of course now there are memories of the Holocaust, so burning a body is a very disturbing idea."

She shuddered. In this pretty street, under a cloudless summer sky, such dark things seemed hard to fathom. She turned her attention to the other side of the road, to the large complex of red brick buildings that made up the crematorium. The arched details over the windows and below the eaves, the diamond patterns set into the brickwork, and the rosette window in the chapel building made her think of pictures she'd seen of Florence. Over everything loomed a square bell tower. She tried not to think about the bare facts of what went on behind the elegant architecture.

It was only as they passed between the imposing brick gate-posts that it struck her. Having told a lie—a white one, surely—about why she was here, how would she explain it if they did come face to face with the American? Now she was torn between desperately hoping to find him, and desperately hoping they wouldn't.

So when Mattias asked who in particular they were looking for, she replied with a rather muddled story about how Gemma's family thought they had a relation in 3P, but weren't sure who. It sounded completely bogus to her, but Mattias (having no reason to doubt, after all) gave his customary nod and turned his attention to the map they got from the office. Once he had his bearings, they set off for section 3P. She dragged her feet just a little at the prospect of Mattias puzzling over having to give Livi's satchel to an American they just happened to meet over the ashes of Gemma's distant relative. Oh, what a tangled web...

They passed the crocus lawn, a broad grassy expanse

this late in the year. She couldn't help noticing how lush the grass was, though it seemed inappropriate to mention it. But Mattias noticed too. "Well fertilised," he commented. She held her tongue.

When they got to the grass of 3P, of course, there was nobody. As she had suspected, known, dreaded. And most recently, with Mattias tagging along, hoped.

He turned the map over. "There's some information about famous people here. So, what about 3P..." He scanned through the list. "Yootha Joyce?"

She was startled by such an unexpected name. "Oh, *George and Mildred!* So funny. An old sitcom," she explained, but he just shook his head. Obviously the Ropers had made it as far as New Zealand, where they were endlessly repeated, but not to Sweden. She had no idea if the programme had screened in the States, but even if it had, it was difficult to imagine why her American would be interested in Mildred. Unless *she* was his relation...

"Anyone else?" she asked, and he continued running a long finger down the list.

"Keith Moon." He looked pleased. "I know who that is."

Another rock star. It seemed a pattern was emerging. "I can't remember which band he was in."

"The Who." He was thrilled to have the answer. "He was the drummer. One of the greatest drummers of all time. So they say."

That's right, she thought. Her dad had an album at home, vinyl of course. Looking at the grass, a thought struck her. "Keith Moon and Yootha Joyce. What a strange pair, to be scattered together for all time. What would they think of that? What on earth would they have to say to each other?"

But with no fond memories of the goings-on in Peacock Crescent, the absurdity of it was lost on Mattias. "I don't think they're chatting down there."

"Do you think they just sprinkle the ashes any old how, so they mix together, or do you think they put them carefully in their own zone?"

"I don't know. Would you like to go back to the office and ask?"

At first she thought he must be joking, but he was straight-faced. "No, that's okay thanks," she answered. She looked around, wondering how much longer she could drag out the visit, just in case the American was on his way.

"Do you think your friend is related to either of them?"

She suddenly remembered the 'reason' they were here. "Um, I don't think so. But maybe, I suppose." To keep up the charade, she took a few token photos with her phone. "I'll send her the pictures, and the map with the information, and she can follow it up."

As she reached out to take the map, their fingers touched, and he clasped her hand, scrunching the paper in between. "Livi…" he began.

Uh-oh. She thought she knew what was coming. Before he had a chance to say any more, she extracted her hand. The map floated gently to the ground, but they let it fall between them.

She presented her most regretful face. "Mattias. My heart is just not in it." Well, it was true. She tried to sound as rueful as she could. "I'm sorry. It's just the way I feel." She held up her hands as though it was a mystery to her too, but there it was, there was simply nothing to be done…

He squared his shoulders. "I understand," he said. "The heart cannot be given orders." His face betrayed his feelings with the same blush she had seen in the restaurant, but he was stoic. "So it is."

Now she did feel properly sorry. But she was grateful for his manners. He would certainly never make a scene or a fuss. She wondered if he'd end up with an ulcer, from keeping everything so determinedly internalised. But he probably had complete control over his insides as well as his outsides—there would be no gastric rebellion allowed under his command. Or if there was, he'd have all the information needed to deal with it swiftly and efficiently.

He bent and picked up the map, smoothed out the

crumples, and presented it to her. "Shall we get back then? It's been a long lunch break for both of us."

She scanned the grounds one more time, in the last-minute hope that a jeans-clad figure would appear from around a corner. But the only person in sight was an old woman, bundled up in a knitted cardigan, stepping carefully down the sunny path with her walking stick. Livi shook her head and turned to follow Mattias back to the gates. As he strode along, the satchel bumped against his hip in a rhythmic reproach: goose chase, goose chase, goose chase...

Chapter Eighteen

All Livi wanted to do that night was get home, put on her pyjamas, and collapse on their least uncomfortable settee, within arm's reach of a bottle of wine and the chocolate-filled shoebox. After the fruitless effort that day, compounded by the awkward Mattias moment, she was going back to sensible. It had suddenly occurred to her on the way home, passing the shuttered ticket office at Blackhorse Road, that she could have just handed the satchel in, entrusted it to the lost property office, and gone on with her life.

What had she been thinking? Or not thinking, obviously. She wondered why Steve and Cass hadn't suggested it. On second thought, she knew why Cass wouldn't have suggested it. But it was one thing to hunt about in London and nearby, another to turn it into a cross-Channel exercise. She wanted to go to Paris one day, sure. But it definitely wasn't in her budget right now. Especially not on such an idiotic, futile mission. Paris ought to be special, magical, enchanting—not a dead rock star in a cold bath.

So tomorrow she'd get rid of the satchel, and the far-fetched idea of the fated man. Now the whole thing seemed so embarrassingly adolescent she could hardly stand to think about it. Tomorrow. Tonight, she was in dire need of a chocolate-induced serotonin boost and some mindless television watching. No reality TV contests—she still couldn't stomach it. Something soothing, involving antiques or archaeologists, or maybe even Rick Stein, in honour of Mattias.

But halfway up the stairs she heard voices, and her heart sank. Her mother's laugh rang out, followed by a hearty belly-laugh she didn't recognise. Thankfully, it sounded like a woman. TV might be off the agenda, but at least there wasn't another Len awaiting her. She carried on up the stairs, leaving her bag and the satchel just inside the door, and popped her head into the living room. "Hello?"

A vision of pattern and colour rose from the sofa. Strappy slave sandals, African-print harem pants, and a muslin peasant blouse, draped with tie-dyed scarves of every colour, led up to a crinkly-kind face topped with flowing grey hair. The woman opened her arms encouragingly, jangling rows of turquoise-studded bangles, and beckoned Livi in.

"Yes, your mother was right," she said, her American accent giving Livi a start—they were everywhere lately. Then she was gathered in for an alarmingly close hug. Long strands of fragrant silver hair stuck to her face as she tried to twist around, sending a 'help me' to her mother. But Evelyn just watched and smiled, entirely pleased.

After what felt like an entire rotation of the Earth, she struggled free. "Um...hello."

"Evelyn!" exclaimed the stranger. "Her aura is very interesting. Lots of pastels—you must be a sensitive soul. No wonder all this upset has been hard on you."

She couldn't think what to say to this, but her mum nodded. "She's always been sensitive. A thinker too. An over-thinker, really."

"Mum!" Now she'd had enough. "What about an introduction?"

"Sorry, sweetheart, this is Journey."

Livi couldn't help the look of surprise that flashed across her face, but Journey was untroubled.

"It's not my real name, of course. My passport says Nancy Eichbaum. But we are all on a journey, after all. It's up to us to choose the way we travel." She gave them both significant looks.

Livi had to make an effort not to roll her eyes, but Evelyn was in agreement. "That's quite right. And you never know where the road will take you next."

Journey rearranged the silk scarves. "Exactly. And today my road has brought me to you." She swept her arms in a great arc, encompassing them both in her expansiveness.

"Via Royal London," Livi guessed.

"Yes. Your mother is a very welcoming spirit." The two of them exchanged smiles of mutual appreciation.

"I know," Livi said. "I'm finding that more and more." Her tone was dry, but Journey took the words at face value.

"Yes, this is a wonderful chance for you to find out more about your mother, as she discovers the truth of her own soul. I'm sure your father would want Evelyn to continue on her path to authenticity."

Evelyn herself didn't seem completely convinced by this last comment, but Journey reached out and patted her hand. "Strength," she added. "Truth."

At the mention of her dad, Livi felt a hard tension begin to spread across her shoulders. "You seem to know an awful lot about us."

She took it as a compliment. "Well, I know a lot about myself. And you know what, at the core of things we're *all* dealing with the same issues. The same desires, the same search for peace. I try to remember the truths of Eckhart Tolle."

Mother and daughter looked blank, so she happily took the chance to enlighten them.

"We only ever really experience the present moment. The past is gone. The future is yet to be. All we have is this present moment. Whatever has happened, or not happened, has brought us to the right now. That's all there is, and we should find the perfection in it." She lay her hands out at her sides, palms up, and breathed deeply, closing her eyes for a moment.

Evelyn was entranced, but Livi felt a growing urge to jump up and scream. It was like a bad episode of Oprah playing out in her own living room. She addressed the Zen-like figure on the sofa.

"So, after this present moment, do you have any plans?"

Journey brought herself back with a little shake of her hands. "Yes, I do. I'm going on a Trafalgar tour of Great Britain and Ireland. Thirty days." She beamed with pleasure at the prospect.

Livi had to laugh. "So you know where the road is taking you for the next month, anyway."

"Well now, I couldn't leave the community for too long. I had to make effective use of my time away."

"Journey is a facilitator for the Living Simply Association in California," Evelyn said. "It sounds so wonderful. Tell Livi about it." And she leaned forward, ready to absorb every word.

Journey began, with the air of someone completely certain of her convictions. "Voluntary simplicity. It's a movement, a belief system. It's about mindful consumption. So many of us have far more than we need, and we're working ourselves into exhaustion to pay for it all, and going into debt, and doing damage to our Mother Earth in the process." She shook her head. "It's not a new idea, but some of us have forgotten what brings real, lasting happiness. It's not consumer goods. We're on a quest for less, to bring ourselves more."

"Livi, don't you think that sounds marvellous?" Evelyn said, her face bright with enthusiasm.

"It sounds very admirable."

She couldn't think of any argument against saving the planet and happiness for all. She might find Journey's flower-in-your-hair California style a bit hippy-dippy for a Tuesday night in northeast London, but her mum was soaking it up.

Journey nodded. "More and more people are embracing it, and not just in the places you'd expect, like California or New Mexico."

"Or Idaho? Livi is searching for a man from Idaho," Evelyn said. Seeing Livi's surprise, she shrugged apologetically. "Cass told me."

"Good luck with that!" Journey let fly a peal of laughter. "Plenty of places in Idaho to get away and follow your own path. A lot of seekers head up there, though I understand you have to get yourself Idaho plates quick as you can, especially if you're from California. I have a great friend who lives in an underground house, out in the wilds. Crazy guy really, but he's in good company out there."

Livi didn't like the sound of that. "Are there lots of crazy people there?"

"Oh, no..." She paused. "Well, sure, there are a few extreme characters. It's not really constructive to comment on other people's choices...I'd only say that voluntary simplicity doesn't consider a firearm an essential item. But then, my Idaho friend had his VW bus stolen, back in seventy-six. Before you were born. And then, it turned up again last year. So you see, things come and go, and come again, just as they should." She smiled at them both. "It's a good lesson."

Livi supposed it was, although four decades seemed a long time to wait for things to be as they should. When she said as much, Journey waved the thought away.

"Time is just a construct. I mean, in Living Simply we're looking forwards and backwards at the same time. Back to the simple, honest ways of the past, for the good of the planet's future."

"But in the present," Livi pointed out.

"Exactly!" Journey looked triumphant. "I knew you'd get it."

Sarcasm didn't seem to be on her radar. Livi decided to give up and go to bed. The leftover egg mayo Pret sandwich she'd eaten on the way home would do for dinner. "Well, it was very nice to meet you. But I'll have to say goodnight, I've had a long day."

"There is one more thing Eckhart says, that you might find helpful. Would you like to hear it?"

She figured the line of least resistance would be quicker in the end. "Okay."

"So, unhappiness isn't caused by the situation you're in, but by what you're thinking about it. A situation is what it is, and your thoughts about it are something separate. The search for happiness is fruitless—we should aim instead for the absence of *un*happiness."

She felt very tired. "I'm sorry, that's all a bit esoteric for me at this end of the day."

"Can I just suggest, then…maybe what you *think* you're searching for is just something to keep you busy, so you don't have to look for what you *really* need to find."

There was a silence in the room. Livi and Evelyn looked at each other, then away.

"Goodnight, Livi," Journey said, satisfied. "May your dreams bring you clarity."

★

She did dream, the kind of anxious, busy dreaming about everything and nothing that seems to last all night long. She certainly didn't feel any clearer when she got up the next morning. Cass was already up, eating jam on toast at the kitchen table.

"Your mum stayed up late last night," she said.

"I hope she didn't keep you awake," Livi said, reaching into the cupboard for cereal. "I'm really sorry about all this. We need our living room back."

"No, I don't mind really. Everyone has their share of family dramas. And it's not forever."

"God, I hope not." She was feeling the strain more than Cass. "I suppose other people's mothers don't have the power to drive you mad like your own does."

"And, look at all the dinners and dishes she's done for us!" Cass pointed out. "That actually counts for a lot in her favour. It's just lucky she's not working until later today, she'll need this lie-in."

Livi sank into a chair and rested her forehead on the cool Formica next to her bowl of Weetabix. "I wish I could stay in bed too. For the rest of the year, preferably."

"That's a bit dramatic, for you. What's the story?"

She sat back up and stabbed at the joyless rectangles, collapsing them into the milk. "Seriously, I have to get my head straight. It's ridiculous to go to so much trouble to find a guy, probably a guy with a freakish death obsession, who I saw for two minutes on the tube."

"But fate! And the bag—"

"Cass. Why didn't I hand it in as lost property?"

"Oh!" Cass looked genuinely surprised. "I didn't think of that."

"Really?"

"I suppose I was excited about finding your man." She paused. "When you first arrived we could see how sad you were. And you never talk about Rob. We hate seeing you still lonely."

"I'm not lonely. I have plenty going on." She ignored Cass's sceptical expression. "Anyway, I've floated along for too long, it's time to get serious. Thirty is looming."

Cass snorted. "No, it's not. You only just turned twenty-five."

"Well, okay. But next I'll be twenty-six, and then I'm on the downhill slide."

"I'll be twenty-six before you, thanks very much."

"Yes, you old tart." She grinned as Cass poked out her tongue. "Anyway, I'm handing that bag in. And then I'm going to do something with my life."

"Like what?"

"I don't know. I don't know if I've ever really known." She reached for the sugar bowl and sprinkled a consoling amount over the Weetabix. "But I do know that I spent far too long working for Mum and Dad when I should have been doing something of my own."

"There's no shame in working for the family business."

She sighed. "I didn't even finish my degree though."

"Well, there's no point in having a degree in something you don't want to do." She shook her head firmly. "And now you're doing what you did originally plan—travelling."

Livi put down her spoon and smiled at her. "Thank you. You keep me sane."

She shrugged, but Livi could see she was touched. "Well, I'm just glad you're here. Now eat your breakfast before it goes soggy."

She obediently took a spoonful. "Speaking of soggy, did you actually meet Mum's latest new best friend?"

"Yes! Talk about the summer of love. Shame she's too late for Glastonbury this year." They both laughed.

"Mum adored her. I could practically see her consciousness expanding."

"Turn on, tune in, drop out…"

Livi sighed. "Better than crazy Len, at least. It was quite funny, but it didn't exactly help. And Mum took it so seriously."

"Mind you, at least your mum has some get up and go. Mine refuses to go anywhere other than Benidorm. She gets that from my Nan. She was happy to go abroad, as long as it was to Jersey."

"Yes, but I dread to think who she'll bring home next. I mean, it's a bit tragic, at her age, latching onto people and their ideas—"

She stopped. Cass was suddenly looking very uncomfortable. She knew immediately that her mother was standing behind her in the doorway. A sick, guilty feeling hit her in the guts. She didn't want to turn around.

Cass got up and left the kitchen, laying a hand on Livi's shoulder as she went past, then Evelyn was sitting in the chair she left vacant. In a fog of shame, Livi couldn't bring herself to look up. After a few moments, her mum began to talk.

"One day, when you were small—maybe about three—you looked at me and said, 'Mum, you look really old'." Livi winced, but she went on. "To you, I must have seemed ancient. But you know, I wasn't much older then than you are now." She paused. "Being a parent is love like you can't imagine. But parents get used to their children hurting them in all sorts of ways. Small and big. Sometimes they mean to, sometimes they don't. I used to think my mother was the most unbearably irritating person in the world. And now I'm almost as old as she was when she died."

"Oh, Mum..." Livi looked up at last. At the sight of her mother in the familiar pink dressing gown, a Mother's Day present picked out with her dad long ago, she began to cry.

"Journey may be slightly mad, but she was right about one thing. We *are* all searching for something. Maybe you and I are not as different as you might think."

She got up, gathering the dressing gown around her. As she passed, she stopped and kissed the top of Livi's head, and she felt like that three-year-old all over again.

"Life is so, so short. I know I'm not doing everything right, and I'm sorry to upset you. But at the end I want to say, *Wow, I can't believe I did that,* not *Why didn't I do that?* I'm afraid of leaving things undone. We all should be."

Then she was gone, leaving Livi sitting at the table with a half-eaten bowl of slushy cereal. She pushed it away. A full helping of remorse and confusion and sadness had taken away her appetite.

★

To: cam.holden@nzuni.ac.nz
From: liviaway@gmail.com
Subject: I am the world's worst daughter

Really, I am. I was awful. There's no other way to describe it. And it's true, what's been said can't be unsaid. Is it written anywhere that mothers have to forgive their children for bad behaviour? I hope so.

You can tell your mum she's lucky to have you, instead of an ungrateful, thoughtless child like me.

xxx

To: liviaway@gmail.com
From: gemgem@outlook.com
Subject: Home update

Hi Livi,

Bex and I saw Cam at the Frigate on Friday night and he told us about your mum. We can't believe it! How are you managing? We're going to FaceTime you when we're both home, just have to coordinate with Bex and her night shifts.

Rob turned up out of the blue a few nights ago. He said he wants to talk to you, but we didn't give him your details. Let us know if you change your mind and decide to talk to him. He says he's not seeing anyone. Not that we care, of course.

Talk to you soon.

Lots of love to you from us two.

xoxoxoxoxo

Chapter Nineteen

As she went into the tube station with Cass that morning, Livi realised she'd left the satchel sitting in the passage at home. Distracted and distressed, she'd walked straight past it, down the stairs and out the door. Well, she figured, he'd done without it this long, another day wouldn't make much difference. It was the least of her worries. She followed Cass through the turnstile.

By the time they got to work she was feeling worse rather than better, having relived the incident with her mum about a hundred times on the journey in, despite Cass's best efforts to console her. Nicolette was coming to check on progress with the list, and although she'd got through it, she didn't feel up to showing the rah-rah enthusiasm Nicolette always wanted to see.

There were still a few minutes to spare, so she went into the bathroom to gather herself together, blow her nose, and put drops in her eyes. But even with freshly whitened whites, she looked puffy and out of sorts. She shrugged at her reflection. Oh well. Without much hope, she put on some lip gloss and smoothed her hair. As she came out again, there was a general sort of sympathy in her direction, and she knew Cass had been updating the others. In how much detail, she didn't know or care.

She checked her email and found a message from Gemma. Well, she wasn't going to talk to Rob any time soon—or any time ever, come to that. There was no point in it. She sent a message to Cam, knowing as she wrote that it was a bit over-dramatic, but also knowing that he'd understand. She sighed and tucked her phone back in her bag.

In the staffroom, she made a pot of Nicolette's favourite coffee, kept in a special tin in the top cupboard, not to be dipped into by anyone else. By the time it was ready, Nicolette had made her grand entrance, sweeping through the door like a queen returning to her realm. After what she judged to be an acceptable amount of effusive welcoming and fussing, they settled themselves at the big lunch table in the staffroom and got down to business.

Livi pushed the memory of the morning out of her head, and forced herself into professional mode. "Katie and I went through the client database and checked everyone we haven't seen for six months or more. A lot of details were out of date, so we might check a bit further forward too, maybe four months. We got lots of bookings in the process, which was a bonus."

"Very good. What about the bathroom?"

"There are three contractors coming in to quote on Friday. I've noted down a few things you'll want to decide on before then, like soundproofing the wall, and what kind of extractor fan. If you have time that day, it would be good to talk to them directly about what you want."

"That should be fine. Next?"

She passed some brochures across and Nicolette took them carefully, slightly hindered by her over-long acrylics. Those wouldn't last a day in the salon, Livi thought. "These are the latest inventory control systems. They look interesting, although I'm not sure if it's worth spending the money to upgrade just yet."

"Right. I'll have a look at them."

When they'd gone through all the items, Livi refilled

Nicolette's coffee and laid another list on the table. Looking at her own handwriting, so similar to her mother's, the sick feeling began to creep in again. She cleared her throat, holding herself steady.

"There are a few other ideas I wanted to give you, too."

Nicolette raised her perfectly groomed brows. "Really? You have been busy."

"Well, actually, these are things I've been thinking about for a while."

Having got to grips with the workings of the salon some time ago, and introduced a range of changes— including better use of social media, despite her own purposefully non-existent profile these days—she'd started to see a lot more areas where things could be improved.

"All right, go ahead."

She launched in. "We really got a lot of bookings when we phoned to check the client details. So it might be worth calling people who haven't been in for a while, instead of just texting. We can keep track using the appointment software we have now. We've seen that if you talk in person you're much more likely to get a definite booking. There are so many places offering special deals now, and our promotions are just as good—we don't want anyone else stepping in front of us and stealing our clients."

Nicolette pursed her lips. "Definitely not."

"It would take more time, but it could be worth it to grow the business. That connection with an actual person can really build customer loyalty, especially combined with the online stuff, like the special offers we've started in the newsletter and on Facebook."

She looked thoughtful. "Yes, interesting. It might be worth a trial. What else?"

"Well, I think we could look at carrying less stock. I know the reps always push for bigger orders, but there's a lot of capital tied up in those boxes of product out the back. And if we weren't using all that area for storage, you could think about converting part of it into a space for beauty therapy. There's not a lot of room, but it could be enough for manicures and pedicures, maybe threading."

"I like that idea."

So far, so good. She checked her notes.

"There's another thing that might be fun. We could set up a really lush, gorgeous picture frame in the waiting area, for people to take an 'after' photo. If they give the okay, we could use it on our Instagram, and repost on Facebook. And maybe Pinterest, if we want to start that too."

Nicolette looked at her as though she was an entirely new person. "I'm impressed. You've been working hard," she said. She seemed to be taking real notice of Livi for the first time. "And you look tired. Is everything all right?"

"Oh, I'm fine. I just had…" Her voice cracked. "I just had a difficult morning." She worked to stop her face crumpling. "Sorry," she managed, pressing her fingers against her eyes. "Really, I'm fine."

But Nicolette shook her head. "I can see you're not. Come on, we're not going anywhere until you tell me what the trouble is."

In the end, Livi's reluctance was no match for Nicolette's insistence. She found herself telling the whole story of her mother's adventures, up to the sorry episode that morning, after which she had closed the living room door and not come out.

"Well, you're only human," Nicolette said. "And you're barely out of your own drama."

"How did you know about that?"

"I'm not here very often, but I do try to keep up with what's happening. The boys told me about your fiancé and the television programme."

"Oh, they didn't." She hid her face in her hands. "I just wanted to leave all that behind."

"That's understandable. I think it was horrendous. Although, at the end of the day, you probably had a lucky escape."

Livi thought of Rob, unexpectedly knocking on her door though she was far away. Rob of the easy charm, the lazy grin, and the tanned, muscle-carved body. Rob of the long, heated nights, when their outright lust for more, more, more overcame any other thought in her head. Funny how, before the show came along, he'd kept her awake night after night, and yet she'd felt more energised than ever before. Now she slept alone, but felt more tired than she could describe. She felt tears welling, but refused to give in to them.

"You're probably right," she said, pushing her shoulders back, determined to keep her composure. Crying in front of the boss was definitely *not* the look she was going for. "And we weren't really suited, anyway." She tried to concentrate on the paper in front of her. "Now, there are a few more things before you go..."

Nicolette reached out and took both lists from her. "Leave them with me. I'm sure I'll like what I see. The boys are always telling me I work you too hard, and now I see they may be right. Why don't you take some time off and get some rest?"

"Time off? I don't know..." Pounds weren't exactly flying in the door, and London rent didn't pay itself.

"Paid time off," she clarified.

"Oh!" After all the complaining they'd done about Nicolette, she didn't see that coming. "Will everyone manage, though?"

"I'll be here," she said. "I don't think I've completely forgotten the basics of running a salon."

"No, of course not," Livi hurried to agree.

"Take a week. Come back in good form. We have lots to do." She looked at Livi, still sitting across the table. "Well, go on! Off you go, before I change my mind."

They emerged from the staffroom, and Nicolette stood in the centre of the salon and made an announcement. "Livi is having a week off. I will be here to keep things running smoothly." In response to the surprised faces, she unbuttoned the sleeves of her silk blouse and began to theatrically roll them up, bravely disregarding the danger of creases. "I *am* the owner, after all."

138

Livi hesitated, but Nicolette was in action mode. She gave a brisk double clap. "Right everyone, back to work! And Livi, go. Go and revive yourself."

Before she knew it her jacket was on, her bag was in her hand, and she was out in the mid-morning street. She looked around with a strange out-of-place sensation, as though everyone was going about their business, but she had no business being there. After a moment she breathed out and started in the direction of the Tottenham Court Road tube, feeling like a child skipping school.

She could have gone anywhere, but she let her automatic pilot take her home. Home, up the stairs into the empty flat, past the damn satchel, into her room and into bed, only stopping to close the blinds and kick off her shoes. She pulled the covers up, and escaped into the blissful respite of sleep.

Chapter Twenty

There was an atmosphere of awkward politeness over dinner that night. Cass had taken a rare turn in the kitchen and cooked her famous spaghetti, hoping good food would lead to good vibes. Livi apologised for what she'd said, and Evelyn apologised for entangling Livi in her crisis. Despite that diplomacy, they tiptoed around each other in the small, small flat.

So the next morning, she waited until the flat was empty, then got up all set to hand the problem of the satchel over to London Transport. But when she was ready to go, there was no sign of it. She looked all over the flat—which didn't take long—before a suspicion began to creep in. She phoned Cass at Peach.

"Where is it?"

In the pause that followed, Livi could tell that she was trying to decide whether to deny it. "I can't tell you."

"Cass!"

"No, you can have it back to go to Paris for the next clue. You've gone this far, I think you should see it through. Especially now you have some time off."

Livi could only shake her head with disbelief and frustration. But a part of her wasn't surprised. Once she got hold of an idea, Cass wouldn't let it go, especially anything romantic, wild, or unorthodox. "You are the world's most infuriating flatmate."

"I love you too. And you know I'm right."

As she hung up, Livi knew she was beaten, for now. But Paris wasn't on her agenda. She'd just have to wait for Cass's conscience to kick in.

So she did as Nicolette had instructed, and rested. It was actually a relief to not answer the phone, be unfailingly polite to clients, keep her makeup perfectly applied, pay too much for sandwiches at lunchtime (though she always *intended* to be organised and bring lunch from home), or use any form of public transport. Cass held her ground on the secret of the bag, but brought work news home that night. Nicolette had declined to do any shampooing or cleaning, lest she risk the acrylics, but she was there, being more or less helpful.

Gemma and Bex FaceTimed her, as promised. They had a good long catch-up, but the sound of their accents brought on pangs. Her own was still slipping inexorably away, steadily returning her to her childhood voice. When she first came back, she'd felt like a foreigner in what was, after all, her own country. Now it was becoming home territory again, and Bex and Gem sounded like the foreigners. The tide had turned. It was a strange feeling.

The following morning, she walked to the local cafe—seeing more of above-ground London at least—and checked her email while she had breakfast. No reply from Cam. That wasn't like him. She'd stayed off Facebook since she left New Zealand, but now she went to his profile to see if there were any clues. But he hadn't posted anything since his bike trip—a picture of himself standing on a high, windswept hillside, all faraway eyes and leather jacket and tousled hair. He looked happy. She hesitated over her phone, but finally decided against sending another message. He was probably away again, or busy, and anyway, she didn't have anything entertaining or cheerful to report.

So she went home, put her pyjamas back on, and was

back in bed by ten thirty. When things get tricky, she thought as she lay down, there's always bed. And chocolate. Some comforts can be relied on.

Some time later, from her refuge under the covers, she slowly became aware of voices in the flat. She struggled up from the depths of sleep, surfacing into that muddled after-nap state. Her mother's laugh floated down the passage again, over the low rumble of a man's voice. Still half asleep, she threw back the covers, a mixture of angry and fed up and indignant. She got up and stomped out to the living room, hair on end. Who had she brought home this time?

In the doorway, surprise glued her to the spot. For a second or two she couldn't quite process what she was seeing. There was her mother, laughing on the sofa in the arms of a tall, dark-haired man. The tall, dark-haired man was...her father.

"Oh!"

They sprang apart like guilty teenagers at the sound of her voice, then laughed at themselves. Her dad took her mum's hand, smiling. "Hello."

Their obvious pleasure made Livi even more mad. She didn't know why. "What are you doing here?"

"We didn't mean to wake you, sweetheart," her mother said, obviously trying to soothe the savage beast in pink flannel pyjamas. She came over and put her arms around Livi, attempting to hug her into a better frame of mind. "Come on, let's go and make a cuppa and we can chat." She herded them into the kitchen, got them arranged at the table, and put the kettle on, a fix for any problem.

"Now, tea, sweetheart, or coffee?"

"Tea, please," Livi and her dad replied, at exactly the same time.

They looked at each other, and there was a glimmer of laughter in his eyes. She didn't feel inclined to see the joke. How could he make them wait so long and then just stroll in, casual as you like, expecting it to all be lovely jubbly, fine and dandy?

"Coffee, please," she said firmly.

Evelyn paused, a tea bag hovering over the mugs. "But you don't drink coffee."

Livi sighed. "Fine," she said. "Tea. Please."

She knew she sounded like that three-year-old again, but her parents let it slide.

While Evelyn bustled, and Livi frowned, her father attempted to make conversation, asking about work, and her friends. She wasn't up for small talk, though—she wanted him, and her mum, to explain what was going on. But before she could ask, he looked at his watch.

"Actually, Ev, thinking about it, now that we've seen Livi we could get that train after all. But we don't have much time."

"Oh, yes! I'll just get organised, and leave you two together for a bit." She gave them a thoroughly meaningful look before abandoning the hot drink project and disappearing back into the living room.

Livi couldn't stand it any longer. "Where have you *been?*"

He smiled, the lines crinkling at the corners of his eyes. "I had to give her a chance to miss me. But it hasn't been *that* long."

"It's felt like it. Although, in one way, I'm surprised you came at all, when she was the one to leave."

Her swirl of emotions made her hard-hearted, but he was patient. "I didn't want her to be embarrassed," he said simply.

That was an unexpected answer. "Some people might expect *you* to be the embarrassed one." She couldn't resist.

"Well, I wasn't happy about it, of course. But someone has to be the first one to reach out. Like they say, do you want to be right, or do you want to be happy? Your mum is going to a lot of trouble to avoid thinking about it, but the truth is, we are both knocking on a bit." He leaned forward. "We've been through a lot together. We have history. She's my past, and I want her to be my future too—for as long as we have."

Tears began to shine in Livi's eyes as she listened, and he reached across the table and took her hand.

"I don't want to spend my old age miserable and alone, just because I was too proud to come and get her. And I wouldn't wish that on her, either."

Her dad was the proverbial man of few words, and this straightforward wisdom was possibly the most insightful speech she'd ever heard him make. She couldn't remember talking to him about matters of the heart before—during the Rob drama he said very little, though she knew what he was thinking. Now she was impressed that he could see things so clearly. Once propelled by necessity out of the La-Z-Boy, he'd turned out to be capable of meaningful action. Finally, she felt her heart shift and soften.

"How did you know she was here?"

"Of course she would be here. Who else would she turn to? You're the most important person in her life."

"Really?" She found this hard to believe. "Me? Not you?"

"She chose me, of course. But she *made* you. Nothing compares. It's okay, fathers know that."

He smiled again. The years in his face were accentuated by the stark light flooding through the window and reflecting off the shiny kitchen surfaces, and she could see the grey in his dark hair. She was suddenly overwhelmed with relief that he was here, ready to make things better. The unpalatable truth, that her parents really were knocking on a bit, was made easier by knowing that her family would be all right after all.

Evelyn came back into the kitchen. "I'm ready. I just threw everything in, I'll be crumpled all over Europe."

"Europe?" Livi was having trouble keeping up with events.

"We have places to go," her dad said, standing up. "And things to think about while we're there."

"What about your job, though?" she asked Evelyn.

"June said she'll take the tours I was rostered for, so that we can go. It was only week by week anyway."

"But won't you spend some time in London?" Now that they were back together, so unexpectedly in her faraway flat, she didn't want to see them go.

"Not yet." Evelyn looked up at her husband, and tucked her arm into his. "First we're going to have some time together, just the two of us. Some proper time, without conveyancing or tax returns or wills or trusts or dishes or laundry or weeding or *anything*."

Her face was light and open and clear, reminding Livi of the old photos in their family albums, images of a young woman and her family in a new country, with a new life and everything in front of her. She wondered what it felt like. For the first time in her life, she realised she was envious of her mother.

"I don't want you to go," she confessed, as she said goodbye to them at the gate.

Her mum hugged her tightly. "I'm sorry I put you through so much upset. But don't worry, we'll see you again soon, sweetheart," she promised, as she got into the waiting minicab.

As he squeezed her in a bear hug, her dad whispered something in her ear. "We'll be travelling for a while, but I don't think you'll be by yourself for too long."

"Really...why?"

But he just shook his head, the glimmer in his eyes again. "You'll see."

She stood at the gate, still in pink flannel, and watched the minicab swing around the corner and disappear. They were off to write the next chapter of their history. Her own story, she felt, was yet to begin.

★

It wasn't long before she found out what her dad meant. As she was tipping out the swampy, over-brewed tea, the phone rang. Assuming it would be Cass, she took her time answering it, tossing the depleted tea bags into the bin before going out to the passage.

She picked up the phone and casually said, "Hiya."

"Hi," said a male voice.

One word was enough to tell her that the caller wasn't English. That one small syllable, uttered by a very familiar voice, held the sweet sound of a home found and lost.

Chapter Twenty-One

"Cam?"

"That's right," he said matter-of-factly. "How are you?"

"Surprised!" And surprised at just how happy she was to hear his voice. The departure of her parents really must have got the better of her. "How are *you*? Why are you calling? Is everything all right?"

"Yes, everything's fine. But I was wondering if you were busy today."

"Um, no." This conversation was starting to seem a bit odd. "Mum and Dad were here, but they just left."

"Yeah, I've been talking to your dad. He said he was going to see you. Well, would you like to get together?"

"What...are you here too?" She pressed a hand to the top of her head, which was spinning.

"I'm at Peach. I was going to surprise you."

"Well, you did that," she said. "And now I know why you didn't email me back."

He laughed. "So, are you free?"

"Yes, and I can't leave you at the mercy of that lot. Shall I come in and meet you somewhere?"

"Meet me at the National Gallery," he said, and her

heart leapt a little. Not an ending after all.

"I'll be there as soon as I can," she said. "At the café?"

"I'll order your hot chocolate."

★

By the time she got herself out of pyjamas again, and put on her makeup and sorted her hair, she figured Cam would already be nearly there. The walk to the tube station felt extra long, and the ride in seemed to go twice as slowly, and have double the usual number of stops. As she travelled, she debated which stop would be closest and where to change, running her eyes along the coloured lines of the tube map above the window. Eventually, she decided to change at Warren Street and get off at Charing Cross. She burst out of the station, crossed the Strand and scooted across to Trafalgar Square. No time today to stop and commune with the magnificent lion statues, her favourites. By the time she scurried up the gallery's wide steps, dodging tourists, she had begun to worry that he'd given up and left. Though where he'd go instead, she couldn't say.

She flew up to the information desk. "Café?" she managed, hand pressed to her chest to steady her breathing.

She must have looked in the flap she felt, because the woman behind the desk swung briskly around in her black swivel chair and pointed, laughing. "Right that way love, through the shop, not far."

In the shop, she paused for a moment amongst the fridge magnets and calendars and toy pigeons to get herself together. But when she went into the café and looked around, there was no sign of him. She checked her watch, more deflated than surprised. How long had it taken to get there?

For a good minute she stood to one side, checking the faces of the people sitting on the long red bench seats and bentwood chairs, pondering cake or croissant at the self-service, and queuing patiently to pay at the counter. No one was wearing a motorbike jacket.

Then it struck her that, as he hadn't arrived by bike, he wouldn't necessarily be wearing one. She sighed and began scanning the crowded room again.

A waitress came past bearing a tower of carefully balanced plates and cutlery. "Do you need any help?" she asked.

"I was meeting a friend here for coffee, but I can't see him."

"Well, maybe you could try the espresso bar."

"Oh! Of course, thank you."

She made her way there and saw him straight away, wearing the jacket, engrossed in a computer screen. She hovered for a moment by the nearest pillar. Although her pounding heart had settled after her rush to get there, it did a little jig at the sight of his familiar profile. Counted in days and months, it hadn't been all that long since she last saw him at the art gallery in Auckland, and told him about her engagement. But it felt like a lifetime ago. In a way, she supposed, it was a *life* ago. Suddenly she felt shy. She put a hand on the pillar. Hello, this was *Cam*. He could probably still do a wicked armpit fart. She shook her head clear, and went and stood next to him.

On the screen was a painting she knew well. A young woman was wearing a richly draped orange dress over a white garment, with a gold-lined blue cloak over one shoulder. There were fresh flowers in her hair, above a clear forehead. She held a palm frond in one hand, and her sweetly beautiful face was strengthened by a determined set to her chin. An angel stood guard at her left shoulder as she looked at something, or someone, just out of view. Waiting, perhaps. Had she known what was coming?

"Saint Cecilia," she said aloud. "She looks so delicate, but she was tough."

"I thought you would remember." He stood up. "Wow, you look different."

She'd forgotten how much her hair had changed since Cass took charge of it. And she was better with makeup, since she'd been forced to glam up every day for work. But maybe she'd put on too much...she put a hand to her face.

"Great different, I mean."

He grinned, and she breathed out and went into the hug he offered. His jacket creaked a little as his arms went around her, and the warm leather smell was just as she remembered. She wanted to stay there, soaking up the feeling of home and safety...and of him. Pressed against him, she suddenly felt a frisson as her body reacted to him in a new, unexpected way. But before she could fully register the feeling, he let her go and stood back. She looked up at him—tall, clever and, yes, flat-out handsome—and remembered what Gemma and Bex had said. It's just Cam, she reminded herself. Seeing her mum and dad had probably sparked a bit of homesickness, and now here was home, and her past, right in front of her.

"You look different too," she said, gathering herself together. "How long have you had those?"

He quickly took off the narrow-rimmed glasses and put them on the table, suddenly self-conscious. "Too many years cross-eyed over textbooks and papers. But they're only for reading."

"Well, they suit you." And they really did make him look different—in a good way. "Very grown-up. You old fossil."

He grinned again. "Okay, slick chick, enough of that cheek. If you still want your hot chocolate."

And they were back in the swing, their old selves. All the emails of the past months had smoothed over the awkwardness of their last meeting. As she sat down, she saw his backpack leaning against the rectangular seat.

"When did you arrive?" she asked.

"Oh, this morning," he said casually. "Early."

And she realised, again, that seeing her was the first thing he'd done.

"Are you holidaying? How long are you staying?"

He shrugged. "No, not holidaying. I have some things to do. A few people to see. Nothing exciting. Nothing in concrete."

She was intrigued, but he wouldn't elaborate. "No. Very dull. Now look. You might remember the lovely Cecilia, but what about this one?"

He pointed to a particularly overwrought battle scene on the screen, and she gave in, knowing that she mightn't be able to get it out of him now, but eventually it would be obvious. All in good time.

Chapter Twenty-Two

L ater they walked to Covent Garden to meet up with the
Peach crowd. In the narrow street outside the Lamb
and Flag, they found Cass, Aidan, and Will amongst the
clusters of people standing around with after-work drinks.
They all squeezed through the door, Cam struggling with
his backpack. He marvelled at the old interior, with its low
beams and dark wood panelling, but Aidan hustled them
through the crowd and up the creaking stairs.

Cass made impressed faces at Livi as they followed the
men up. "Very nice," she mouthed, but Livi shushed her
and waved her on.

They managed to find a place to sit just as some others
were leaving, and Cam squished the backpack out of the
way as much as he could. "Great place."

"Ah yes, the old Bucket of Blood," Will said. "Seen a
bit of action in its time."

"Oh, really?" Aidan enquired, eyebrow raised, but Will
gave him a squashing look.

"Not that kind of action, as you well know. Could we
please keep it seemly this evening?"

He was chastened for only the briefest moment. "Well,
I'll get the first round then, and we'll see how seemly it

stays. Things go downhill all too quickly with this crowd." He leaned confidingly towards Cam. "I hope you are of sturdy disposition."

While he was at the bar there was a surprise arrival—Steve, neat as a new pin, looking nervous and hopeful in equal measure. When she saw him Cass went a little pink, and stood up, then sat down, then stood up again.

"So, everyone, this is Steve..." She sat down again abruptly, leaving Steve to manage his own introductions to the men.

Livi took her chance. "Quick, *tell*," she whispered to Cass.

"He phoned me at the salon today," she whispered back. "I forgot I'd told him where we work. And I thought, he could just come along tonight."

"Wow, he's brave. But poor Steve, talk about baptism by fire."

Just then Aidan came back with their wine. Steve's obvious nerves made him too soft a target, and Aidan couldn't resist.

"Does this mean I have to go back *again*?" he sighed, on being introduced. "I'm practically wearing a *ditch* in the floor here." He swept a dramatic arm towards the bar.

Steve looked aghast. "Sorry mate, sorry." He fumbled for his wallet. "I'll go, don't you worry."

But Cass stood up again, firmly this time. "Aidan! Leave him alone! Steve, just ignore him. Honestly, he can't help himself."

"Ah, Cass, that's okay, I'm just fooling around." Aidan gave Steve a slap on the back. "Come on, give me a hand with the pints. I've heard you're a bit of a hero." And they went for the rest of the drinks, Steve relieved but clearly not entirely convinced.

"Poor Steve is right," Cass said to Livi. "But did you notice his fingernails? They look completely unbitten." She watched approvingly as he seemed to manage Aidan's banter at the bar.

"Look at you," Livi said. "After all those test runs,

maybe you've finally found one you like enough to keep on."

Cass looked coy. "Yes, maybe...I think so."

"Well, I approve. He's a sweetheart. I want to see *you* happy, too."

Cass gave her hand a squeeze, and they smiled at each other.

When everyone was settled with their drinks, Livi told the story of her eventful day, to much exclaiming. Then there was the inevitable comparing of Cam's accent to Livi's almost non-existent one.

"Remember that time you suddenly regained your English accent?" Cam asked her. "You sounded far more posh than your mum and dad ever did."

There was laughter as she shook her head. "No," she insisted, suddenly very conscious of how English she sounded now. "I don't remember. You must be thinking of some other terribly British New Zealander." And she gave him a wink, which he returned with a knowing smile.

"It's good that they sorted things out," he said, and everyone murmured their agreement.

"It's such a relief," she said. "Although I shouldn't have let it affect me so much." She sighed and looked into her glass. "I mean, I'm not a child any more."

"You're *their* child," he said gently.

He was there, all those years. He knew. She smiled gratefully at him. Around the table, her friends looked at each other, all obviously wondering if this sweet moment was the beginning of something.

But the moment passed, and one round eased into the next, and the next. While Steve kept a low profile, Cam more than held his own with the in-jokes and teasing. Sitting next to him, her wine slowly going tepid, her foot sticking to a tacky spot on the wooden floor, the hum of voices and the close, warm air pressing around them, she was suddenly acutely aware of how good he smelled. She relaxed a little to her left, imperceptibly closer, she thought. But he put down his pint with a bump and threw his arm around her shoulders. "That's my girl," he said, and squeezed her against him. Then he leaned across the table to join Will and a more animated Steve in a vigorous debate about the merits of Harley versus Triumph. She breathed out and took a careful sip of her drink, not wanting to show any sign of the unexpected shock of pleasure she'd felt when he put his arm around her, or the disappointment when he let her go. Distracted by her own thoughts and his proximity, she lost track of the conversation around her.

She was jolted back to attention by her friends' laughter.

"Jack Dee! That guy looks like a swear word." Aidan's face was scrunched in disapproval.

"He does not!" Cass laughed. "But which swear word?"

"No particular word, but you know what I mean. And the shiny suits...no."

Cam looked curious. "Does he swear a lot?"

Livi shook her head. "No more than the next comedian. But he has that seventies cop show look about him. Why are we talking about Jack Dee?"

"Embarrassing celebrity crushes," Cass explained.

"Really? That's not especially embarrassing." She looked across at Aidan, who had his hand up like an eager schoolboy. "Tell us yours then."

"Easy. Christopher Plummer, *Sound of Music*. Such authority. So well-groomed."

Will nodded in agreement, and Aidan gave him a nudge. "Come on then. Your turn."

"All right," Will said. "I'll admit it. Russell Brand. There's a superb brain behind that wanton exterior, you know."

But Cass wasn't having it. "No, no, he doesn't count. Even the sneery people who claim not to fancy Russell Brand, secretly do."

"I don't think any of you are in the spirit of this," Livi said. "I thought it was supposed to be *embarrassing* crushes.

Try again."

Will looked reluctant. "Well, then...I suppose it would have to be Alan Titchmarsh. He really is desperately lovely." When Aidan laughed heartily, he retorted, "At least I told the truth. We all know that *your* greatest love is yourself. You won't be happy until you're permanently installed on the fourth plinth."

"Don't be snippy," Aidan said. "I know you love me just as much."

Will rolled his eyes and turned to Livi. "So, now that you've embarrassed me, what about you? Apart from George, not embarrassing. And the American, of course."

"Oh no, not the American!" she said hastily, feeling Cam's eyes on her. "No, I don't have any. Apart from George."

"And Hugh," added Cass. "You know, Livi, we have a laugh about Nicolette and her old-age pensioner, but now I realise you're just as bad."

"They're not that old! Leave me alone." She couldn't bear to look at Cam, who was laughing along with the others. Now she was very glad she'd never confessed her lingering affection for Captain Jean-Luc Picard of the Starship Enterprise.

But Cass wasn't done. "Actually, there is someone of a reasonable age. You were just telling me the other night."

It was true. "Fine. Okay. David Tennant. Are we finished now?"

"She doesn't like the latest guy," Cass told them, as Livi blushed.

"When did you start watching *Dr Who*?" Cam said, intrigued. But before she had time to reply, Aidan was holding his hands out to Cam and Steve.

"Now that we have demolished poor Livi, that just leaves you, our guests of honour," he said, the drinks making him extra grand. "Visitors are not exempt."

But Steve wouldn't be coerced. "Nothing to confess," he declared, glancing sideways at Cass, who looked pleased.

Then Livi held her breath as everyone turned to Cam.

He smiled. "It would have to be the marvellous Miss Olivia Callaway, of course. World famous in New Zealand."

A collective 'aah' went round the table, and Livi felt her cheeks flame. If he was joking, it wasn't very funny. She didn't want to be reminded of her brush with fame. But if he wasn't joking...

She gave a dismissive wave, trying to look casual. "That doesn't make me a celebrity. My fifteen minutes are well over."

But as she said it, Cam looked awkwardly away.

"What?" she said, a horrible feeling starting to take hold. "What is it?"

"I thought you would know," he said.

There was a kind of suspended tension at the table as the others waited, riveted, leaning forward over their glasses.

"Know what?" Queasiness grew in her stomach.

He was plainly reluctant to say anything more, but with all eyes on him he had to continue.

"The footage from that night, when you saw...you knew it was all over the news. Then there was a debate in the media about the ethics of reality TV. Nothing exactly like that had happened before in New Zealand."

"No *Big Brother* for you," Will said, and Cam nodded.

"But that was ages ago," Livi said, although to her ears it sounded more like a plea than a statement.

"It was, but auditions for the second season are starting soon." He looked pained to have to say it. "And they're using the clip of you in all the promotions."

As her past came rushing in, the queasiness turned to a violent, stomach-twisting urge to throw up. She pushed the last of her wine away, unable to bear the smell. The voices in the pub were suddenly much too loud, and she put her elbows on the table, holding her head, knowing they were all looking at her. Was that why Rob had suddenly turned up at her old flat?

Cass was enraged on her behalf. "They can't do that! Surely they don't have the right to use that without her permission?"

"I don't know." Cam sounded despairing.

Sitting up, she could see he looked despairing too. She tried to give him a smile.

"I'm sorry, Livi," he said.

"Don't they *think*, don't they realise she's a real person, with *feelings?*" Cass fumed. "That's so freaking *classless.*"

"Not exactly *Strictly*," Will commented.

"No." Cam shook his head. He took her hand and they all sat in silence, the merry mood ruined.

But, with the recharging warmth of his hand, Livi gathered herself.

"Oh, screw them. Why should I care anyway? I'm on the opposite side of the earth, and I'm never going back. It was yesterday's news once before, eventually it'll be yesterday's news again." And she slugged back the remains of her wine.

Said firmly enough, it sounded quite convincing, and everyone stirred and nodded and sat up a little straighter.

"Good for you," Will said.

"Yeah, screw them," agreed Cass.

Cam put his arm around her shoulder again. "That's my girl," he said once more.

She looked around. "I think someone could buy me another drink now."

Chapter Twenty-Three

B y the time they went unsteadily home that night, Livi had drunk more than enough to dull the sting of her distant fame. Or notoriety. No, she supposed that was Rob, who, after all, was in the footage too and was still there in the middle of it all. Quite a satisfying thought. She wondered what had happened to sequins girl, and Jasmine. Ironic that not one of the three of them had turned out to be his perfect match.

It seemed surreal to be sitting in one of the now-familiar tube carriages with Cam next to her, his backpack on the floor between his legs, as though he'd been transported not just from another place, but from another time. Which, in a way, he had been. The plastic arm rest pressed into her side and separated their bodies, but, further down, his knee sat comfortably relaxed against hers, as though their limbs had always been this closely acquainted. He didn't seem to notice.

Walking home from the tube station, Cam and Steve went ahead, deep in motorbike talk, while she and Cass wandered behind, deep in their own thoughts. Then Livi caught Cass looking at Steve's behind. Cass said, "Well?" and pointed at Cam's, just visible below the backpack.

Livi hissed "No!", slapping her hand down, causing them both to fall into giggles. The guys turned around curiously, making them both laugh even more.

"Cass, *don't*," Livi whispered, as they turned back to their manly discussion, shaking their heads. "You know it's not that way with us."

"But it could be," Cass persevered. "Why do you think he's here?"

Livi grabbed her arm and slowed down, letting the guys get further ahead. "He said he had things to do...people to see...I don't exactly know."

"And by people, he means you. He was quick enough to come and stay with us."

"That's because I invited him! It's only polite."

That was actually true. When she invited him to stay that morning, she had the purest of motives—good manners and friendship. Since then, it seemed like things had got more complicated.

"Yeah, right." Cass clearly didn't believe it. "Although, I don't know why I'm encouraging you. I mean, you're going to Paris to find your American next." She considered Cam's behind. "But maybe I like this one better..."

"Just stop, *please*," Livi begged under her breath as they looked around again. "Let it go."

Cass shrugged, but her expression made it obvious she would do no such thing.

When they got back to the flat, she wasted no time. "Well, I am *extremely* tired," she said pointedly, as soon as they went into the living room. "What about you, Steve?" He, of course, was knackered. They said goodnight.

"Be good, you two," she sang over her shoulder. "Or not."

"No," Livi started. "We're—"

But she was gone. They heard her bedroom door shut. For a moment they looked at each other, then Cam broke the silence.

"This couch looks all right," he said heartily, going

over and bouncing in a positive manner on the slightly less lumpy sofa. He took off his jacket and folded it up into a pillow. "This'll be great."

"We can do better than that," she said. "I'll get you some pillows and blankets. Oh, and a spare key. Mum left hers behind."

She busied herself getting the things, aware of him watching her go out and come back in. There's no reason to be self-conscious, she told herself. An over-emotional night and too many drinks and your imagination gets away on you. Focus now. She passed him a blanket.

As they worked together to turn the sofa into a bed of sorts, he said, "Steve's a nice guy."

"Yes, he really is. Cass thinks so too, especially after the Len thing." She took the back cushions off the sofa to make more room. "I think it took her a while to get used to the idea of someone who works in a garage though. She usually goes for guys in suits and corner offices."

Cam took the pillow she offered. "But he's not just a grease monkey. He's a motorbike designer—an independent consultant. He's quite well-known."

"Really? I don't think he told her that—he just let her assume he was a mechanic. She'll be impressed." She stood back and looked at the bed doubtfully, comparing its length with his six-foot-plus frame. "I don't know how comfy you'll be."

"I'll be fine," he said. "I can sleep anywhere."

Was it her over-charged imagination, or did that last word hang in the air? He was smiling now, waiting for her reply, but she found herself completely distracted.

"Okay then...well, make yourself at home. You know where the bathroom is, and the kitchen, if you need anything. Nothing's hard to find in here. But if you need anything you can't find, just let me know, you know where to find me."

Oh God, she was babbling. She forced herself to stop. Damn that last drink too many, and Cass for creating this awkwardness, throwing her off-centre. What was the goodnight protocol in this situation?

"Thanks," he laughed. Then he stepped towards her, and they were hugging goodnight. He seemed to hold her extra close, so that she could feel the length of his body pressing against hers. Or maybe it was just the wine making her acutely aware of the breadth of his chest and the warmth of his breath in her hair. She swayed a little. If she just looked up now...

Then he let her go. "I'd better get some sleep," he said. "Early start tomorrow."

"Oh," she said, snapped back to reality. "What are you doing?"

"People to see," he replied, opening his backpack. "Nothing exciting."

"Maddening man! Goodnight then." And she left him to it.

Lying in bed after cleaning her teeth and giving her face a very perfunctory wash, she could hear him get in the shower. She'd forgotten to give him a towel, but he must have found one. She tried not to think about it. Soon the water stopped, and there were shaving sounds. She was almost asleep, the wine working its soporific magic, when she heard him come out and pause in the passage outside her door, open just the tiniest crack.

"Sleep tight," he called gently. "Stay strong."

★

She got up the next morning feeling every single one of the previous night's consoling drinks. Cam was gone, leaving a stack of pillows and neatly folded blankets on the floor next to his backpack, but Cass and Steve were there, a picture of domesticity over the kitchen table.

"I think you had a bit too much," Cass observed, as she gingerly came through the kitchen door. "Maybe you should have paced yourself," she added, conveniently overlooking her recent carnival excess.

Livi decided to ignore her. She silently got a large glass of water and eased herself into a chair.

Steve looked sympathetic. "I've got a bit of a headache too."

"Where's Cam then?" Cass asked suggestively. "Still in bed?"

Livi didn't have the energy. "He wasn't in my bed, as you well know. I don't know where he's gone."

"I saw him this morning, early," said Steve. "He didn't say where he was going, just that he had—"

"People to see," Livi finished for him, and he nodded.

"I don't know about that," Cass said. "I think it's all a good story to cover for coming to see Livi."

"He's gone to a lot of trouble to make it believable then," said Steve. "A big black car came to collect him."

They both stared at him. "A big black car?" Livi repeated, suddenly much more awake.

"With a driver?" Cass said.

"Well, obviously with a driver," Steve laughed. "But if you mean a driver with a uniform and a peaked cap, then no. He was just a guy wearing a suit."

Livi and Cass looked at each other. "I can't even begin to guess what he might be doing," Livi said. Where could he be going that was substantial enough to warrant a big black car and a driver? He was an economist, not a movie star. Her head ached even more trying to imagine what he might be up to.

"Wow," said Cass. "Impressive. Livi, you might have something big here."

To distract her, Livi changed tack. "Speaking of impressive, Steve, I hear you've got some serious credentials in motorbike circles."

He blushed, reminding her of how shy he was the first night Cass brought him home. "Oh, well, not really."

But Cass was onto it. "Credentials? Don't be modest, tell."

Livi took her glass of water and left them to it.

Some time later, as she tried to wash away the

hangover fug under a hot shower, she heard Cass call out goodbye. "Bring me that satchel!" she replied over the sound of the water, using her sternest voice. "I mean it!"

But Cass just laughed. "Not until Paris!" she yelled back.

Livi could hear her talking animatedly to Steve as they went down the stairs, then there was peace. She took her time to wash her hair, standing with her head tipped back under the water, rinsing away the stale feeling, letting the steam soothe her tired eyes.

Finally she turned the mixer to cold for just a few moments, turning quickly around under the water, gasping as the chill hit her body. It was brutal, but apparently it was the secret to good circulation, better skin, shiny hair and, best of all, a pert bust, so she figured it was worth a go. Unlike some beauty secrets, it was free. Plus, she'd heard that James Bond always finished his shower with a cold blast. What better recommendation could there be?

Feeling much better, she wrapped her hair in a towel turban and slathered herself with moisturiser. Funny how she always washed from top to bottom, but moisturised from bottom to top, she mused. Did everyone do the same? She must ask Cass. She swung another towel around her body and then, tucking it in securely at the top, went out into the passage.

Her heart lurched. Len Mortlock was standing in the entranceway.

Chapter Twenty-Four

He stood still, legs apart, blocking her only exit. She looked wildly around, clutching her towel with both hands. Despite her entire body being in a screaming state of alert, she was unable to make any sound.

"Hello, love," he said, a hard smile on his face. "Just us. Your hero has gone out with your little friend." She noticed that his once carefully styled beard was ragged, stubble growing up through the gaps. He was much taller than she remembered.

"Shall we?"

He started towards her and she backed away, desperately trying to think what she could defend herself with. If only she had some James Bond moves now. She couldn't remember a damn thing from her mum's self-defence classes. The towel turban teetered and started to fall sideways, and she tore it off, flinging it uselessly at his head as she turned to run down the passage. It hit him in the face but he cast it aside and kept coming.

At the end of the passage she made a split second decision and swung into the living room. Plenty of implements to use as a weapon in the kitchen, but plenty for him too. She pushed the door closed behind her, but he was already there, forcing it back open. Fear made her strong, but he was stronger.

"Not quite fast enough, love," he said as she shot around to the other side of the coffee table, cracking her shin on its corner in the tight space. She barely registered the pain as she turned to face him across the small room.

He looked her up and down, taking his time. It wasn't a warm morning, but her goose-bumps were not only caused by the temperature. Legs shaking, she held the towel together tightly, horribly aware of how small it was. For a fleeting, ridiculous moment she remembered standing in M&S with Cass, debating whether to pay more for bath sheets or settle for regular towels.

"Sit down," he told her. "No need to be so formal."

She started to obey, but as she lowered herself to the sofa the towel began to part at the front. "I'll stand, thank you," she said, keeping her voice as strong and steady as she could.

He shrugged, shut the door, and took a seat nearby. Arms across the back of the sofa, legs spread, he made himself comfortable in the same spot where she'd first seen him. This Len was calm compared to the shouting, spitting creature Steve had removed from their garden, but more menacing. He had regained his smooth manner, but the well-groomed exterior that had impressed her mother was long gone. The neatest thing about him now was the perma-crease running down the legs of his synthetic trousers.

He saw her glance at them, and raised an overgrown eyebrow. "Like what you see, love?"

A small, disgusted noise was her only reply. At this he stood up, his face reddening, and began to come towards her. This is it, she thought, bracing herself for who knew what. But when he saw the fear that flashed across her face, he laughed, satisfied, and sat down again.

Relief added to shock made her even weaker than before. Her heart was still pounding, and she felt sick from the adrenaline charge. She said nothing, afraid of antagonising him, and fixed a neutral expression on her face. Time seemed to slow as he sat, and she stood. Cold drips of water from her wet hair ran down her spine. She stood her ground, waiting, and Len smiled as he watched her. He was in no hurry.

After the longest time, a dog barked, and the sound broke the impasse. "I wonder why you think I'm here," he said. "Maybe you think it's for you." He leaned forward, stroking the wayward growth around his lips, narrowing his eyes as he considered her. "This is actually between me and your mother. But now that I see you again...so much of you... Yes, I could thoroughly enjoy myself."

His tongue crept out, pushing aside the damp whiskers that threatened to curl into the corner of his mouth. "There's no rush, everyone at work. We always knew there would be another time, didn't we love?" He stood up, rubbing his stubby-fingered hands together. "Always a party when Mortlock's in the house..."

She had never been so scared, or so desperate. She tried to judge which way he would come, so she could escape in the opposite direction. But then he stopped.

"No, business first. Where's Evelyn?"

"She's gone," Livi managed, thankful that it was true. "She's gone with my dad."

Her words were a slap in the face. He raised himself up, his chest puffed out.

"She has *not*," he insisted. "She's finding herself. She's being her own woman for once. She's not going to do that with *him*." The last word was a venomous spit.

"Yes, she is." This time the satisfaction was hers. But it didn't last. He flew at her and grabbed her by the hair, yanking her head around.

"Where is she? Where the hell is she?"

Spittle landed on her face and she tried to twist her head away from his rage and his fetid breath, but he held her hair too tightly. Struggling to keep hold of the towel as he forced her down to the sofa, she kicked out blindly with one leg. By sheer luck, it struck his grey polyester crotch. He let go of her hair and lurched backwards, hard against the corner of the coffee table. Then, with a roar of pain and anger, he set upon her, tearing at the towel she was gripping with all her might.

As she fought back, she heard herself scream, the kind of sound she'd never made before. She stabbed at his face with one hand, and felt the fleshy orb shift under his eyelid as her fingernails connected with his eye. He covered the eye, cursing, and she ducked away, so close to escape.

Just as she reached the door, it flew open and crashed against the wall. With one look, Cam took in the scene— Livi freezing and desperate in her towel, Len crazed and wild right behind her, a long scratch across his left eye. He turned tail, but Cam was on top of him in two strides, dragging him back across the coffee table, past Livi and out to the floor in the passage. She followed, holding her towel securely, and got there just in time to see Cam land a resounding punch on the side of Len's sweaty, dishevelled head.

He was lining up for a second hit when they heard an exclamation from the entranceway. Aidan and Will stood there with incredulous faces.

"The key was in the door," Aidan said, holding up the spare key she'd given Cam. "Livi! My God, what's happening?"

Len took advantage of Cam's momentary distraction to attempt a punch of his own, but Cam caught his arm and forced it across his chest. Then he lifted him up and twisted both arms behind his back. "You can probably guess," he said grimly. "Livi, get some clothes."

He pressed Len hard against the wall as she passed by. Even in her shaken state she noticed the beautifully cut black suit he was wearing. "Thank you," she managed, and he gave a dark nod.

She threw on her dressing gown and came straight back out. None of them had moved, although Cam now seemed to be crushing Len almost completely flat against the wall. Aidan and Will were still agog, fixed to the spot.

"What are you doing here?" she asked them.

Will suddenly remembered. "God, Livi, this is terrible timing. There's a reporter and a cameraman from New Zealand looking for you. They came to the salon."

"What? Are they coming here now?"

"Yes, but they were driving. We hoped we'd beat them by tube. Aidan was home, so I phoned him to come too. We thought you might need back-up, if you were home, but we didn't expect..." His voice faded as he waved at Len, subdued for the moment but looking defiant.

"We did call you," Aidan added, "but Cass remembered she left the phone in her bed this morning, so you might not have heard it. And you didn't answer your mobile. Now we know why." His nose crinkled. "Who *is* this?"

"Someone bloody lucky he's still in one piece," Cam said, giving Len a shake-up. "Let's put him in the kitchen. Livi, you'd better call the police."

She went and rummaged in Cass's bed and found the phone. For a moment, she sat on the rumpled batik bedcover, thinking about what to do next. When she got back to the kitchen, Len was seated at one end of the table, with the three men standing guard, arms folded like three Corleone brothers. She might have laughed if she wasn't so stressed.

She went around them and peered out the open window. Nothing yet.

Cam took one eye off Len. "Go ahead and ring."

He wasn't going to like this. "Um...I can't."

She had all their attention. Len sat up straighter in his enforced seat.

"You have to, Livi. He's not getting away with this."

"No, not if there's a film crew arriving here any minute. Imagine how much they'd love this drama. There's no way I want *this* on television."

Cam took her arm and steered her out into the passage. "You're not safe with him around," he said in a low voice. "He could come back at any time."

She looked away, but he put a finger on her cheek and

turned her face back to his. "He's dangerous, Livi. Think what could have happened."

"I know. Thank God you were here. But I just don't want anything for them to film."

"Really? You'd put pride before your own safety?"

"It's not pride! It's avoidance of humiliation. Cam, please."

He sighed. "Well then, we'd better get rid of him before they arrive."

But it was too late. Will gestured towards the window as they went back in, and Livi caught a glimpse of a reporter and a cameraman getting out of a white van before she ducked out of sight.

"Damn!" She pressed herself against the worktop, out of view of the street. "Did you two close the door behind you?"

When they nodded she relaxed a little, but not much. Now she knew how the fox felt, hounds just on the other side of the fence. She'd always been a believer in drag hunting.

Just then the phone rang in her hand, making her jump. It was Cass.

"Are they there?" she asked urgently.

"Yes, they're outside. How did they find out where we live, do you know?"

"Absolutely no idea. But it seems like you can find anyone online, if you know how. Mia says so, anyway. Are the boys there?"

"Yes, they both are, and Cam too." She paused, not really wanting to worry Cass any more. "And Len."

"Len? What's he doing there?"

As she was about to reply there was a loud knocking on the door, and, taking advantage of the open window, Len yelled, "We're up here!"

Cam reached out and shut the window in a swift movement. He was ready to take aim at Len again, but Livi went across and grabbed his arm.

"Don't, it's not worth it," she said, while Cass's voice

came down the line, desperate to know what was going on. Cam stopped, but gave Len a look that would split a stone in two.

"We're just having a bit of drama here," Livi told Cass. "Len was a bit...upset." Despite the presence of three big men, she didn't want to set him off again.

"Upset like last time you mean? As in, a complete lunatic?"

"Pretty much, yes. And now we're stuck here with our own paparazzi outside."

The sound of knocking came again, and Cam eyeballed Len.

"Shit. But Livi, I know what to do. You were supposed to go to Paris tomorrow. Rue Beautreillis, right? Just go a day early. Get out of there."

"Paris? But..." Too late, she saw Len's focus snap onto her, and wished she could swallow the word back in.

"Why not? The trains run all the time. When the boys get back I'll meet you at St Pancras and give you the satchel, you'll need that."

"Okay." This time she was careful not to give anything away. "Thanks."

"See you soon."

She hung up, trying to ignore the persistent knocking from downstairs. "They can just wait," she said. "I need to put some clothes on. And Cam, can you do something for me?"

He was reluctant to relinquish his Len watch, but left the boys on duty again and followed her into her bedroom, where she pulled her wheeled suitcase from under the bed and began flinging clothes into it.

"I have to go," she told him in a low voice. "Cass is right, I'm just going to get out of here."

"To Paris?"

She shrugged and threw in a pair of shoes. "Might as well. I wanted to see Paris one day anyway." Not like this, admittedly.

"But the reporter...and Len will know where you've

gone."

"From Cass's room I can go out the window and down the fire escape. It comes out on the street behind ours. They won't even know I'm gone. And I doubt Len is going to follow me to Paris. It's my mum he's really interested in, anyway."

"Then I'll come too." He took off his tie and stuffed it in his suit pocket. It was final. He wouldn't listen to any argument.

Five minutes later, they were out in the back street and heading for the Blackhorse Road tube. Cam carried her little suitcase while she texted Will as they went, explaining Cass's plan. She imagined them there in the kitchen, still waiting for her and Cam. Hopefully they could manage Len and get him past the waiting camera without revealing where she was going. Hopefully she and Cam would make it to the tube station without a white van finding them. And hopefully, by the time she got back from Paris, they would have given up and gone back to New Zealand, and she would have peace again.

Chapter Twenty-Five

They finally made it to the tube station and fell into a westbound train, heading for St Pancras station and the Eurostar. "I don't think I'm going to breathe again until we hit the Continent," she said, collapsing into a seat.

Cam took off his backpack and sat next to her. "Lucky I was already packed."

"True." She ran her fingers through her hair, hanging down her back any which way. Her head hurt where Len had grabbed her hair so hard. God knows what she looked like. No time for makeup or blow-drying or even a comb. She sighed, and Cam looked sideways.

"You look lovely," he said. "Like I remember you before you grew up."

In her flustered state all she could do was make a disbelieving noise, but he just smiled. Then she could see the boy she grew up with too, even in the quietly sophisticated black suit.

"What about you, all dressed up—where have you been?"

But he stuck to the script. "People to see. Nothing exciting."

"Would these people have a big black car, by any chance?"

"They might."

He smiled again, impenetrable, and she sighed. Eventually.

As they arrived at St Pancras, a text came from Will. They had phoned for a minicab and then frogmarched Len out without a word, straight past the crew, and left. Livi had to laugh as she told Cam. Never explain, never apologise. That summed those two up. They'd dropped Len at Hackney Marsh, a decent walk from any kind of transport, and were going on to Leyton tube station.

"Wonder what the taxi driver made of it," Cam commented.

"Me too. This is probably the only time I'll be glad of dodgy London cabbies."

St Pancras was busy with workers, tourists, frazzled-looking mothers with children, and, around the edges, lost souls with nowhere else to be. They ordered hot drinks from a kiosk, and found a seat out of the hustle and bustle. Although she knew he was probably still out in the wilds of Hackney, she couldn't stop scanning the passing faces for any sign of Len.

She sighed. "We might have a long wait, by the time the boys get back and Cass makes it here."

It was tempting to go without the satchel—couldn't Cass just hand it in to lost luggage here? She was even less keen to find the American with Cam in tow than with Mattias. Actually, she was starting to forget what he even looked like, let alone that intoxicating feeling that had started all the trouble. But the next Paris train was delayed so there was no option but to wait, and then Cass was there.

She flung herself upon Livi, crushing her in a repentant hug. "Oh my God, Livi, I'm so sorry! The boys told me everything. It's all my fault—I can't have closed the door properly when I left with Steve this morning. You were so *brave*. You could have been killed! I'm *so sorry*..." All the while squeezing just about hard enough to kill Livi herself.

"It's not your fault," Livi said, patting her back. "How could we have guessed he'd do that?"

"I suppose so," she said, letting Livi go and wiping her eyes.

"It might be a good idea to see if Steve can stay for a night or two, though. Just to be safe."

Cass nodded. "I'm pretty sure he won't mind that." And a little twinkle was back in her eyes. "Oh, now, here's the bag." She held it out to Livi.

She hesitated. "I don't know...I think it would be better to hand it in to lost property."

But Cass pressed it upon her. "No, you're taking it," she insisted. "It's been here all along, in the lockers, and it cost me good money. If you don't find him in Paris, then you can hand it in."

"You're such a bully," Livi said, trying not to look at Cam.

"Is this another bag I'll have to carry?" he teased.

After that night at the Lamb and Flag, he knew all about the clues and the search so far. Livi herself hadn't felt the need to share, but Aidan and Cass wouldn't let a good story go to waste.

"Oh...are you going too?"

Cass looked from one of them to the other, her face reflecting the awkwardness Livi felt. Taking one man on the hunt for another was less than ideal. She'd got away with it at the crematorium, when the American was a no-show. And Mattias had survived her rejection, chatting about third-rail versus fourth-rail electrification on the way back. But this time, it seemed *she* was the one with feelings—a complication she'd be keeping to herself, until she knew what they meant.

Cam was standing firm. "Just making sure she's okay."

"Well, she has been through a trauma. It'll be good to know she's out of Len's way."

"Thanks, you two, but I'm fine," she said. "Honestly."

The two of them exchanged glances, as though over a delusional child. Livi decided not to say anything more. It actually was nice to have company.

Then the train was announced, and they had to go. As

they hugged goodbye, Cass whispered to Livi, "I hope you find him. But if not, it doesn't hurt to have options. I like that suit."

Going through check-in and security and passport control, Livi realised that the stress of the morning was receding, eased out by the excitement of going on an adventure.

"I feel like we're really going somewhere," she told Cam, as they went up the travelator to the sleek, yellow-trimmed train. She tipped her head back to take in the huge arched roof. "I haven't been out of England since I came back."

"Paris is definitely somewhere," he agreed. "How's your French?"

"I think I've forgotten almost everything I learned at school."

How embarrassing to realise that the first French words to pop into her head—apart from menu French—were the old *Voulez-vous couchez avec moi, ce soir,* like the song. Despite her newly confusing feelings, that phrase seemed unlikely to be of any use. She'd had her moments, but Lady Marmalade she was not. She looked sideways at Cam, half expecting that he could tell what was in her mind. Surely she could remember something more appropriate. "*Bonjour,*" she tried. "*Un café au lait, s'il vous plaît.*"

He laughed. "There, you sound like a native. Just a shame you don't drink coffee."

"Maybe the French me *does* drink coffee."

He raised a sceptical eyebrow. "We'll see."

They found their seats on the train and settled in. The first part of the journey wasn't especially inspiring, but the 'somewhere' feeling bloomed as they emerged from the Channel Tunnel into France. The train rose and dipped gently with the countryside, and church spires dotted the landscape. And when they pulled into the Gare du Nord, her 'somewhere' was in full Parisian technicolour. They gathered their bags and went out through the grandeur and bustle of the main station. Then, just like that, they were standing out in a Paris street.

"Paris." Livi breathed. "Wow."

The late afternoon light was beginning to soften into evening. Old iron lamps stood tall and proud along the street. Workers hurried past, taxis came and went, and some of the buildings were just starting to glow with the famous golden lights. From their spot on the broad promenade, by the columns standing guard along the station entrance, Livi could count three small dogs trotting along with their smartly dressed owners. She could hardly take it all in.

Cam broke the spell. "We'll need to find somewhere to stay."

So they went back into the station, changed some money, bought a guide book, and googled a moderately priced hotel. Then they found a taxi, and Livi gazed out at the street while Cam gave the driver the address.

The drive there was better than a movie. She was aware that her nose was practically pressed against the glass the whole time, but she didn't care how much of a tourist she looked. She'd spent years saving up, dreaming of all her travels. She'd made it to London, but that was reality—commuting, and dishes, and paying-as-you-go to keep warm.

And now here she was in Paris. Never mind that the circumstances weren't exactly what she'd imagined. She wasn't missing a second of it.

They passed eateries big and small, outdoor seats turned to face the street so patrons could people-watch with ease. Tobacco shops announced themselves with red neon cigars, and pharmacies with green neon crosses. Effortlessly stylish people strolled past crepe stands, the iconic Metro signs, and scooters parked on the pavement. If the occasional Starbucks intruded on the scene, she didn't mind. The people within were Parisian, after all. Well, some of them surely were, amongst the tourists.

When they reached their hotel, on the Île Saint Louis, she just about fell out of the taxi in surprise. "Are you sure this is moderately priced?"

It was gorgeous. The warm stone façade looked timeless in the evening light. The substantial door, worked in carved wood and wrought iron, was flanked with clipped topiary and matching lanterns. A small red carpet lay in the entrance, hinting at exclusivity without the need to boast.

Cam just shrugged. "It's Paris. You can't come here and stay in a dive."

Checking in, she suddenly wondered what they would do. But Cam got in first, asking the concierge for two rooms and sliding across his credit card. There was a brief to-and-fro when she insisted on paying half and he refused, and she insisted and he refused. Then she saw the expression on the concierge's face. Obviously it was unseemly to argue about money in such a refined setting. She backed down and thanked Cam graciously, but resolved to even things out later.

The building was so old there was no elevator, but the concierge snapped his fingers and an underling appeared for their bags. Their climb up worn stone stairs to the third floor was rewarded when the porter opened the door to her room with a flourish. Cam thanked him and gave him a tip while Livi went in, captivated.

"This is amazing."

The little room was so richly furnished it felt like stepping into Aladdin's cave. Although the fabrics and furnishings were all sorts of colours and patterns, the whole effect was glowing and elegant, even in such a small space. Tapestries hung on the walls, rugs warmed the floor, and a starry chandelier glimmered above them, while richly upholstered chairs sat on each side of the window. She went over and looked out between the heavy, embroidered drapes. Outside lay the hazy-soft city, postcard perfect. And beyond the trees lining the river, Notre Dame was right there, gothic and glorious, just as it had been for hundreds of years.

"Is that..?" She turned to Cam, incredulous.

"Apparently." He smiled as he leaned against the door

frame.

She turned and flung herself onto the carved four-poster, sinking into the ruby-red bedding. The canopy above was lined with tiny tassels, and the gold brocade on one of the many cushions tickled her cheek. "I feel like a princess."

"Watch out for peas."

"No danger. This is ridiculously comfortable."

Suddenly, nestled on the bed, she was swamped with tiredness. "I hate to waste an evening in Paris, but I think I have to sleep. I'm not even hungry."

He came over and sat next to her. "I'm not surprised. You've had a hell of a day."

"It wasn't the greatest. But this is an improvement." She smiled.

He was a stranger in the expensive suit, now slightly rumpled from travelling. A real grown-up. And yet he was still so familiar. His dark hair was unruly across his forehead and he looked a bit tired after the day's dramas, but his greeny-hazel eyes were warm as he smiled back at her. Lying on the sumptuous bed, the events of that morning hardly seemed real, as far away in time as in miles.

"Thanks for everything. I didn't know you had such a mean right hook."

He grimaced. "I'd be in trouble if my old karate instructor knew about that."

"Well, he might not approve, but I certainly appreciated it."

She let her shoes fall to the floor, pushed the cushions aside, and got under the covers, too tired to think about changing into pyjamas. It was a relief to lay her head on the downy white pillow. "I wonder what Len's doing now."

"Don't think about him. You're safe and sound here. My room's next door." He took the extra cushions and put them on a chaise longue in the corner. Then he leaned over and smoothed a stray lock of hair from her cheek. "Goodnight, princess."

As he shut the door, she felt sleep start to overtake her.

Chapter Twenty-Six

The next morning, Livi found Cam in the vaulted stone cellar that served as the hotel's dining room. When he saw her come in, he put down his phone and came around to pull out her chair.

"That's very gentlemanly of you," she said.

"Well, when in Rome. Or Paris. How did you sleep?"

"Like a very sleepy baby. Apart from getting up in the middle of the night to put on my pyjamas. I'm absolutely starving now." She looked at the beautifully laid table, silver cutlery shining on a whiter-than-white tablecloth, crisper-than-crisp napkins nestling on white porcelain. "No breakfast menu?"

"No. The waiter is bringing a proper French breakfast."

As if by magic the waiter in question appeared. Without a word he set down his offerings of coffee, hot chocolate, orange juice, pain au chocolat, croissants, and jam. Livi was halfway through an appreciative thank you when he turned and disappeared back to the kitchen.

She shrugged. "I don't care how rude French waiters are if they bring me food like this."

Cam pushed her hot chocolate across. "I know you

were expecting to wake up transformed into a Gallic coffee-drinker this morning, but I ordered hot chocolate just in case. No marshmallows though."

She looked at his coffee, black and serious in a tiny cup. Maybe the French her could drink hot chocolate after all. She was about to thank him, when his phone rang. He looked at the screen. "Sorry, I won't be long," he said, and abruptly left the room.

She looked at the feast in front of her and decided not to wait.

By the time he got back, she'd eaten almost all her half. "You'd better hurry."

"Sorry," he said again. "I had to take that."

"That's okay." She waited, but he didn't say anything more. Although she was dying to be nosy, she held her tongue. Cam as a man of mystery was a new concept. She realised that she didn't think much of it.

When they finished breakfast, he stood up purposefully. "Come on, you have a mission to complete."

"Oh..." She wasn't enthusiastic.

"I don't want to get in trouble with Cass. Go and get that bag."

So she went reluctantly, and met him again downstairs by the concierge's desk. "Okay, I'm ready."

He took the satchel from her and slung it across his body. It rather suited him, she thought. He offered her the guide book, but she waved it away.

"I'm just going to absorb everything."

Although it was still quite early, the streets of the little island were already busy. They came to the Pont Saint Louis, where camera-draped tourists, in happy holiday mode, were easy pickings for buskers. Teenagers on skateboards made a menace of themselves, weaving between sightseers, and the wicker chairs outside the cafés were already filling with people-watchers.

Livi looked across hopefully in the direction of Notre Dame, but Cam turned her and steered her away, down a small street lined with bicycles and scooters. "First things first," he said firmly. "We'll be back later."

As they crossed the Pont Louis-Philippe, she looked back at the island. Grand townhouses stood proudly along the edge, untroubled by the petty activities of the tour parties at their feet. Further below, along the lower, tree-shaded quays, she could see people reading books and newspapers. A couple lounged against the warm stone walls, and two small children were feeding the ducks that swam close to shore.

She sighed. "How civilised to be a Parisian duck."

But, just like a man, he didn't see the romance of it. "Yeah, until you end up on a Parisian plate."

She gave him a shove, but turned her attention to the Right Bank. The road they followed along the Seine was busy, and they began to wish they'd walked the length of the island instead. But soon they turned into quieter, narrower streets.

Cam checked the map on his phone. "Okay, here it is. Rue Beautreillis, the scene of Jim Morrison's final bubble bath."

"I don't think you're bringing a sufficiently reverent attitude to this," Livi told him. "This is pilgrimage territory, apparently."

He grinned back at her, and she shook her head, laughing.

Although there were cars parked along one side, the little one-way street was quiet enough for a couple to stroll down the middle of the road with their baby in a pushchair. Livi and Cam stopped on the narrow flagstone pavement opposite number seventeen, and looked up.

Above the dark, oversized doors, a stately building rose up, its finely worked wrought-iron balconies underpinned by ornately carved scrolls and wreaths. Like so many Paris buildings, its creamy tone was slightly tarnished with age. A black bicycle leaned against the building, looking like it had been carefully placed there by a set designer.

A few feet away, a knot of black-clad Jim Morrison pilgrims were also staring up. No one said anything. Soon they were joined by a grey-haired couple, who with their leather jackets and faded tattoos were obviously Doors fans from the same vintage as Jim himself. Livi thought they could well be comrades of Journey. They all gazed up at the third floor, clearly very moved to be there.

"This feels like one of those tricks, where people stand and look up at nothing and see how many others they can get to join in," Livi whispered, not wanting to ruin the atmosphere.

Cam laughed. "Are we doing the tricking, or being tricked?"

"Good question." She rubbed her neck. "I don't know what they're hoping to see up there." Or what *she* was hoping to see.

Then his phone rang again, the sound shrill in the street. He hurried to answer it as the Morrison pilgrims shot dirty looks in their direction.

"Sorry, sorry." He waved apologetically in their direction before turning and walking down the street away from them. "Hello…"

Livi couldn't hear any more, and it obviously wouldn't do to follow him, ears flapping. So she hovered about until he came back.

"You're in demand today." It was more a question than a statement, but he wasn't playing.

"Mmm." He looked up and down the street. "Still no sign of this American?"

"No."

Same old story, of course. He might not be there now, at eleven in the morning, but he might be there at eleven thirty. Or at five o'clock. Or…he might be up in Jim's apartment, looking out the window, wondering why the hell she was standing in the street like an idiot, with some guy wearing his satchel. She looked up again, but the grand old building was giving nothing away.

Once again she felt ridiculous. If it wasn't for the repulsive Len she wouldn't be here at all—she could blame him and Cass both for this one.

After a while they sat on the footpath and leaned against the cool stone of the building opposite number seventeen. Time ticked by as tourists came and went, but none of them were the American. Finally Cam said, "Well, we'd better go and see him."

"Who? The American?"

"No, the other American. Jim."

"Oh! I suppose we should. Pay our respects. Mia said he's somewhere at Père Lachaise cemetery."

"Come on then, let's try the Metro."

She cast a last glance over her shoulder as they left. So much for that. Cass would be disappointed, but she was actually kind of relieved.

They figured out the Metro without any trouble, and made it to Père Lachaise, where the steps took them up between cast iron balustrades to one of the classic art nouveau *Métropolitain* signs. Livi felt like she was in a movie, and wouldn't have been surprised this time to find a film crew waiting—just as long as it wasn't the New Zealanders.

They crossed the road. There was only a small gate, right at the end of the stone cemetery wall.

"Do you think this is the right way in?" She looked along the road. The wall stretched as far as the eye could see, with no sign of another entrance. So they ventured in through the gate, and found a vendor selling cemetery maps.

But when she told him which grave they were looking for, he shook his head.

"Non non non," he insisted, pointing back out the gate and up the street. *"L'autre façon. L'autre façon."*

So they turned to go the other way, thanking him, but he insisted they buy one of his maps first. Livi looked at it, then at the wall going into the distance.

"La cité des mortes. The city of the dead. It must be huge."

As they set off down the road she had a déjà vu moment—walking to cemetery number two, another man in tow carrying the satchel. Madness. This trip was definitely, absolutely, the last stop on the American trail.

They got hotter and hotter in the summer heat. Now she was glad she'd worn Sketchers with her sundress instead of ballet flats. They would've been very Parisian, but not so good for hiking the city streets. Finally, they came to the main gate, with a monumental entranceway of stone befitting the stature of the permanent residents inside.

"This is more like it," said Cam.

They went through onto a wide boulevard. On each side, grand family tombs and more modest graves sat between tall trees. She was surprised to find that the cemetery was quite hilly. Cobbled roads led on to narrower lanes and uneven paths, where some of the tombs were immaculate, but others were blackened and broken. In places, so many trees rose up between the graves that they made a green canopy high above. She was captivated.

"This is really, properly beautiful. What a place to spend eternity."

They followed a winding route, backtracking once when they thought they'd taken a wrong turn down a leafy lane. Then they passed a tree marked with an arrow and 'Jim. This way.' Further on, a tomb was inscribed 'Break on through to the other side.'

"We hardly need the map now," Cam said.

In the end, a cluster of people gathered on a small byway told them where Jim was. They stopped in front of the barrier. The grave was nothing more than a plain, square headstone with a simple plaque, behind someone else's large tomb. A few flowers had been flung over, landing awkwardly on the next-door plot, or upside down between the graves. But some determined visitors had obviously clambered right in. The dusty plot was scattered with Doors memorabilia, photos of Jim, tea-light candles, and flowers, some alive, some dead or dying in their plastic wrap. More pragmatic visitors had offered plastic blooms. Here and there was a cigarette butt.

They stood for a moment amongst the mourners. "It's

not much, is it?" Livi said. It seemed a shabby, mawkish memorial for anyone, let alone the object of so much adoration. The nearest tree and the tomb in front of the grave were covered in graffiti. "I feel a bit sorry for the people who have to spend their eternity next to Jim and his entourage."

"It is pretty tacky."

They looked around at the motley group. Someone began quietly singing 'Riders on the Storm'. Equally quietly, Cam started to hum 'People Are Strange'.

"Shhh!" She shoved him, hard, but he just laughed.

"I think Jim has enough company. Let's go."

After Père Lachaise they played tourists. For lunch they ate baguettes and cheese in a pocket-handkerchief park. They visited the Arc de Triomphe and strolled down the Champs-Élysées (giving the McDonalds a wide berth). In the Tuileries they admired the flowers and stopped to watch the children dangling their feet in the round pond. Around every corner, there seemed to be a pair of lovers, unashamedly kissing and caressing as if determined to prove the 'City of Love' label true. At the Louvre, they took one look at the ribbon of tourists queuing in the hot sun and decided to keep walking. The queues at the Musée D'Orsay were shorter, so they went in for some culture, and some air-conditioning.

Livi enjoyed herself so much that the American barely crossed her mind. She might almost have forgotten why they were there, except that Cam spent the whole day with the satchel slung across his body. As evening approached, they found a small bistro nearby.

"I think seeing all that van Gogh made up for missing the Mona Lisa," she said, as the waiter set down steaming bowls of onion soup. "And seeing Camille Claudel's work. Although, to be honest, I probably wouldn't know about her if it wasn't for the movie. Sad stories, both of them."

"Genius and madness," he replied, blowing gently on his soup. "We had to do one art gallery, at least. Keep up tradition."

"This whole day has felt like *being* in a painting," she said. "Like the children being pulled into Narnia."

"It is a bit unreal," he said. "But then, this is just everyday stuff for the locals."

"I could do this every day."

She raised her glass, and they clinked in agreement. His gaze lingered on hers, warm and amused, and she felt herself blush and look away. The romance of their surroundings was going to her head, she thought, even before the wine.

After dinner they decided to make one last tourist stop, at the Eiffel Tower. It had to be done, they agreed. Their taxi found a space between two tour buses to drop them off, and they paused on the wide pavement to take in the view. A grassy avenue stretched out in front of them, lined with tall, square-clipped trees. At the end, the tower was a beacon reaching for the sky, twinkly from tip to toe, its searchlight a beckoning beam across the city.

Even now, at almost ten o'clock, people were enjoying the still summer night. Couples lay on blankets on the grass, basking in the reflected romance of the fairy-lit tower. Well-to-do tourists spilled out of a coach and mingled with sandal-clad backpackers, all taking photos, all equally rapt with the magical scene. Even the usual unruly skateboarders clattering about didn't spoil the atmosphere.

They wandered out onto the grass and found a spot to sit. Not far away, a couple of young guys were sitting on backpacks, strumming their guitars, singing 'Let It Be'. A crowd of tourists was gathered around, singing their hearts out, feeling the lyrics, swept up in the moment.

Livi watched them, enjoying their heartfelt enthusiasm. "This should be too cheesy for words, but actually it's perfect."

Cam laughed, and she looked up at him. "Thanks for coming with me."

"That's okay." He smiled and put his arm around her. "I've got your back."

She leaned into the warmth of his body, relaxing into

her own moment. London and Len, the reporter and the cameraman were a distant memory, the whereabouts of the American irrelevant, the dramas of New Zealand nothing but a faint recollection from a past life. Here, now, however temporary, was a somewhere she was pleased to be. She let her head rest against his chest, welcoming the feeling of peace.

But all at once he jumped up, leaving her to fall sideways on the grass. He strode across to the singing tourists, the satchel bouncing against his body. For a moment she wondered if he'd been struck with the urge to join in, and was racing across to whisper words of wisdom too.

But then, standing up, she saw what he must have noticed. Slinking around the edge of the group, in the shadow of the good will glow, two quiet figures were waiting for a chance to dip in for wallets and purses.

Cold reality swept back in.

She watched as he quietly said something to an older lady whose bag, on a long strap, had slid around to her back. Livi couldn't hear what she said, but she was obviously grateful as she clutched the bag safely in front of her. Next, keeping an eye on the pickpockets, he tapped the shoulder of a man whose back jeans pocket had an obvious wallet-shaped bulge. Then he turned and came back, as casually as he could. She anxiously looked to see if anyone would follow him, but he made it back without incident.

She was torn between wanting to hug him and shake him. "That was a really, *really* good thing to do. But, God, you could have got in trouble."

"No, no." He shrugged.

"I can't believe it. Everyone was having such a beautiful time." She shook her head, embarrassed now at being taken in by the false display. "I really am a sucker."

"Don't let that ruin it," he said. "All the more reason to hold on to the magical bits. Look."

He took her hand and turned her around. Suddenly, countless thousands of white lights were flashing all over the tower, a crazy firefly riot against the gold backdrop. All around them, people broke into spontaneous applause, whistling and whooping in appreciation.

It was perfection. Not even slightly cheesy. She focused high up on the tower, blinking hard, not wanting him to see that she was moved to tears. He squeezed her hand, looking at her under the scatter-gun brightness. His grip was firm and his hand was warm. They were so close. If she looked around now... For a moment, she hovered on the brink. Then, with the hypnotic sparkles of light reflecting in her eyes, she couldn't hold back any more. She turned to him, her carefully guarded resolve forgotten, and in an instant his lips were on hers, her arms around him. His warm breath mingled with hers as he gave an audible sigh, and she laughed in the kiss, all caution gone. The satchel slipped around between them as he leaned down, but she pushed it aside and pressed against him. As she stood on tiptoe to meld further into his kiss, the crowd seemed to be clapping only for them. In that moment, the city's magic was as real as the grass under her feet and the tingle of sunburn on her bare arms.

As if on cue, his phone rang again.

Instantly, she felt him tense and pull away. She opened her eyes, dragging herself back from the far-gone, hazy place she'd fallen into. That she thought they'd both fallen into.

"Sorry," he said, stepping back. He took the phone out of his pocket and looked at the screen. "I really have to get this."

Before he lifted the phone to his ear, she saw the name that was showing on the lit-up screen. It was upside down, but she could read it clearly. Well, she thought, there you go—the mystery caller. Sasha. Sasha Fernsby. She phoned, he jumped.

He turned and walked away as he answered the call.

As she stood alone, waiting on the grass, the light show finished. The crowd dispersed and the pickpockets sauntered past, looking her up and down. They laughed and said something to each other that she couldn't understand. But scorn sounded the same in any language. She remembered now. The world was full of fancy light shows, sleight-of-hand, smoke and mirrors, waiting for the naïve and hopeful. Search high and low, around the world if you like. Finding something to believe in doesn't make it real.

Chapter Twenty-Seven

Going back to London was not a happy prospect the next day, especially as it meant facing the possibility of more Len madness. But her time off was coming to an end. Cam said he had things to do too, though he wasn't leaving the country just yet.

Neither of them mentioned that moment, the night before, when something shifted between them. It was better that way, she told herself. If she'd developed an unexpected crush, and got caught up in a Paris moment, it wasn't his fault. Maybe they'd crossed a line, but it was easy enough to step back over. After the phone call, she'd been determinedly brisk. They'd taken a taxi back to the hotel, gone up the stairs, and said goodnight at her door. They were friends. Cam had helped her when she was in trouble, and then helped her look for another man. And soon he was going home, to the other side of the world.

So that morning, it was back to the Gare du Nord. They'd managed to fit in a flying visit to Notre Dame—she couldn't leave Paris without seeing it up close. But now, of course, the train was running dead on time. She wouldn't get even an extra half of a Parisian hour. No fighting it.

They went through the usual check-in procedure and

found their carriage. She went ahead down the aisle, wheeling her small suitcase behind her, and he followed with his backpack and the leather satchel.

She looked back. "That damn bag had as good a tour of Paris as we did," she said. Poor guy, he'd carried it around all day, uncomplaining. She had to laugh. But, as she turned back to check for their seats, she came to an abrupt halt. Behind her, Cam dodged sideways to avoid stepping on her suitcase.

Sitting in a window seat, looking right at her, was the American. A hot rush whipped around her body. Her stomach turned, her cheeks flamed, and her heart hammered. Jelly-legged, she held on to the back of a seat.

He stood up, knocking his denim-clad thighs on the table in front of him. His dark hair was as shiny as she remembered, his tan even deeper. He grinned, teeth as bright as last night's flashbulbs on the Eiffel Tower.

"This is a surprise," he said. "A great surprise. Trains must be our place."

She unsuccessfully searched her head for two meaningful words to put together. "Uh...yeah."

Now, jolted back to that Saturday night on the tube, she couldn't believe she'd started to forget. He was disarmingly, alarmingly handsome, a bit older than she remembered, the stubble and a worn check shirt giving him a rugged, indie edge. Still, he was so obviously, glossily American that he could have just stepped from an episode of his own reality show. But being out of place was clearly no discomfort for him.

"The mystery woman." He ran his eyes over her, taking his time, taking her in. Then he looked right at her, his dark eyes mischievous and appreciative. "You look beautiful."

Caught in his direct gaze, for a moment she was oblivious to anything around her. But then he looked over her shoulder, and she suddenly remembered Cam, and the satchel. Oh, God. Here it was, the embarrassing moment she'd desperately hoped to avoid. And worse, trapped on a train.

"We should sit down," Cam said from behind her. "We're causing a traffic jam."

"Sorry, yes." With a physical effort she shook herself out of the American force field, and rechecked their seat numbers. They were right across the aisle. "We're just there."

But the people sitting in the seats across the table from the American were listening. With terribly British politeness, they insisted on swapping, so the three of them could sit together. Her heart sank as Cam ushered her into the other window seat, and returned the satchel to the American. "This must be yours."

"Thanks," he said. "I'd kind of given up on it."

They eyed each other. Cam was younger, but he had the height advantage. There was definite man-tension in the air.

"I'm so sorry," said Livi as they sat down, trying to lessen the atmosphere. "Everything's in there. I should have handed it in to lost property, but Cass wanted me to find you, and then she hid it when I decided I would hand it in, and then there was a bit of a nightmare so it seemed a good escape to come to Paris, but we didn't find you..." She bit her tongue, forcing herself to stop blathering on. From paralysis to verbal diarrhoea. Smooth, Livi.

She felt Cam looking at her sideways. Then he held out his hand to the American. "Cam Holden."

"Ryan Velez." They shook hands manfully, then both turned to her.

"Oh, right." She held out her hand. "Livi. Livi Callaway."

He smiled at her as they shook, his eyes daring her to hold his hand a little longer. Painfully aware that her pink cheeks were obvious to both men, she removed her hand quickly, putting it on her lap under the table. It seemed to reverberate as she covered it with the other hand, so she tucked it between her thighs.

There was an awkward silence as the train started to move.

Then Cam's phone rang. He pulled it from the pocket of his leather jacket., but this time he was less keen to answer. For the briefest moment he considered the screen, just giving Livi time to see the name—Sasha Fernsby again. Then he excused himself and answered it, glancing back at them as he went away along the aisle. "Hello...no, no, that's okay..."

Ryan Velez looked at her across the table. "Everything okay?" he asked.

"Yes," she said firmly. "It's fine. It has to be."

He let the cryptic comment go. "You came to find me."

There was no denying it. "Well...I wasn't going to, but..." She didn't want to remember what had made her leave London that day.

He grinned. "But you did."

"Things kind of got out of hand. And out of *my* hands." She held them up in front of her, as though the physical action would push away the memory of Len.

He waited, but she wasn't saying any more, so he changed the subject. "You know, I saw you at the carnival. But when I made it to your side of the road, I couldn't find you."

"It *was* you!" So she hadn't imagined it.

"I thought it was a pretty crazy coincidence. And now, seeing you here...meant to be."

His words gave her a little shock. "That's what Cass said."

"Well, whoever Cass is, she's right."

"Maybe." She looked at him, wondering. A romantic would call it fate. A cynic would call it coincidence. Once she would have been firmly in the first camp...these days, not so much.

"So now I know it's not Australian, but that *is* a cute accent you've got. Not completely British."

"Thanks. My family moved to New Zealand when I was a kid. I'm back now though."

"Really? I thought it was like paradise down there.

You didn't want to stay?"

"Oh, it's a big wide world, lots to see," she replied vaguely. She was definitely not going there. When it came to her TV drama, she operated on a need-to-know basis—and he definitely didn't need to know. "But what are *you* doing in England? You said your mum was English?"

"Yeah, she was from Dorset. You know, the Jurassic Coast."

Now it was her turn to wait, but nothing more was forthcoming. "I haven't been there yet, but I hear it's really interesting. How did she end up in the States?"

He paused before answering. "She was a geologist. Dad said she grew up messing around with rocks and fossils from the beach. She met him in Idaho, when they were both working on a big dam project for a hydroelectric power plant. He's from Puerto Rico. He's an engineer."

He looked out the window. For the first time, his cool confidence slipped away, and she saw vulnerability reflected in the glass. There was obviously more to tell.

Very gently, she said, "What happened?"

"I was only a few weeks old. She'd gone up to see him in his lunch break, as a surprise. It was the first time she'd left me with anyone else." He looked at his phone sitting on the table between them. "He didn't know it, but she was already on her way when the dam collapsed. Even if he had known, he couldn't have warned her—not everyone had mobile phones then. And anyway, there was so much water..." He stopped.

"I'm so sorry." She didn't want to imagine the rest. The young woman washed away, the tiny baby motherless, the husband left behind.

"He blamed himself. He was on the engineering team that designed the dam."

"That's so awful. I'm really sorry." It was the only thing to say.

But he shrugged, one shoulder at a time, as though pulling the real world back on. "Well, life's hard. A lot of people have it much worse. You get on with it."

He looked at her properly then, straight and level. She knew her eyes were glistening with emotion, but she looked right back. For a moment, the air hummed between them. Then he winked at her, the bravado back, and it was over.

"Where's your sidekick?" He looked pointedly up and down the carriage. "Or should I say boyfriend? I don't want to step on any toes."

"Oh, well...no, it's okay."

"Really? What's wrong with him?" he teased. "Paris, the city of love, and no romance?"

She was back to blushing. Parisian romance was surely to blame for the night before's kiss, but it wouldn't be leaving France with them.

"It *is* romantic," was all she could say.

He was going to push for more, she could tell. But then, mercifully, his phone rang. He went to answer it, but stopped, giving it a dismissive wave. "They can wait."

The implication was clear—*he* wasn't a slave to his phone. *He* wouldn't rudely interrupt their conversation. But she could see he was itching to pick it up. She sighed. Men could make a competition out of anything.

"No, honestly, that's okay. Answer it."

"You sure?" But before she could reply, he'd already answered. She looked out at the French countryside, trying to give the impression she wasn't listening.

"No, Tuesday...yeah, Wiltshire...if we don't, someone else will, might as well get in first...yeah, damn right he's earned it..."

When he was done, he took a business card out of his wallet and slid it across the table. In red lettering on a black background, it said 'Ryan Velez. What needs doing.' She turned it over but there was nothing more, only a handwritten phone number. She looked at him, questioning.

"Ring me when you're free of your sidekick," he said. "I'm not here much longer, but we should see each other again." He sounded star-spangled confident, but there was a hint of doubt in his eyes as he saw Cam coming along the aisle.

Then Cam was sitting next to her, and Ryan picked up his bag, and the satchel. He'd leave them in peace, he said. He was spending the rest of the trip in the bar. Cam was obviously relieved, but Livi wasn't sure how she felt. She tried not to watch him go.

It was only then that she realised she hadn't found out why he was tripping around after dead rock stars. He didn't *seem* dodgy or ghoulish. A tease, sure…but dangerous? She fingered the rectangle of his card in her pocket. What needs doing. That told her absolutely nothing. Tuesday. Wiltshire. She thought of the folding map of Wiltshire, the last clue from his bag. Which expired rock star might have lived in Wiltshire? Or died there?

Well, it was nothing to do with her now.

Unless…unless she wanted to see him again.

Chapter Twenty-Eight

Back at St Pancras, Cam apologised and said he had to go, and that he'd be busy for a few days. Livi knew better than to ask where. If he had people to see, they would obviously be Sasha Fernsby. Which was fine. *Fine.* She had Wiltshire and Ryan Velez to think about, anyway.

"I don't want to leave you to go back to the flat by yourself," he said as they stood in the station, people stepping around them and their luggage.

Livi realised she didn't want that either. "I'll ring and make sure Cass is home. Without reporters or crazy people."

"Good. Hopefully Steve will still be there. Or if no one's home, you could go to Aidan and Will. Maybe I'd better wait and see."

"No, I'll be fine." She sounded more confident than she felt.

He looked at his watch. "Right, if you're sure."

"I'm sure."

He paused. "Last night—"

She leapt in. "Oh, no, that's okay." He looked doubtful, but she waved a hand, trying to seem casual. "What happens on tour, right?"

"Well...okay then."

He gave her a hug and she held on, suddenly feeling the loss of him. They might have stepped back to the friends side of the line, but her heart wasn't completely convinced. "Thanks for looking after me."

He let her go and smiled, hoisting his backpack over his shoulder. "Well, you know. I've got your back."

She watched him make his way through the crowds, off to who knew where. Despite the kiss, there had never really been a beginning of anything, she knew. So why did this feel like yet another ending?

As she turned to go, her eye was drawn upwards to the statue of lovers embracing under the station clock. "Oh, get a room," she muttered, and turned to make her way back down to the tube, back to reality.

★

Cass was there when she phoned, and thrilled to hear she was back in one piece. When she got home, Livi found her waiting in the doorway. She hustled Livi in and locked the door firmly behind them. There had been no sign of Len or the reporter, she said, but best to be careful. She was desperate for every detail of the trip. So they sat in the kitchen, drinking tea and eating chocolate Hobnobs, and Livi told all. The Île Saint Louis, Père Lachaise, and the Eiffel Tower. Jim Morrison, the pickpockets, and Ryan Velez.

Well, almost all. Not everything needed saying. If even Cam had been caught up in the cinematic romance of Paris, that was understandable. One impulsive Parisian kiss didn't change anything in the real world. The American was every bit as gorgeous as she had remembered, and Cass had hoped. And it was very nice of Cam to help her find him, after all, so what he did with Sasha Fernsby after that was none of her business. If she'd been looking at him in a different way, well, things had been a bit crazy lately. A person could be forgiven for being drawn to a friendly face from simpler times. Still…she wondered where he was now, and what he was doing. And with whom.

Come to think of it, maybe another opinion wouldn't hurt.

She cleared her throat. "Cass…how did you know? About Steve?"

Cass smiled. "Well, it wasn't like love at first sight or anything. But he was so nice, and I felt so relaxed. So *myself*. And then, you know, he turned out to be so much more *manly* than I expected." She grinned. Then she sat up straighter. "Wait—are you thinking about Cam, or the American?"

"Well…" If she said it out loud, would that make it real? "Maybe Cam. But I don't know. I think being in Paris played with my head. It was ridiculously romantic." She wasn't going to mention the kiss—not until she knew what it meant, or didn't mean.

"Maybe it was romantic for a reason," Cass suggested. "Maybe you just needed to see him out of your ordinary surroundings."

"Maybe…but he's going home in a minute, remember?"

"They both are," Cass pointed out.

"True."

"I never thought I'd be a cheerleader for the nice guy," Cass said, "but now I realise, they do have a lot going for them."

"I take it Cam is the nice guy here," Livi said. "But the thing is, I think he's got someone on the go already." She told Cass about all the phone calls.

Cass decided she was unimpressed by the persistent Ms Fernsby too. "Sasha Fernsby. Sounds too fancy by half."

"I know." Livi crinkled her nose. "For a moment there, it seemed…" She sighed. "But I suppose not."

There was silence as they both pondered the situation. Then Cass steered them towards the positive. "But anyway! This American," she said. "Tell me more about *him*."

Livi handed her the black and red card, and she

studied it carefully, front and back. "This is so cryptic! You are absolutely hopeless. I can't believe you didn't find out anything more."

"Well, there wasn't much time. And it was uncomfortable, to say the least, with the two of them there."

"But the—Ryan—was he still completely to die for?" She leaned forward, eager for the juicy details.

Livi laughed. "Actually, yes. He looked like he'd just come off the set of a Levi's ad. I practically fell over in the aisle when I saw him."

Cass was delighted. "Well then, you *have* to phone him." She turned the card back over and pointed at the number.

"He's supposed to phone me, really." Livi feigned disinterest.

"No, don't be so old-fashioned!" She couldn't bear it. "And anyway, he doesn't have your number! Although, I suppose maybe you should wait a day or so. How long is he here for, did he say?"

"Definitely until Tuesday, we know that much. Now the last clue makes sense. Can you think of any dead rockers from Wiltshire?"

Cass shook her head. Neither of them had any idea what the connection could be. They decided to talk to Mia about it tomorrow.

But that night, curled up in front of the television, too sleepy to channel surf, a story on the late news made her sit up. Fleet Donnelly, the chaotic and controversial singer, was being released from prison on Tuesday. He would be returning to his country home in Wiltshire, and despite credible threats to his safety, he was understood to have refused additional security arrangements.

Ryan Velez's words rang in her head. *Tuesday…Wiltshire…if we don't, someone else will, might as well get in first…yeah, damn right he's earned it…*

Surely not. Surely not. And yet…what *had* been in that weighty, bubble-wrapped package? She looked again at his card. 'What needs doing.' What, exactly, might need doing on Tuesday?

★

Livi had her hands full the next day getting the salon back in order after her time away. It was ridiculous how a place could fall into disarray in such a short time.

But all day the idea niggled at her. Should she ring him? What the hell would she say? "Um, hello, I was just wondering, are you planning to knock off a rock star tomorrow? If so, could you please not?" As though any decent would-be assassin would confess immediately and cancel his plans.

By the end of the day, she was almost convinced that she was the only thing standing between Fleet Donnelly and an untimely end. How would she feel if she was back on the couch watching the late news on Tuesday night, and the story was now 'Fleet Donnelly victim of transatlantic killer'? Brian Jones, Keith Moon, Jim Morrison...would that trail lead to one more headline? Okay, maybe it was delusional—but could she take the risk?

Cass, of course, thought absolutely not, when Livi asked her that night. Something had to be done. And if it meant Livi seeing the divine Ryan Velez again, all the better. When Livi pointed out that the divine Ryan Velez could, after all, be a twisted, dangerous madman, Cass said really, she thought probably not, but did Livi remember any of her self-defence moves?

She thought back to Len. Maybe she'd play it safe after all. The police knew what they were doing, surely.

On Tuesday morning she made sure to watch the news before she left for work. She yelled out for Cass to come and see. A reporter was outside the prison as Fleet Donnelly was released, wearing his signature jaunty hat, but looking less drug-addled than usual after his stint at Her Majesty's pleasure. He stopped to light a cigarette and give the waiting cameras a peace sign. Time away clearly hadn't dampened his swagger at all. Then she was reassured to see several very large bodyguards get him safely to an anonymous black car.

"He'll probably be all right," she said. "Don't you think?"

Cass nodded. "Oh, I think so. More than likely."

Neither felt a hundred per cent convinced.

Naturally, when they got to work Cass couldn't resist telling Aidan and Will about Livi's concern for Fleet. They both laughed like drains, but Cass shushed them.

"It's not completely silly," she said. "You know he's had all kinds of dodgy things go on around him. And this American is persistently mysterious." She elbowed Livi. "Show them the card."

So Livi took out the card and passed it to them. They agreed it was, indeed, mysterious.

"I do keep wondering why he was going around all those dead rock stars," she said. "What's that all about?"

Aidan wasn't one to mess around. "Just ring him. Then you'll know." She looked reluctant, so he gave her a little push. "Go on, I dare you."

So she went into the staffroom, and sat in front of the telephone. After a few moments gathering her courage, she dialled—and got his voicemail. In true man style, it was short and to the point—can't take your call, leave a message—and gave absolutely nothing away. She hung up.

Then, without giving herself time to second-guess, she looked up the number for the Wiltshire police and dialled again. A no-nonsense voice answered. As she was explaining about the American and the phone call and the bubble-wrapped package that may or may not have contained a weapon, it sounded mad even to her, but she pressed on. When she finished, there was a moment's pointed silence.

"We have had a number of calls this morning from concerned...young ladies." His tone made it clear that 'young ladies' was not his first choice of description. "Mr Donnelly has accepted responsibility for his own security, which I think is only right given the amount of police time he has taken up recently. Wouldn't you agree?"

She was comprehensively squashed. "Um, yes, I suppose so, but—"

"Thank you for your call, Miss." And the conversation was over.

For a moment she sat at the table, quietly steaming at being so thoroughly dismissed. Then she made a decision. She dialled again, Mia's number this time, and filled her in on the latest developments.

"Wow, you've had some drama. I was half expecting you to ring anyway. Cass texted me about the Wiltshire clue—I thought she might have talked you into going today."

"It's mad, I know. I'm getting to be as bad as her."

"Well, I can't go with you today, but you can take my car if you like."

"Really? Thank you."

After Livi's week away, Nicolette had entirely disappeared again, so she'd be able to sneak away one last time. Everyone agreed that Nicolette was probably sorting out her chipped acrylics, and catching up on emails to Jake. With all the drama lately, Livi had been increasingly grateful for that hands-off approach. After today, though, she'd have to settle down and get on with things. It would probably be a relief to get back to the regular routine. But first, Fleet Donnelly.

"I thought maybe I could pretend to be a stylist, to get past his security."

"Blag your way in?"

"Exactly." How exactly, she didn't know, but she'd have an hour or two in the car to figure it out.

"You can take my other equipment case then, as a prop. Do you know where he lives, though?"

This was, admittedly, a flaw in the plan. "Not exactly."

"Leave it to me." Mia loved a challenge. "I'll bring the car as soon as I can."

Chapter Twenty-Nine

I t was an easy drive to the little village in Wiltshire, and armed with Mia's research, Livi found Fleet Donnelly's house without any difficulty. There were cars parked in the narrow lane, so she went around the corner and parked the Saab in a safe spot, then walked back along to the high white gates.

A gaggle of girls, each carefully made up to look carelessly made up, were hanging around in the hope of getting through to their newly freed idol. Each shot dirty kohl-rimmed looks at the competition as they staked out their territory.

Barring them from their goal were two security guards, black t-shirts stretched across their unfeasibly large shoulders. Both had necks wider than their chrome-domed heads.

She held the silver equipment case in front of her, and tried to look as stylish as possible as she pushed through to the front. Not for the first time, she wished she had a few extra inches. She could have been ten years older than any of the leggy, bohemian-themed girls, who were probably lucky the release date fell in the school holidays. In her leggings and wrap top, both in salon black, she felt glaringly conservative. At least she had her strappy beaded heels on. The guards ran their eyes over her, appraising, and she pushed her shoulders back a little more.

"Hi. I'm from Peach, in London. I've come to style Fleet. I mean, Mr Donnelly."

"Is that what you girls are calling it now?" said one, giving her a look. "Did you order a girl?" he asked the other, who shook his head, eyes fixed on her cleavage.

Suddenly she realised what he meant. Urgh. She wished she had some buttons to do up. "No, I'm from Peach salon." She held up the silver case.

"Ha, ha, Peach is right," said bald head number two, finally removing his eyes from her chest. "What tricks do you have in there? You can style me next, darling."

Her stomach turned, but she stood firm. At least they weren't turning her away.

"Now then, my love, don't mind him," said number one. "Some people have no class, no class at all. But you know we can only let in authorised people."

She felt her chance slipping away. "Did you let an American in today?" She could tell from his face that they had. "Please, I have to go in. I think Fleet's in danger."

Number two snorted. "In danger of what? Blue balls?" He guffawed with appreciation at his own humour. "Ratty little tosser, he can do it himself..."

Yuck. She felt properly grubby now, but gave it a last try. "Please?"

"All right, all right," said number one. "At least you're legal. Wouldn't let my sister in there, but I suppose it'll be worth your while. God knows what you girls see in him."

She decided to press her advantage, and gestured to the gates, smiling at him as sweetly as she could. "Would you mind?"

So he let her in, much to the disgust of the fan-girls, and she crunched up the narrow driveway, heart pounding as she heard the gates close behind her. On each side, the lawn was like a hay field. The stone patio in front of the red-brick house was cracked, and a creeper was having its way with the stonework. What had obviously once been a manicured garden was now brambly and wild. A cat eyed her warily from a windowsill.

There was no sign of anyone, so she knocked on the peeling front door and waited. And knocked again, and waited. After a bit she tried the door, her heart thumping. The hinges groaned with the effort of opening. As she stepped inside another cat scooted away, dodging through a mess of clothes and papers, books and bric-a-brac, random objects jumbled amongst furniture sitting any which way. A faded Union Jack hung from the ceiling, blocking the light from the window, and there was a dank, stale smell.

For a moment she stood in shock. The garden should have given a hint of what was coming, she supposed, but still, it was not what she'd expected. Then again, maybe it reflected the inner life of the occupant.

She clutched the case to her front and picked her way across the room and into a hallway. Eventually she came to the kitchen and found a door into the back garden, which was as dilapidated as the front. Weeds sprang from an old bird bath and a mouldering sofa sat in a patch of grass. In front of it was a rickety table with a half-empty bottle of whisky and an abandoned glass.

She looked away down to the bottom of the long garden. Just beyond the alley of oak trees, where the garden met waving fields, she could see two figures. In the knee-high grass, Ryan Velez was pointing something at Fleet Donnelly. Her heart was suddenly in her throat. From this distance she couldn't see what it was, but Fleet seemed to be leaping about, his arms in the air...

In the next instant she was racing down the length of the garden, waving her own arms, yelling "Don't! Ryan! No!"

At the very moment she caught sight of the cameraman lurking in the trees, she stepped into a hole, and went down with a cry of horror and pain. The strap on one of her delicate shoes tore away from the sole, and she hit the ground hard. Sprawled in the summery grass, she knew her ankle was ruined, but she held her breath. Like a child hiding in a cornfield, if she made not a peep, maybe they wouldn't find her. Were all of them in danger from Ryan Velez? She curled herself up between the grassy walls, ankle throbbing, wishing herself invisible.

But within seconds her mortification was complete. Ryan, Fleet, the New Zealand reporter and the cameraman—through his lens—peered down at her. Their faces were a mixture of concern, confusion, amusement and, for the reporter, satisfaction. This footage was gold.

"Oh my God." She hid her face in her hands, pain mingling with humiliation. The camera kept rolling.

Then she heard Ryan tell the camera crew to get the hell away. There was a kerfuffle, followed by serious voices some distance away. She still didn't want to look, but then Fleet said, in his gentle voice, "Come on. It's okay."

She opened her eyes again and saw him reaching down to her. He helped her up, holding his hat on with one hand. When her foot with its dangling shoe touched the ground she gasped with pain, but he put his arm around her and helped her towards the house. Looking back, she could see Ryan talking to the reporter. The cameraman was not filming.

Finally they reached the house, passing the now-dented equipment case, lying where she'd dropped it on the paving stones. Fleet sat her in an old rocking chair in the kitchen, her foot up on an amp. He seemed entirely unfazed by her unexpected—and melodramatic—arrival. He dug some ice out of the freezer and wrapped it in a slightly manky tea towel. She took off her shoe, and pressed the tea towel to her ankle. Even the lightest touch was agonising.

"I've got whisky, somewhere," he said, looking around. He went back out into the garden, then came back and offered her the smudgy glass of amber-gold liquid. She took it gratefully.

He slopped a generous amount into a teacup for himself and tucked the bottle under his arm. "Sorry, do you mind?" He opened a corner of the tea towel and fished out a couple of ice cubes, then dropped them into his drink. "Thanks. Are you okay?"

With the whisky warmth inside, her ankle was starting to improve, but the agony of her media ambush was not. It was bad enough that they'd found her at all—how much worse that she'd made such a spectacle of herself. Thinking about it made her want to crawl into a hole, or under one of Fleet's piles of detritus. She held out her glass for more whisky, and he topped her up, then lowered his skinny frame into an under-stuffed armchair.

"I seem to have a habit of embarrassing myself," she told him.

"That's not embarrassing," he said. "Not really. You should see half of what I've been up to." He reflected for a moment. "Though I can't remember a lot of it, to be honest."

He took another sip of whisky and gave her a sweet, resigned smile, and she could see, then, a little of what the tousle-haired girls saw in him.

She laughed, despite her ankle. "Maybe you should google yourself."

"I probably already pay someone to do that for me," he said vaguely, fingering the beads around his neck. "Do *you* google yourself?" He made it sound almost erotic.

"Hell no, too scared." It was the truth.

He looked at her with interest from under the brim of his hat. "Really? What have *you* been up to?"

But then Ryan put his head around the kitchen door. "Fleet, can I have a word? Won't take long." He disappeared again, and Fleet levered himself out of the armchair and followed, taking his teacup with him.

She waited, sipping her own drink and holding the now-soggy tea towel against her ankle. A cat wandered in and sat just out of reach on the flagstone floor, giving her a disdainful catty look.

"I know," she said. "Did you see that? What an idiot." She sighed.

It was very quiet. Where were they? She was suddenly

acutely aware of how stuck she was. In the kitchen of a notoriously off-the-rails rocker—albeit a supposed creative genius—and at the mercy of a death-obsessed American. Add a reporter who'd come around the world to...to what, actually? Get more footage to promote the humiliation she'd already been through?

Well, she didn't have to sit here like a sack of potatoes and wait for more. She might have time to sneak away before they came back. The keys for the Saab were in her pocket, but her phone and other belongings were in Mia's case. She'd just have to retrieve it from the back garden, and shuffle her way out.

She pushed the tea towel off her ankle and put her glass down next to the rocking chair. As she struggled up her head spun, either from the pain, or whisky on an empty stomach, or both. She only made it a few hops across the kitchen, scaring the cat out the door, before she was overcome and crumpled to the floor. The awkward landing twisted her ankle again. It hurt like hell.

For a moment she sat gathering herself together, holding her head in her hands. Then she heard footsteps. All four of them were back, looking down at her from the doorway. Damn, damn, damn. She sat up as straight as she could.

"Could someone please help me up?"

Ryan and Fleet helped her back into the rocking chair and gave her back her whisky. She held the glass firm and her dignity firmer. "Thank you."

The kitchen was crowded now. "I wasn't expecting so many visitors today," Fleet said mildly.

Livi drained her glass. Now she knew what to do with two of the unexpected visitors. She may be stuck, but at least she could get some answers.

Chapter Thirty

Time for the truth, for better or worse. She eyeballed the reporter. "How did you know I was here?"

"How do you think? We followed you from London. While you were simpering at the gates with the other girls we just went around the back and climbed a few fences."

He obviously wasn't setting out to make friends, so she held her ground. "And why exactly *are* you following me?"

"The network's putting together a programme to promote the next season of *Dance 'til You Drop*. Where are they now, blah blah." He sneered. "Back to obscurity, most of them, where they belong. It wasn't hard to find you."

She decided to ignore the insult. "How *did* you find me?"

He sighed. "Rob knew you were working at a hairdresser somewhere in London. We just did some research." His tone implied that he was talking to a simpleton. "The salon's website didn't have your photo, but it had your first name. When we saw you coming and going with the other girl, we guessed you lived together. And once someone has their name on a few bills, the right person can find them. It's not rocket science."

"So Rob talked to you?" Even though she'd expected

better, it wasn't that big a surprise.

"It's in his best interests. Contractually. They've asked him to go on the show again this season."

"What, so he can be the ladies man again?" She couldn't hide the disgust in her voice, didn't try to.

He rolled his eyes. "As if that was *his* idea. That Therese is a cunning bitch. She knows what makes good television, and she knows ratings. She doesn't give a shit who gets caught in the crossfire."

Livi sat still while everything shifted in her head. Therese. She could believe it. She'd lost count of the times she'd heard 'Therese says' from an enthusiastic Rob. What had Therese been saying about her? Or about Rob himself, the newly minted golden boy? In the end, maybe he'd begun to believe Therese's version of his own publicity.

But then, even with Therese as puppet-master, it wasn't like sequins girl forced herself on him. The image was still right there in her head. The girl on high-heel tiptoe, Rob's fingers buried in her hair, his hand cupping her neatly curvaceous bottom. He was remorseful enough afterwards, but remorse wouldn't undo what was done. And broadcast to the nation, splashed across the papers, debated on talkback radio, and discussed online. She'd never seen the footage of herself, caught in shock, and she never wanted to. What she had wanted, was to know why. Let's just play the game, he'd said. In the end, maybe the game played him. She'd had her doubts, but she never guessed how that game would end. How they would end.

Now she shook her head. "I just don't know why he had to do it." By the time the end did come, she knew they couldn't have lasted—but it was a spectacularly public finish.

"Why do people do anything for fame or money? They get a little whiff, and it changes them. Look at this guy." He gestured at Fleet. "Do you think he was such a wreck before he got his big break?"

She waited for Fleet to react, but he just shrugged and raised his teacup.

"Maybe that's why they call it that," she said. "Because it actually can break you."

"Maybe," the reporter replied. "Anyway, it's not going to happen to me. I'm going to get my break, and I know what to do with it. I'm not chasing after nobodies like you my whole life."

If she wasn't temporarily crippled, she'd have got up and slapped him. She had to make do with leaning violently in his direction. "I'd rather be a nobody in the media and a somebody in real life, than the other way around."

But Ryan stepped in. "That's enough," he told the reporter. "You can go. I'll be in touch."

"You'd better be, Captain America. If I don't get what I came for, I have to reimburse the network for all our expenses. Believe me, I will not be happy."

The cameraman trailed out after him.

"I'm going to see them out," Fleet said. "And I'd better see who's at the gate. Rude not to, if they've come all this way."

He was clearly relishing the prospect of the gate girls. Well, he'd been away a while, Livi thought, as she watched him follow the other two out. Why wouldn't he? When they were gone, she sat, processing. Despite her best efforts, her past had caught up with her.

Ryan leaned against the chipped Belfast sink and waited, his arms folded across his artfully faded flannel shirt. Even in her current state she couldn't help but admire him. With his dark eyes and effortless charm, he was absolutely magnetic. Maybe it was his aura. She wondered what colour Journey would see.

Finally he broke the silence. "So, that was a dramatic entrance." He laughed as she squirmed with embarrassment. "I have to ask—what are you doing here?"

She shook her head, putting off the inevitable. "You first."

"Okay then." He sat in Fleet's armchair. "From the beginning. I live in Silver Lake, in LA."

"Not in Idaho?"

"Idaho's still home, but there's no work there for me. I'm kind of a go-to guy for filmmakers, but I specialise in the music industry. Locations, research, making connections. Greasing the wheels. Whatever needs doing, you know. One of my clients is doing a documentary for MTV about how rock stars live on after they die—their legacy—and they want Fleet to front it."

"Ah." That explained Brian, and Keith, and Jim. "Are they expecting him to go next?" It had to be said.

"Well, obviously it wouldn't be right for them to *hope* for someone's death..." He gave a wry grin. "Anyway, they want him to film some segments himself. That's why I was showing him the camera."

"Oh. That makes sense."

"What did you think?" He was going to make her say it.

"I thought you were..." She pressed the whisky glass against her forehead. "I thought you were going to shoot him."

He had every reason to be offended but, to her relief, he laughed. "With a camera?"

"No, obviously not with a camera. I thought maybe the package in your satchel was a gun." No thanks to Steve for putting that idea in her head.

He raised his eyebrows. "I don't think you would have got a gun through Eurostar security."

"Oh...no." Of course not. She knew that. Where was her head at? God, she'd been all over the place lately.

He shook his head, amused. "I knew you were a bit crazy the first time we met."

"No, actually, I'm really not at all," she said, but he looked unconvinced. "It's just that things kind of...got away on me."

"That's okay, it's a charming kind of crazy."

"I don't know if the viewers will agree." She imagined the glee with which Therese would receive the footage of her mad gallop and subsequent tumble. She must have looked completely unhinged.

"I can help you there."

"Really?" She couldn't think how.

"He told us the story, what happened to you in New Zealand. And we did a deal. He's deleted the footage of your grand entrance, in return for an exclusive with Fleet."

"Thank you!" Sheer relief made up for him knowing her inglorious backstory. "That's amazing."

He shrugged. "With his ego, it was an easy sell. He thinks he's too cool for the local news round. If he plays it right, an exclusive could launch him into a new career."

She hoped not.

"And some positive PR wouldn't do Fleet any harm at the moment—he's earned his reputation." He paused. "But the reporter has still got the assignment. So you'll have to do an interview."

"Oh, no." Her heart dropped again.

"At least now it's on your terms. No ambush."

"Okay." No escape after all. She sighed. "I don't know how things got in such a state. I seem to be lurching from one mishap to another these days."

"Well..." He seemed to be considering whether or not to say something. "If it's all too much, come back to the States with me."

She laughed. "Don't be silly."

"Why not? You might be a bit unpredictable, but you're a breath of fresh air compared with the kind of California craziness I'm usually surrounded with. And you seem like the kind of girl who'll take a chance."

This was so far from how she saw herself that she had to laugh. But then, recent events had proved otherwise. "I suppose it might look that way, but I think the California craziness has rubbed off on *you*."

He shrugged again, his smile teasing, and for a moment she let herself consider the idea. Another step across the water. Was there any point in keeping on moving, when her previous life had already tapped her on the shoulder? On the other hand, if she had nothing more to lose, why not make a leap for that next rock in the stream? She looked at him—legs outstretched, his easy, sun-baked confidence making even the shabby armchair look desirable. The company would be pretty good. Although when it came to the crunch, surely he wouldn't really follow through on such an impulsive proposal.

She imagined telling Cam. At least she wouldn't have to do it in person this time, with him going home any minute. He wouldn't say anything much, she knew. But she also knew he wouldn't think it was a good idea. Charisma had no power over him.

Well, he wouldn't be here to say it, or not say it, and make her second-guess herself. She put him firmly out of her mind, along with her Parisian memories, and focused on the man in front of her.

"You might have fun."

His eyes held the wicked suggestion of all kinds of fun. Maybe he did mean it. It was a tempting idea, she had to admit. Mad, but tempting. She was only human, after all. "I might..." She leaned back in the chair, accidentally making it rock, and winced with pain.

He left the question unanswered. "Come on, I think we'd better get someone to look at your ankle."

"Thanks, Captain America."

His grin was superhero dazzling. "Glad to be of service, Ma'am."

Chapter Thirty-One

R yan went down the road and got the Saab, then helped a barefoot Livi back down the path. She was too distracted by her ankle to fully appreciate being held so near. Chrome dome one and two were still at the gate, but only a handful of girls were left, looking despondent after Fleet's selection of a fortunate few.

Getting the dodgy ankle into the car proved a bit difficult. The front seat was too uncomfortable, so with some careful manoeuvring Ryan helped her into the back. She stretched her leg out along the seat, and took a sip of whisky from the near-empty bottle he handed in. Despite being famous for his recreational drug taking, there wasn't a single paracetamol to be found in Fleet's house. In desperation, Livi made do with self-medication of the liquid kind.

Waiting at the local medical centre, she noticed that the other women in the room kept glancing at Ryan, in between dealing with grizzly children. He was oblivious, or maybe ignoring them. Well, he'd be used to it, she assumed. Even with the ankle, she couldn't help glancing herself. He propped her leg up on a plastic chair, and found her a magazine.

"We're going back to London tomorrow," he said, sitting down next to her with a dog-eared copy of *NME*. "Maybe I can drive you in your car, instead of going with Fleet and his guys, and meet them there."

"That would be great, thank you," she said. She was starting to feel decidedly queasy now, and her ankle was an alarming size. Driving herself back to London, even tomorrow, was obviously out of the question.

She texted Mia and Cass to update them. Replies came straight back, Cass's punctuated with exclamation marks. She saw the whole thing as a perfect opportunity to get to know Ryan better...much, much better. Livi couldn't deny that the thought had occurred to her, especially as the whisky bottle emptied—but the deep, throbbing pain in her ankle was a definite hindrance.

When they finally saw the doctor, he confirmed that it was sprained, but not broken. She gripped the edge of the bed tightly as he flexed her foot, testing.

"This is a reasonable sort of sprain," he said. "Keep it elevated as much as you can, until the swelling goes down. You can take paracetamol, but I've prescribed you codeine, for the pain. It can cause drowsiness." He handed her the prescription. "Take it with food. And *avoid* alcohol."

She suddenly realised that he must be able to smell it on her. She decided not to admit that she was moderately whisky-tipsy already.

"Alcohol increases swelling. *And* increases the risk of falling over again," he added, unsmiling. She could only nod obediently as the nurse came in to bandage her up, and he left to deal with some real emergency.

By now it was getting late. They found a Boots with a late-night pharmacy, and then stopped for pizza. She waited in the back of the car, her leg up and her head heavy against the seat back. With an empty stomach, and only the whisky to wash down the codeine, she'd had to wait for her first dose of painkillers. It felt like a very long wait indeed. Finally Ryan came back with the pizza and a can of Sprite, and she thankfully downed two tablets. She went to put the lid back on the little bottle, then paused. Her ankle was pounding in its bandage, the smallest movement still excruciating. There wouldn't be any harm, surely... She shook out one more tablet and popped it in her mouth, then lay back again. Prescription or otherwise, she was grateful for any helpful substance tonight.

★

By the time they made it back to Fleet's house, she was completely used up. They settled into the kitchen to eat, Livi back in her rocking chair. But before long, they realised that Fleet was still entertaining his (possibly illegal) houseguests in the room next door. The unmistakable, rhythmic sound of mattress springs in action was punctuated by squeals and giggles.

Oh, no. She tried not to look at Ryan, but when she caught his eye they both had to laugh.

She held her hands over her ears. "Is his bedroom next door?"

"Yeah. He said he likes being close to the fridge."

The giggles were now replaced by theatrical moans and gasps. Livi was torn between embarrassment at overhearing, and wonder at the ostentatious sound effects. "How many girls does he *have* in there?"

Ryan grinned. "More than enough. Do you want to sit somewhere else?"

She closed the lid on her pizza box. "No, I don't think I can eat any more anyway. I'm so tired."

"Come on then." He helped her up again and put his arm around her. In her worn-out state, she leaned gratefully into him. Now, with the lusty chorus coming from next door, she was acutely aware of his hard body under the soft flannel shirt. They made their slow and careful way along to Fleet's room, and he banged on the door. "Fleet! Where can Livi sleep?"

The theatrics stopped suddenly, but the giggles

returned. After some time, a reply came. "You've got a bed, put her in there."

They looked at each other for a moment. The possibility hung in the air, along with Cass's exclamation marks. Then Ryan called back through the door. "No, she needs a proper rest, with her ankle."

There was a chorus of giggles and shrieks from within. He sighed, and banged on the door again. Finally Fleet's voice could be heard.

"Sorry mate, try upstairs, at the other end of the house. My mum's room, when she visits..."

They started to go, but then the door suddenly opened. As they both turned to look, Fleet stepped out, buck naked. Livi's first instinct was to close her eyes. When she came to her senses a millisecond later and reopened them—she'd never have another chance to see that, after all—a bed-haired girl peeked out from behind his bony shoulder, curious. Livi recognised her from the gate.

"Hang on mate, I've saved something for you. Just a second."

He disappeared back into the room, leaving the girl lounging against the door frame. One long, smooth leg had escaped from the sheet she was wrapped in. She stared boldly at Ryan, unbothered by Livi's presence, clearly liking what she saw. Livi, on the other hand, was surprised to find that she felt quite bothered. In fact, she felt a strong desire to shove the tantalisingly dishevelled girl back through the doorway.

Fortunately, at that moment Fleet reappeared—not with another girl he'd saved for Ryan, as Livi had half expected, but with a small plastic bag. "This is too good not to share," he said, pressing it into Ryan's hand.

He started to decline, but Fleet insisted. "Go on. Least I can do."

So he took it. "Thanks mate, that's very generous."

Then Fleet and the girl disappeared back into the bedroom, the girl giving Ryan one last provocative look before she shut the door.

Livi looked at the little bag. "Is that...?"

"Yeah." Then he had a thought. "Is that what?"

"Um..." Hello again, country mouse. She wasn't *completely* unworldly—but there was obviously plenty she didn't know. "Never mind."

"Okay," he said, tucking it into his shirt pocket. Then he looked at her. "I try not to turn anyone down. If they think you're on the same page, everything flows more smoothly."

"Oh, right. Yeah." She was none the wiser, but she wasn't going to draw attention to how un-streetwise she was. "Let's go up and find this bedroom, leave them to it."

They came to the bottom of the stairs, and her heart sank—they seemed to stretch a mile high. He saw her face. "No problem," he said. And before she knew it, he picked her up and set off.

"Oh no, I'm too heavy," she protested.

"You're kidding, right?" He went steadily up the stairs. "You're no more than a doll."

Along the passage, they were surprised to find a beautifully furnished, tidy room. He gently put her down inside. The curtains matched the floral canopy over the bed, and there was a little en-suite bathroom with a vintage bathtub under the window. While he went back down for her abandoned shoes and the equipment case (luckily full of hair and makeup products she could use in the morning), she used the toilet as quickly as she could, and splashed her face with water. There was toothpaste and a newish-looking toothbrush in a tumbler. After some consideration, she rinsed the toothbrush in scalding hot water and used it. Needs must.

When she hobbled back out, she saw that he'd pushed the window open. A small lamp glowed on the bedside table, and the warm evening air brought in the scent of climbing flowers. She took off her shirt, avoiding his eye, and got into bed wearing her leggings and silky cami top, leaving her bandaged foot uncovered. With her head on the pillow, she could see out into the long garden where she'd embarrassed herself that day. Now the grass swayed silvery and inviting in the moonlight. The only sounds were crickets in the garden, and the regular punctuation of a frog somewhere in the distance.

He sat on the bed alongside her. Another mad day, another strange bed. She felt herself begin to drift in and out of an unreal half-sleep. In the dim light, he was a broad-shouldered silhouette. He didn't seem in any hurry to get to his room. As her eyes fought to close, she wondered if Cam was sitting on someone else's bed right now...Sasha Fernsby's bed, to be exact. In her mind, the sound of crickets merged with the sound of clapping at the Eiffel Tower lights...

★

She awoke suddenly to find Ryan lying next to her, on top of the blankets. He smiled lazily as she struggled to wake up.

"How long was I asleep?" She felt completely disoriented.

"Not very long."

She had no idea if that was true. But the little lamp was still on, and he didn't look like he'd been asleep too. "Sorry...I couldn't stay awake. Maybe it's the tablets."

"You just need to sleep."

She did. She felt decidedly off-kilter. But although her body was heavy with tiredness, and her brain was fuddled, his nearness focused her attention. This close, she could see the flecks of gold in his dark eyes, and the way his scar tapered around under his jaw. Her finger itched to trace along it, down the side of his neck and beyond.

A random thought popped out before she could stop it. "How do you always keep that same stubble? Do you have some special shaver?"

He laughed. "No, I just usually shave every couple of days, before bed."

The temptation was too great. She reached out and lay

a tentative finger on his jaw, where the scar interrupted the dark shadow. "Oh, right. Five o'clock shadow in the morning. Very rock 'n' roll."

"Ha, yeah, that's me." He made the 'rock on' sign, then let his two raised fingers fall on the bare skin at her collarbone. He trailed them softly down to the edge of her camisole, then paused. Her drowsy body was now awake and humming, waiting for where his touch would travel next. But he stopped, and propped himself up on his elbow.

"So, are you coming?"

She worked to gather herself. "Coming where?"

"Back home with me."

"You're not serious."

"I am. I have to go—you should come too." He made it sound so simple.

"I do have a life, you know. For starters, there's my job. I can't just up and leave."

"You did last time," he pointed out, daring her.

"This is different." How, she couldn't exactly say. His warm proximity wasn't making clear thought any easier.

"I don't see why."

She sighed, knowing what any sensible person would say. "I have no idea who you are. I mean…I don't want to end up on the side of a milk carton."

"Don't worry about offending me or anything," he said. "Anyway, you'd probably be stuck on a lamp post."

She thought back to Steve's words. She hadn't seen him chew gum so far, he obviously wasn't an evangelist, and there didn't seem to be any wives. And who knew whether gun-toting was commonplace back in Silver Lake.

"I'll have to google you. There are no real secrets any more, apparently."

"You won't find much."

"Why not? Don't you advertise to the rich and famous?"

"No. The opposite. They like it better if you're hard to pin down. If you're elusive, they feel like they're getting something exclusive."

"But how do I know you're not, I don't know...an exclusive, elusive axe-murderer?"

"Take the chance."

His face was teasing, challenging her. She took in the curved mouth, the all-American teeth, and the complexion that would put Enrique Iglesias to shame. All just a breath away. Sensible was in danger of losing the fight. Cling film and tea bags stood no chance against this. Probably not a good idea, she knew, but...

He leaned down, and she closed her eyes as his lips met hers. For all the stubble, his kiss was surprisingly tender, and she gave herself up to the heady pleasure of what she'd imagined so many times since that night on the tube. Then he took her face in his hands and kissed her harder, parting her lips, delving deeper, and any thought of sensible behaviour melted away in the reckless heat of her body's response to his confident, seeking mouth.

"Live dangerously," she murmured, as he pulled back for a moment to look at her.

"Exactly." He gathered her in, pulling her hard up against him, and went to kiss her again. But with the sudden movement, pain flared in her ankle, making her cry out.

He stopped. "Sorry," he said, letting her lie back on the pillow. "Hurts, huh?"

"Yes." She gritted her teeth, waiting for it to ease.

"This is no good. I'd better let you sleep." As he got up, she wanted to weep with both frustration and pain. He let out a long breath and ran his fingers through his hair. "Don't know how much sleep I'll be getting though."

He bent down and kissed her gently on her passion-bruised lips, his eyes still heavy with the heat of their encounter. Then he turned off the little lamp and went out, leaving her flustered and fidgety, wondering what, oh what, she'd just missed out on.

Chapter Thirty-Two

S he woke the next morning feeling less than rested. Everything was quiet in the house, so she limped into the bathroom. There was no shower, and she couldn't begin to imagine getting in and out of the old high-sided bath. So she did the best she could with her own little makeup bag and the contents of Mia's case, and took another couple of painkillers. She'd have to find some breakfast. It seemed unlikely that Fleet would be well-stocked with groceries— maybe leftover pizza would have to do.

By the time she went carefully out into the passage, Ryan was waiting at the top of the stairs. They smiled at each other, and she was suddenly self-conscious, remembering the heat of the night before, feeling the warmth of a blush in her cheeks.

"How's the patient this morning?" he asked. His voice was concerned, but his smile held a knowing tease, and she knew he could read her thoughts.

"Okay thanks," she said, putting down her bag and Mia's case, and holding onto the railing. "A bit sore."

"I bet. I hope you got some sleep, after…"

He left the rest unsaid, but she felt the blush intensify anyway. Despite that, she kept her voice steady when she answered. "Some. What about you?"

"Yeah, some," he echoed. "I had something on my mind."

Under his steady gaze, heavy with implication, she was acutely aware of the open door to the bedroom only a few steps—or hops, in her case—behind them. She couldn't help looking over her shoulder, tempted. But as she moved, she let her weight fall on her sprained ankle, and the pain made her suck in her breath.

"Sorry," he said. "Shouldn't leave you standing here." And he sprang into action, taking her things and helping her back downstairs, the moment over for now.

It was quiet in Fleet's room as they passed. "No more athletics this morning," he commented.

They went into the kitchen in search of breakfast. On the worktop were the pizza boxes (empty) and the familiar leather satchel—and the little plastic bag, with only a smudge of white dust left in the bottom.

Fleet came in right behind them. "Let's go," he said.

"You're up early," Ryan said. "Thought you'd be sleeping in."

"Sleep?" He waved the suggestion away. "I'm keeping going while the going's good. Sleep when you're dead. Thanks for the pizza, by the way, great breakfast. Now come on, let's go." He jigged with impatience.

Ryan and Livi looked at each other. Judging by the expression on his face, he was thinking the same thing she was—he didn't want company for their trip back to London.

"Aren't you going with your security guys?" he said.

"Nah, they didn't get any more interesting while I was inside. I'll come with you, and we can talk about this project."

So it was decided. Fleet was going to see his manager, so they'd drop Livi and the Saab at Peach, not far away. She sat propped up in the back again, the satchel on the floor next to Mia's case, while Fleet talked on and on, sometimes about the documentary project, sometimes going off on long, rambling tangents. Ryan nodded and made all the right noises, while Livi snuck glances at him, wondering anew what she'd missed—and whether she should give herself the chance to find out.

She texted Mia and Cass to say she was on her way, and ate one of the pastries Ryan bought from a bakery they passed. After a while, she felt herself getting sleepy again. She had no idea who had taken what, or not, or whether she even gave a damn. Who was she to talk, anyway, dosed up on codeine? She closed her eyes. She'd have to trust to fate that, between the two of them, they'd get her safely back to London.

★

At Peach, Cass came out to meet her, but she could see the others trying to watch through the window. She hoped there wouldn't be any hair mishaps caused by distracted scissors. Fleet went straight from the Saab to his black Range Rover with tinted windows, pausing only to take a long appreciative look at Cass. "Hello, love," he said—and with just those two words, she was lost. She blushed and giggled as he got into the Range Rover.

On the pavement, Ryan gave Livi the car keys and kissed her one last, lingering time. "Let me know," he said, and she could only nod as he followed Fleet into the Range Rover and closed the door.

Between Fleet's ogling and the sight of Ryan, with his effortlessly hip good looks, Cass was overcome.

"Wow," she said, as they pulled away. "You've obviously had quite a time."

"Yes, I have." She laughed, holding onto Cass's arm as she balanced on one foot. "I really have."

"I'm totally jealous. Come on, I want to hear about it. One of the boys can move the car. *And* a package arrived for you this morning, we're all dying to know what it is."

She got Livi inside and settled on the salon sofa.

"Welcome back, wounded warrior," said Aidan, taking the chance to come over between clients. "You were a bit obvious out there," he added to Cass.

"No, I wasn't! I was very composed."

"You weren't," Livi said. "I think you actually fluttered your eyelashes."

"I did not! I don't even know *how* to flutter my eyelashes." She demonstrated with mad spasmodic blinking. "See?"

Livi laughed. "It must have been involuntary eyelash fluttering."

"It could have been," she conceded. "But you can't blame me. I was completely unprepared. I never fancied Fleet Donnelly before, but seeing him in person...and your American is dangerously attractive."

"Oh, I know," said Livi. "But it's the amount of dangerous versus attractive that I'm not sure about."

She looked at the large, square parcel that Cass pulled out from behind the sofa. "What *is* this?"

"That's what *we* want to know," Cass said.

Livi tore off the brown paper wrapping, and then used the scissors Cass offered to cut away several layers of bubble wrap. "Oh!"

It was Saint Cecilia, beautifully mounted and framed in heavy antique gold. And it could only have come from one person.

"It's gorgeous!" Cass exclaimed.

Aidan nodded, impressed. "That's classy."

It was both those things—a grown-up version of the teenage print stuck to her wall, now rolled up and packed away along with the rest of her previous life. She considered the gold-framed girl, composed as she awaited her fate. Cam, too, was now looking like a grown-up version of himself. A very attractive grown-up version, going back to his real life far away. She sighed. Saints and devils each held their temptations. But now she knew that, whichever way you were inclined, the choice might not be easy to make. Or there might not be a choice at all.

Chapter Thirty-Three

"**D**o you ever have times when you *just don't know* what you should do?" Livi despaired into her drink at the Lamb and Flag the following night.

The Parisian memories were proving harder to squash than she expected, especially after the arrival of Cecilia, but her Silver Lake superhero wouldn't lie down and die either. One known quantity, leaving. One unknown quantity, also leaving. Each so different from the other, but with one thing in common.

"She doesn't know whether to say something to Cam, or go across the Atlantic with her American," Cass explained for Aidan and Will, as they came back from the bar with their post-work drinks.

They assumed matching expressions of sympathy. "Cam or glam," Aidan said. "That *is* tricky."

Will came around the table, carefully avoiding Livi's bandaged, propped-up foot, and sat next to her. "Anyone could see how special Cam thinks you are. And you seemed so comfortable together."

"Special, smeshal," Livi sighed. "Anyway, the whole thing is hypothetical, isn't it? I mean, 'I've got your back' is hardly a declaration of undying love. And he actually insisted we try to find Ryan in Paris."

"But there were sparks, right?"

"Well…it seemed that way." She still hadn't told any of them about the kiss under the Eiffel Tower, when her crush got the better of her. "But it was Paris! Who wouldn't feel romantic in Paris? I've never seen so much blatant public fondling. Plus, it's probably just a side-effect of seeing someone from my past. The happy part."

"Do you fancy him, or does he represent something in your psyche?" Aidan teased. "Deep."

Livi threw a crisp at his head, but it fluttered down to the table.

"In any case," she added, "I haven't talked to him since. When I phoned to say thanks for Cecilia, I had to leave a message, and he just sent a text back." She sighed. "The mysterious Sasha Fernsby must be keeping him busy."

"The *evil* Sasha Fernsby." Cass remained unimpressed.

Aidan couldn't help himself. "Ooh, the Madonna and the whore—how Freudian."

"Aidan!" Cass said.

Will shushed him. "Aidan, do you mind? *Very* inappropriate."

"Thanks, at least, for making *me* the Madonna in that scenario," Livi said, finishing her wine. "I think."

"Anyway, we don't know the whole story there," Cass said. "He did send you the saint…that must mean something. It might be you he'd rather have."

She was unconvinced. "No. Come on. Why would he trek around Paris looking for another man, then?"

Cass shrugged. "I don't know. And then, that other man is no slouch, either. Oh, I'm torn!"

"He's definitely no slouch—but then, I'm not completely sure what he is. Or who he is."

Will persevered, showing his bias. "In that case, I don't think you should just rule Cam out. You've known each other for so long. How nice to not have to start at the beginning again. He knows why you are the way you are, because he was there. You can just relax."

"Just because he's been around the longest doesn't mean he should be the one," Livi retorted. She banged her empty glass on the table. "I don't want comfortable, I want the rush, damn it!"

But for a moment her mind was filled with the glittering lights of the Eiffel Tower, and she remembered herself turning to him, her guard down, her heart open and her desire obvious. If she was honest, it wasn't hard to tell who she really wanted. She groaned and leaned her head on the table.

"Anyway, he's leaving, and I'm not going back there," she said, her nose pressed against a damp coaster. "I'm just not."

They all looked at her. "How many drinks has she had?" Will asked Cass.

"Just a couple," Cass replied. "Over-emotional..." Everyone nodded.

"I am still here, you know," Livi said, looking up and waving at them.

"Maybe you're over-thinking things," Will said. "You do tend to do that."

"Yes, think like a man instead," Aidan suggested. "Think with your...well, maybe not that."

"Va-jay-jay," Cass substituted for him. "Oprah," she added, by way of explanation.

Will looked incredulous. "Do you mean to say that woman is telling us what to call our equipment now? My God, is there no end to it?"

"Stop!" Livi said. "I think this is a conversation to have after considerably more drinks than this."

"But if your va-jay-jay was in charge, it would pick Ryan, right?" Aidan persisted.

"It doesn't operate independently of my other body parts, unlike you men," she replied. "My brain and my heart keep functioning at the same time. Although..." Something occurred to her. "That would explain Rob."

"An a-ha moment!" exclaimed Cass. "See, Oprah knows."

"There you have it. She is omniscient," Will deadpanned.

"But the only thing is," Aidan said, pointedly ignoring him, "lovely though Cam is, Ryan has stepped up and, let's face it, Cam has not."

Livi realised he was right. For years Gemma and Bex, and probably everyone except her, had expected Cam to step up, but he never did. And here he was now, not stepping up, off with the unrelenting Ms Fernsby. It obviously just wasn't going to happen. Why was she even factoring him in? Just because she'd now discovered some very unexpected feelings of her own, it didn't mean he was suddenly going to—Paris or otherwise.

"You're right," she said to Aidan. "Of course you are." Better to blame the whole thing on her Parisian imagination getting carried away.

For once, he didn't look pleased to be right. "I'm sorry, my love, I don't want to sound harsh, but it's true. So we're not choosing between two, we're really choosing yes or no to Ryan."

"We?" she said.

"It's too late, I'm *invested* now," said Aidan. "Like it or not, I care."

"As do we all," said Will, and Cass agreed.

"Thanks, you guys," said Livi, feeling slightly misty. "With friends like you, who needs a man?"

As she looked at their familiar faces, something dawned on her. Actually, who *did* need a man? Did she desperately need a man, right this minute? If things weren't falling into place with either of these two, maybe she should just let it go. She did have other things to think about, after all. The interview, heaven help her. But on the positive side, friends, travel, and a not-quite-yet glittering career to work on.

"I think," she said slowly, the idea solidifying as she spoke, "I will choose...*not* to choose a man right now."

"Oh." Cass was disappointed. "But I wanted you to find your true love."

"No, it's good," said Will. "Because we want you to be

happy, but we don't really want you racing off to another country. We like having you here."

If home was the place where you looked around and found the people you loved, here she was.

"That's so sweet," she said, as he reached out and patted her hand. "But you know, even if I give up on men for a while, there's still the question—what's my next move now?"

★

Having decided to go it alone, she had to tell Ryan. When they got home that night she phoned his number again, and this time left a message. He rang back a few minutes later.

"I'm sorry," she said. "It's bad form to tell you on the phone."

"No, no problem," he said easily. "It would've been great, but I knew it was a long shot. Maybe I am as crazy as you."

"Hey!" she protested, and he laughed.

"If you're ever stateside, look me up."

"I will. And thanks again for your help with everything."

As she hung up, she knew she'd made the right decision. If her a-ha moment explained Rob, it also explained Ryan. The cowboy put his hat back on, and turned and walked away, boots kicking up dust as he went.

In the background, a figure sat astride a motorbike. She averted her eyes. No point in flogging a dead Kawasaki.

Chapter Thirty-Four

O ver the next few days, she grew increasingly anxious. Ryan might have negotiated the interview on her terms, but she feared she'd be no match for a fast-talking reporter determined to push his own agenda. She was glad he'd agreed to do the interview in Trafalgar Square. If she had scuttled away around the world, at least let them see it was to somewhere spectacular. And it felt better to be public rather than private. Didn't they used to say that if you sit in Trafalgar Square long enough, everyone you know will eventually pass by? Safety in numbers...she hoped.

So when Nicolette asked her to meet for lunch at a restaurant on Dean Street, she was glad of the distraction. It would be good to talk about plans for Peach. It would be good to talk about her long-overdue pay rise, too.

With the bandage now off her ankle, she carefully walked the short distance to the restaurant. Going in, she could see that Nicolette had the best spot in the place. As usual, her loud voice carried above the hubbub of the other patrons, and her ostentatious arm waving put passing waiters in danger. So far, so normal. But then Livi saw who she was talking to. Rachael Radner and Helena were sitting across the glossy black oak table, laughing over their glasses of wine.

She knew it couldn't be a bad thing that they were there, but her pleasure at seeing them again was tempered by a sudden anxiety. It was the same feeling she'd had as a child being called to the headmaster's office, even if she knew she'd done nothing wrong. What could be going on? She went over, half on edge, but they all looked up and smiled.

Rachael stood up. "How lovely to see you again," she said, taking Livi's hands and giving her a kiss on each cheek.

"You too. This is a surprise." There were kisses all round, then they settled into their seats, and Helena poured Livi a glass of wine.

She looked at Nicolette. "I thought we were just having a meeting."

"We are." She raised her eyebrows, obviously enjoying the anticipation of whatever was coming.

"It's a meeting with a proposal," Rachael said, getting right to business. "While you were away we had some discussions, and we have a project we'd like you to be involved in."

While Helena was glowing with excitement, Nicolette was nearly bursting, so Rachael let her go ahead.

"It's a new salon," she announced. "A place for Americans to feel at home when they're in England. British quality and service, with the best of American style and comfort. We'll cater for the Hollywood crowd, visiting actors and actresses, industry players, singers, any kind of celebrity. And a select few who want to mingle with them—if they can afford it." She winked at Livi. "With backing from Jake and Rachael, we can make it happen."

Livi looked at the three of them, her own excitement growing. "And you want *me* to be involved?"

Rachael nodded. "Yes. We'd like to offer you the manager's job. And we'd like you to be involved in choosing the stylists, and determining the look of the salon. If it all goes well, in the medium term we'll look at expanding into LA. The best of British and American combined."

235

Helena was bouncing in her chair. "Livi, isn't it so exciting? I'm going to be the receptionist. I can't wait."

"It *is* exciting!" Suddenly her career looked a little more glittering. "I can hardly believe it."

"Well, believe it, darling," said Nicolette. "You made it happen by working hard and doing a damn good job. And those ideas you left with me were top-rate. You've earned this opportunity."

Her head was spinning as she processed what they were telling her. "Wow...thanks." And from the many thoughts whirling in her head, one emerged clear and strong: she couldn't wait to tell Cam.

Nicolette held up her bejewelled hands. "Not to mention, look at the state of my nails. Thank God you're back."

Livi laughed and looked at the contract on the table in front of her, a few pages holding the promise of so much. "It all sounds amazing. Thank you."

But Rachael shook her head. "It wouldn't be professional of us to ask you to sign now. Take the contract and read it through, see what you think, and we can negotiate on the details." She smiled. "But I do hope we can do business together."

Their eyes met and Livi knew she was dealing with a straight shooter. "Me too."

Maybe she did have something to thank Therese for, after all. Even without the TV show, if she'd stayed with Rob she would have realised their mismatch eventually— possibly too late. And then, how different her life would look now.

Rachael signalled for a waiter. "In the meantime, I still owe you a lunch. Let's order."

★

That night, Livi and Cass stopped at the off-licence on the way home and bought a bottle of bubbly. They agreed that the occasion deserved more celebration than the shoebox of chocolate under the coffee table.

"Funny to think that this whole thing is thanks to Mattias, in a way," Livi said, as she poured the sparkly liquid into champagne flutes. They didn't match, but they were real crystal, at least. "Now I feel a bit bad that we hardly see him any more."

Cass raised her glass. "To Mattias." They both laughed as they clinked their appreciation. "Oh, and Steve said to tell you congratulations from him."

"Thanks!" She took a sip. "And to think I was on the verge of leaving."

"I'm *extremely* glad you're staying," Cass said. "I really didn't want the drama of finding someone else for your room." She grinned.

"And where would you ever find someone saintly enough to put up with you the way I do?"

"Irreplaceable, and modest."

"Absolutely." They smiled at each other, and secretly Livi thought how lucky she was. She'd lost Bex and Gemma along with her Antipodean life, but Cass was an unexpected and very welcome compensation. "Mind you, you'll probably be replacing me soon anyway," she added. "Three is a bit of a crowd in this wee place."

"Oh, we're not at that stage yet, not really," Cass said. "Not yet..." And she smiled to herself.

"Well, when you are, I won't be offended if we have to make alternative arrangements." It would be sad to break up their team of two, but Livi was glad to see one of them finding love, at least.

Then the phone rang, and she left her glass on the table for Cass to top up while she went to answer it. "Hello?"

"Hi."

Cam, out of the blue again. Her heart jumped, but she kept her voice casual. "Oh, hi! How are you?"

"Good...busy."

Vague as usual. She knew better than to press him. In any case, she didn't want the details if they involved the fancy Ms Fernsby. "Thanks again for Cecilia."

"You're welcome. After your battle with Len, I realised she wasn't the only brave one."

She laughed. "I don't think we quite compare—but thanks. You never know what you'll do in a situation like that, until it's upon you."

"You did very well."

She paused. "That was a really...thoughtful gift." She waited to see what else he might say.

But then Cass was there, curious. "Is that Cam?" she whispered. When Livi nodded, she called out, "Hi, Cam! We're having champagne, you should be here."

Livi shushed her, and Cam said, "That sounds good. I was ringing to say congratulations on the new job."

"Thanks!" Livi said. "But how did you know already?"

"Steve told me."

"Ah. Your spies are everywhere."

He laughed. "We've kept in touch. Bike stuff. So...does this mean you're not going with your American then?"

"Oh!" She was pink, and it wasn't the champagne. "No. That wasn't the right thing for me. Did Steve tell you about that too?"

"Men talk too, you know."

"So it seems. I thought you two seemed to hit it off."

"Yeah. I'm going to try one of his bikes. Too good a chance to miss."

"Are you back in London, then?" Back from wherever...and whoever.

"Just for a couple of days. I'm staying in a hotel while I get a few things sorted out. I'm not looking forward to that long flight."

So he was going. In her mind, she'd already farewelled him off to Sasha Fernsby anyway. And she always knew he'd be getting back on the plane sooner rather than later. As Aidan had pointed out, there had been no stepping up, no beginning, and the framed Cecilia obviously didn't hold any romantic significance. So there was no point in confessing her feelings at the last minute. But, now that it came to the crunch—was that regret, that heavy feeling in her chest? She stifled a sigh, held her line. "When are you leaving?"

"My flight's booked for late Saturday night. I just have one thing to do on Saturday morning. Would you like to have a last coffee-and-hot-chocolate after that, back at the National Gallery?"

Yes, she would. Now that he was going, she absolutely knew it. She really, really would.

Chapter Thirty-Five

They met under the portico outside the grand, square doors of the gallery. It was an uncharacteristically hot day, and the usual London crowds had been replaced with a summery new bare-limbed cast, many of whom were lolling on the broad white steps. Happily, none of them were disrespecting Livi's lions today, clambering all over their noble backs.

She put her sunglasses on her head as she skirted around a pair of sunbathing tourists, and jogged up the last few steps, her ankle recovered from its Wiltshire injury.

"You look lovely," Cam said, bending down to give her a kiss as she reached him at the top. She closed her eyes as his lips met her cheek, savouring the moment.

"Thanks. You look nice too."

He was wearing the suit again, a crisp white shirt open at the neck, making her feel underdressed in her floaty cotton dress.

"One last meeting." He looked around, distracted. "Let's go in."

She'd given up asking about his mysterious meetings. The only thing left to do was make the most of her last time with him. "Would you like to get a coffee now?"

"No." He looked over her shoulder, towards the entrance. "Let's find Cecilia first. We didn't see her last time."

"Oh, okay." She followed him in, grateful for the coolness of the air-conditioning. He was obviously still in efficient business mode. Whatever the business was.

"Let's ask this guy," he said, making a beeline for a uniformed guide. He explained that they were looking for Saint Cecilia.

"Ah, Italian. I believe some of those paintings have been moved recently," the guide said. "Would you like me to show you where she is?"

"That would be lovely," said Livi. It wasn't as if Cecilia was very famous or extravagant or dramatic. In fact, she was quite modest, unremarkable even. But she was a bit special. After admiring all the reproductions, it would be nice to see the real her.

The guide led them through a large room hung with canvases small, large and enormous, past earphone-clad visitors awed by the history within arm's reach. Then they followed him along a smaller corridor, until they came to a closed door. He got out a heavy ring of keys. Livi raised her eyebrows at Cam, surprised at the high security, but he just shrugged. The guide unlocked the door, and told them he would wait outside, then Cam stood aside so that she could enter first.

She only made it two steps in.

On the jewel-red walls in the little room were six ornate gold frames, each one glowing in a soft waterfall of light. But there were no great works of art. Instead, each frame held a single word, beautifully inked on parchment-coloured paper. 'Livi' said the first. She slowly turned, her mind hardly processing what she was seeing. 'Will' said the next. Then 'you'. Her pounding heart knew what was coming next. Her eyes travelled across to 'marry' and 'me'. In the last frame was an artful question mark.

She turned around and he was on one knee, a small pale blue box in one hand. She caught her breath. "Really?"

He smiled. "Yes."

"But...how did you do all this?"

"Sasha's wife is on the board." He shifted a little on his knee on the hard parquet floor, his hand poised to open the little box.

She couldn't quite put it together. "Wait. Sasha is...a lesbian?"

"What? No. He's an economist."

"Oh! I thought you and Sasha...all those phone calls..."

He laughed. "Right, the name. His mother's family was Russian. And he's a nice old guy, but I'm not especially attracted to nose hair and false teeth. He's one of the last great eccentrics—whenever he has a thought, he calls to tell you about it, and you'd better be available to hear it. Especially if something's riding on it."

He stood up again and put the still-closed box in his pocket. Then he took both her hands, and a deep breath. In the lights, his greeny-gold eyes shone almost the colour of her own as he looked at her.

"Livi. I let chances slip away because I thought we would just happen, because we were meant to be. You are the greatest work of art I can imagine. They could fill every frame in this building with paintings of you, but none of them would do you justice. Nothing but the real you is so beautiful and sweet and honest and maddening. I can't be on the opposite side of the world without you any more."

She looked back at him in amazement, blown away by the beauty of his words and the strength of his emotion. Bex and Gemma were right after all. Now his passion was clear on his face.

"I never knew," she said, shaking her head. "But, why did you traipse around Paris to help me find Ryan?"

"I needed to know if it was something real." His fingers were warm and steady around hers. "Until you followed it through, you wouldn't know. And if it wasn't real, then you could let it go. I was hoping, anyway."

"Since you got here, I've started hoping too," she

admitted, and all at once that hope was reflected in his face.

"I didn't know what you'd think, especially after that night in Paris," he said. "I mean, we've been friends for so long. It might have been too late. Or too weird."

She shook her head. "It was Sasha who caused that confusion. It does feel a *bit* strange—but in a good way." He smiled, and she hated that she couldn't say what they both wanted to hear next. "But now—my new job. And going back there..." She looked away at the frames, wishing things were different.

"Is that the only thing stopping you from saying yes?" He gently turned her face to his, and as he waited for her answer, she could see the reflection of her own face in his searching eyes.

She remembered how right it was sitting next to him in the pub, laughing and joking. His rage as he tore Len away from her. The perfection of leaning into him on a Parisian summer night. Rewinding further, the memories stretched back to school days. She'd taken his constancy for granted, a steady presence, a best friend. Now here he was, a grown man in a well-tailored suit, handsome and smart and kind, telling her, Livi, that he couldn't live without her.

She thought of the times she'd watched him leave her. Years before, when he'd gone off travelling. At the art gallery, when she told him about Rob. At St Pancras, when she thought he was being summoned by a glamorous Sasha Fernsby. How could she bear to watch him walk away again?

He reached into his suit pocket and pulled out an envelope. "You're not the only one with career news." He took a piece of paper from the envelope, and held it up for her to see. "The tome is finished, and this is a job offer. I've got a post at the New Economic Institute. I had to visit with the affiliated professors in London, and in Oxford and Cambridge, to get their approval, but we finalised the last details this morning."

"Really?" Hope lifted her heart. "So this...institute... it's here?"

"In London." He put the letter away again. "It's an independent organisation, a sort of think-tank. They work with the London School of Economics, the World Economic Forum, that kind of thing."

"So all the phone calls were about work."

"Sasha's the founding director. If I wanted the job— and I did—I needed to jump through every hoop. But he was willing to make some effort for me, too." He pointed to the golden frames.

She looked at him. The perpetual student now had a real life, and an impressive one at that. "You are properly clever."

He shrugged. "Clever enough, anyway."

Simply acknowledged, without ego. It was, she realised, one of the things she loved about him.

"So you're staying."

"I have to now, whether you want me to or not. I've just signed a contract."

She took a step and threw her arms around him. "I want you to." With her ear pressed against his chest, the words were loud in her head. They sounded clear and sure and *right*.

"Is that a yes, then?"

"Yes," she said. "*Yes*. But you'll have to sign another contract."

He laughed, and she felt his whole body relax. She looked up. Standing in the little jewel-box room, their words still hanging in the air, she felt like she was seeing him anew. This was another Cam, a man she didn't really know at all. In that moment, she was struck with shyness. As he tangled his fingers in her hair and tilted her head, never taking his eyes off hers, her heart suddenly seemed a size too big. Slowly, he leaned down. She could hardly breathe. Then, unhurriedly, he kissed her. Purposefully, with the intensity of years of waiting for the things they'd just told each other, but with such restraint that she found herself pressing into him, wanting more, every part of her seeking its home against the matching part of him. When they parted she felt blurry, swimming in the heat of their connection.

"You do want it," he said, his voice both satisfied and wondering. "It wasn't just Paris."

All she could do was nod, too overcome to be shy now about her desire. She'd wanted the rush, and she got it. But here was something more than the Rob rush, or the Ryan rush. Everyone talked about chemistry, and electricity. She'd experienced it herself, the fervent charge of two people who can't keep their hands off each other. But this, she thought, was beyond voltage. What she hadn't expected was the depth-charge of their history, all the years of sharing and friendship and—yes—having each others' backs. It was something elemental—like the poles had suddenly switched, with the step they'd taken, and everything was rearranged. Which, in a way, it was.

She thought she knew him.

Now she realised, with delicious anticipation, how very much better she'd be getting to know him.

She reached into his pocket and took out the little blue box. "Could we try that again, please?"

He took it from her and got back on one knee, his face serious. Slowly, he opened the lid to reveal a sparkly, princess-cut solitaire, set in a narrow gold band. But before he could say a word, she was down on her knees too. He slipped the ring on her finger, where it glittered and shone in the gallery lights.

As she looked at Cam, and the ring, and back again, she still didn't feel grown-up. She just felt like her most real self, with nothing to prove, and nothing to hide from. Home wasn't just about *where*, but also about *who*. And this—the two of them together—was her own true home.

★

They finally found Saint Cecilia, high on the wall amongst the other seventeenth-century Italians in room thirty-two.

She was just one of many artworks in the room, and she was more than a little overshadowed by an enormous painting of shepherds adoring the baby Jesus. But...she was lovely.

Once, a platonic Livi and Cam had whiled away their time in Livi's childhood bedroom, beneath her poster Cecilia. And now another version of her was leaning against the wall in Livi's London bedroom. Here, though, the real thing gazed out of her heavy gold frame, still watching and waiting for what lay ahead, while beneath her, very unsaintly thoughts of what lay ahead were running through Livi's head.

The unfamiliar sensation of the ring on her finger was nothing compared to the sensation of standing close alongside him, her hand firmly in his and the memory of their kiss burning in her mind. She turned and pressed herself against him again, threading her arms around his waist under his suit jacket.

"If we were alone in here, all the saints would have to close their eyes," she said.

He smiled at her, and pointed to the deep-buttoned leather seats in the centre of the room.

"If we were alone in here, I would have to throw you onto those and—" He stopped suddenly as a group of tourists stopped to admire the shepherds next door.

"Nice guys can play dirty, huh?" she teased, keeping her voice low.

"Who said I was a nice guy?" he threw back.

"Live in denial if you like, I know the truth about you."

"You might be surprised at what you don't know about me," he replied, ignoring the tourists and kissing her with all the promise of what she was going to find out.

As she closed her eyes, she marvelled at how right it was. How could *she* have been in denial all this time, so blind to what was right in front of her? Ironic that Cecilia was the patron saint not just of music, but of the blind. Maybe she'd been looking out for Livi all along—bringing her, when the time was right, to this very spot. Cass would certainly think so.

"Beginnings, endings, and beginnings again," she said over his shoulder to the painted Cecilia, when he finally let her go.

He gave her a quizzical look. "What?"

But she just laughed, and shook her head. It could be hard to tell whether an ending was good or bad, but now she knew one thing for certain: sometimes you have to go full circle—all over the place, maybe—to get back to the right beginning.

Epilogue

Trafalgar Square. Interview day. It was breezy at the top of the steps, but the view over their shoulders was impressive. As Livi took her place, the diamond on her finger caught the sun. She drew from the bronze strength of the lions in the square behind her, and stood tall. Inside was Cecilia, as strong and true as Livi aspired to be (but more saintly than she would ever aim for). She thought of Cam, tidying up the endings of his life far away, but soon getting back on a London-bound plane.

Now the reporter fussed a little more with his hair, then gave the cameraman a nod. But he shook his head behind the camera. "Move over mate, Nelson's column is coming right out the top of your head."

He shuffled a little to the side. "Okay now? Right." He cleared his throat and reassumed his news face.

"Here I am with Livi Callaway, who has bounced back from abject humiliation at the hands of last year's *Dance 'til You Drop* heart-throb to find success in London, and love with her childhood sweetheart. Livi, first tell us about your new business venture…"

She smiled right into the camera. It was going to be fine.

Thanks for reading *All Over the Place!*
For more information about Serena and her other books,
visit www.serenaclarke.com. While you're there, sign up
for her VIP newsletter to receive new book news, special
offers, and exclusive extras.

*Reviews help other readers find the kind of books they love. If you
enjoyed All Over the Place, please do consider leaving a rating and
comment at your favourite online retailer or review site.
Your review is greatly appreciated!*

Acknowledgements

Huge thanks…

To all the writer friends I've been lucky to find—online and in 'real life'—for the support, advice, and steady stream of happy distractions.

To the RNA in the UK, and their wonderful New Writers' Scheme, for guidance on the first draft of *All Over the Place*.

To Alice Hoffman, for generously allowing me to quote from her amazing book, *Practical Magic*.

To my friends and family, for your love and support through all the ups and downs, near and far away.

And most of all, to Adam, Nate and Zach, my heroes big and little. Wherever you three gorgeous guys are is the place I want to be.

Also by Serena Clarke

A North So True
The Same But Different
One Distant Summer

About the Author

Serena Clarke writes escapist romantic fiction set all over the world. Readers have described her books as engaging page-turners, with sigh-worthy happy endings that will leave you smiling.

Her own story? She's lived in thirty-nine houses, in seven cities, in four countries. She's been a riding instructor, edited a medical journal, worked at a London law firm, and taught English as a second language to wayward teenagers. And now she's found her own happy ending—living near the beach in beautiful New Zealand with her family, writing the kind of feel-good books she loves to read. She hopes you'll love them too!.

Find her online at www.serenaclarke.com.